Saint Gabriel's Gospel

J. L. Harber

This novel is a work of fiction. Names, characters, places and incidences are the product of the author's imagination or are used fictitiously. Any resemblance to any person, living or dead, or to any institution currently or previously existing is a coincidence.

In cases where references are made to actual institutions, places, or events, public or private officials, they are used fictionally to the benefit of the story and are not meant to represent facts about them.

The front cover art was created by www.digitaldonna.com.

ISBN:-10: 1482568276
ISBN-13: 978-1482568271

Acknowledgements

This book is the result of a long time dream, a nagging idea, and the support and encouragement of good friends. I especially want to thank Ellen Prewitt who read the first few chapters and offered good advice and encouragement to keep writing. She then read my "final draft" and offered more ideas and encouragement. Thank you, Ellen for the generous gift of your time and talent.

Judy Dean, Dennis Clark, Carol Duke, and Mike Harber are among my other first readers. The very positive response each made was the best kind of encouragement. When Judy emailed me and said she was up until 1:30 AM the previous night finishing it, I thought I might be on to something.

The unnamed men and women who spurred me on are found among the hundreds of authors who have entertained me over the years. I'm pretty certain that I absorbed a lot about writing a novel from reading theirs.

Miss Dorothy Wolf, my high school English teacher for three years developed my early interest in writing. I hope she's able to look down from heaven, where she surely is, and feel pleased with my efforts.

Many of the locales and facts about the locales are a result of the Internet and browser searches and are accurate—for the most part. Even fifteen years ago, much of what I learned couldn't have been done so easily. I didn't always stay faithful to details I found there because the story was more important than the details.

Finally, to Carol, my wife of many years, thanks for your patience and love.

PROLOGUE

Jerusalem, 61 AD

Mariamne dipped her reed pen into the shallow wooden bowl of charcoal and olive oil ink and began writing her last entry on the parchment page in front of her.

"Because Yaakov told us to write down our memories, I have decided to share what I have kept privately all these years. These pages contain all that I have seen and heard since the first day with Yeshua. Each evening before I slept, I wrote as much as I could remember of what he said to the people who came out to see him and hear him. I have written his private sayings to we who are his friends, as well as what he does of importance. I have tried to be a faithful witness to our beloved Yeshua. I pray that all who read these words will tell others as we await the future."

She lay down the pen and carefully gathered all the sheets of parchment together that were stacked on her rough writing desk. She laid her fresh sheet on top of the stack and then began to thread leather strips into the holes already punched into each page. When she had secured the pages together and was satisfied with her work, she turned a page and began to read what she had begun writing more than thirty years before, feeling the memories come rushing back as if no time at all had passed.

"The beginning for me was a word on the wind. People from the area around Nazareth came to my town to trade. They did not bring only goods, but they brought stories--wondrous stories of a man who works with his hands who had left his tools and begun preaching and doing wonders. They told how at a wedding in nearby Cana he turned water into wine. Marta, a godly woman who worked for me in my business of selling dried fish begged me to go to Nazareth and find this man whose name was Yeshua."

"I knew why she urged me. I was beset with sadness after my husband had died in a storm soon after our young baby died in his sleep. My parents were dead long ago and I was completely alone. My nights were tormented by terrible visions and some days I could not rise from my bed to go to the store I felt so deadened. I was losing weight because I could not eat. My blood flow was irregular. Often my head would be filled with pain and I would see lights with my eyes closed. When I was at my shop, I seemed in a daze, thinking of my husband and our baby. I did not hear people speak to me nor could I concentrate on what they said. Some days I thought it would be better if I just walked into Lake Gennesaret and kept walking until it consumed me."

"Marta wept for me and urged me all the more to seek out this Yeshua. She had heard stories about more than turning water into wine. She had heard that he cast out demons and cured the sick. 'You must go, you can not live with this pain much longer,' she implored. Perhaps I would, I thought, but I wasn't sure I was strong enough to endure the four hour journey to Nazareth. I told Marta so and she urged me even more and begged me to go by cart. 'You are a woman of means. Get a cart and a driver. When you arrive, this will impress the healer and he will not turn you away.' And so I set about to meet Yeshua Nazoraean. My life would never be the same."

CHAPTER 1

A Dig Site In Jerusalem

"Doctor Gabriel! Come quickly! We've found something at the dig!"

I looked up from the pottery shard I was examining to see one of the volunteers from the dig, standing in the door of the trailer. She looked red faced and excited, a little like a heat stroke about to happen. My first thought was that having poorly trained volunteers has its drawbacks. Sure, aside from shelter and food, they don't cost anything, but their enthusiasm about every little find can be distracting. I wasn't ready to hop up and leave the cool trailer on her say so. Jerusalem summer was unseasonably hot this year and I wasn't ready to sweat for nothing. Not able to remember her name, I said, "What is it? Another piece of pottery?" sounding skeptical of the find's importance.

"No sir. It's better than that and Marty says you've got to see it!" her enthusiasm still very evident.

Since Marty is my co-director on the dig, mentor, excellent field archeologist and my friend, I decided maybe I should go. Marty and I had worked together my entire field career. He was older than I, probably around 60 I'd guess. There was none better in our profession. He could almost sense where to dig on a site before any surveying had even been done. He hated classroom work, and when we weren't on a dig, he was in the lab looking at finds and making incredibly good educated guesses about what we were uncovering. I had to push him to publish results, though. Even though he is tenured, our field requires that others learn what we have discovered. We have to add to the knowledge out there so other can benefit and, perhaps, build on it. So, if this somewhat rumpled man, whose tanned face was wrinkled from too many years in the sun and who was loyal to me and our work to a fault, if that guy thought I needed to take a look, well then, I did. "OK. Let's go," I said as I reached for my hat. "What is it?"

We were digging in a first century residential area of the Old City. We were there because a construction project of some kind had unearthed a wall of what appeared to be a building. We decided to use ground penetrating radar to scope out what we had before any digging would take place. We had been able over the past several seasons to squirrel away enough funds, so that with the help of a special grant, we now had a serious state-of-the-art instrument, which I had been eager to try. We had snagged detectors that included two different antennas. One was the 400 Mhz GPR antenna. It produces 60 electromagnetic pulses per second and can reveal structures more than 12 feet below the surface if the soil is dry enough. We also had a 40 Mhz antenna that can scope out soil and rock structures up to a depth of 130 feet--an amazing breakthrough and incredible time saver. I thought the 60 was good enough for our site, and if the results were not adequate, we could always switch it out for the 40. The results were great. We had something good. Something physically large in keeping with that area of the Old City. It was a building of some kind--almost certainly a residence.

"It's a sealed jar, Doc, and it's intact!" she answered.

This is a big deal. Ever since the Qumran cave finds, the so-called Dead Sea Scrolls and the Nag Hammadi finds, every sealed jar seems unusually important and promising. I was becoming a little excited. What if we were to find more manuscripts? That should make a splash. And what good is a splash? Pots are just pots, bones are just bones, but the "right manuscripts" opened the vaults of those who like to support archeology. The "right manuscripts" in this case were anything written in the first century AD. Especially texts. Especially religious texts. Manuscripts equal funding and we always need funding and first century ones would probably equal serious funding. I hate to sound mercenary, but I work for a university in the States. Grants are vital to our work. And big grants are always nicer than small ones. As we walked away from the trailer and toward the find, there was no guessing where it was because everybody in the dig was gathered around it. As I shouldered my way through and jumped a few feet into the excavation pit, I said, "Okay, Marty, what've we got?"

Marty was standing in one of our pits which was about five feet deep. He pulled off his filthy hat, took an equally disgusting handkerchief from his back pocket, and swiped at his sweaty face. "Gabby, we're still pulling away the soil around it, but it's clearly a sealed jar of some size--as you can see."

What I could see was a niche in a stone wall. In that niche, still partly covered in dirt and debris was the jar Marty pointed to. Marty kept talking.

"Based on what we can see so far, it looks a lot like the Qumran jars. There are no handles like grain or liquid storage jars might have. It appears to be about 40 centimeters in diameter and I'm guessing it will be around 90 centimeters tall. The lid is about 25 centimeters in diameter, so if I'm remembering correctly, the proportions are about the same as Qumran."

Marty went on, "The lid is sealed with pitch which would indicate it was not a regular household jar. If it were a normal household jar the owner would seal a jar like this with wax or tallow because that would be easier to open. I'm guessing the pitch was to provide a more durable seal as if it had to last a longer than the usual time."

The reason Marty is standing in a pit is once we used the detectors to discover the general layout, we began our work by digging two meter square test pits at the locations of the four corners of the building as shown by the radar. We quickly had success. In one corner we found what was probably the kitchen or hearth of the house. Carbon dating from this area indicated a date somewhere in the first century. We dug a pit in the middle of the building, and we found what was probably a courtyard because it was paved with stone. We also had a rare find of a Roman first century coin from that pit. These things together nailed down the opinion that this was an especially important find. We hadn't really found much else: some pottery shards mostly. We put a small crew in each pit and had them begin to dig down farther and to widen the pit as well.

Our theory was the residence had been destroyed at some point, we now thought in the first century, and others built over the ruins. We didn't much care about the earlier layers; our target was the first century layer. We thought it very important to establish this as a first century site because of the politics of archeology in Israel.

Sadly, though archeologists aren't always called for these kinds of finds in Israel, especially in Jerusalem, we are seldom given all the time needed to study the site carefully. The construction project was being delayed and that was costing somebody *beaucoup* bucks as well as inconveniencing the hell out of many people. God knows, fixing those problems is more important than learning more about our ancient history. Not that I'm bitter. Now if we'd found bones, we might have been given more time, but no bones--so far.

Ordinarily the Israeli government is in charge of digs such as this, using their own people, at least in the early stages. It was our good fortune that we were, one, working nearby already and two, the IAA--Israeli Antiquities Authority--didn't have anybody they could put on it. So they asked us and, always eager to please Big Brother, we agreed and shifted about half of our team over here, resulting in our trying to manage two sites at once.

Our dig team consisted of three groups. Graduate

students in archeology, primarily from Vanderbilt, but a few other schools as well were the bulk of the team. The second group was volunteers composed of people of all backgrounds who had an interest in archeology and signed on for fun and paid much of their own expenses. The third group was locals whom we had to pay the going wage for experienced dig workers; some were laborers, others much more talented and experienced. We tried to use as few of this group as possible for economic reasons, but dealing with two sites meant we had several on each site this season.

The finds had been tantalizing so far, especially the size of this house, which the radar showed us. But we needed more than a coin and a few other artifacts to be given all the time we wanted. However, nothing spectacular had emerged and we probably didn't have a lot more time to work here before IAA pulled the plug on us. As I stood looking at the jar, I was very excited. Maybe here was our ticket to stay long enough to do the work we want to be able to do on every dig.

As usual, Marty's summary of the find was spot on. Marty had a tidy mind, if you will, and he likes to get all the facts clear and unadorned as possible. I valued that in him; that kind of precision is essential for good archeology. I got down on my knees to look at the find more closely.

"Look at the shoulder of the jar right here," as

Marty pointed to the right side of the jar as I faced it, "there's some faded writing. Maybe two words. I can make out a few of the letters a little and they appear to be Greek."

Everybody at the dig was hovering over our shoulders, almost literally breathing down our necks. "Give me one of the softer brushes," I said to no one in particular and quickly had one slapped into my hand like a scrub nurse slaps a scalpel into the hand of a surgeon. Gently I dusted dirt away from two of the other letters, but they weren't appreciably clearer. I stopped, afraid I'd disturb the medium in which the letters were written, probably charcoal based ink. At this point I suspected we were going to have to do some digital enhancing to see what we had. We didn't have the equipment to do this on site, but we could take digital photos and e-mail them to the lab at Vanderbilt, our home base.

"Trevor, use the high res camera on this, please; I want some shots of this inscription."

Trevor jumped into the pit with us. I stood up, not even bothering to brush the dust from my knees and Marty moved to give Trevor room. Trevor is the official dig photographer and has been with me for several years. He's nearing the completion of his degree and when he leaves, I'll really miss him.

"Listen everyone! You cannot, I repeat, cannot

discuss this find with anyone. We don't know what we have so we don't know its value. But one thing is sure; in this town discoveries such as this can fuel a lot of speculation and that speculation can lead to problems. You must not speak of this even among yourselves here at the site and when you head for the local watering holes after we knock off, you need to forget you were even here today. Don't talk in your rooms, and certainly, no pillow talk with anybody. I mean this. Leaking this information is a killing offense--well not literally, though I'll want to kill you." There was some nervous laughter.

"What I mean is it will kill your career because I will rat you out to anyone who even thinks about hiring you. Anybody who can't keep a confidence in this profession doesn't belong in it. Am I understood?" My voice had inched up as I talked. I needed them to get it.

I think the stock phrase to describe their reaction would be "the natives were restless." They murmured among themselves and shot looks back and forth, perhaps a little unsure if my threat was real. Or maybe they wondered if I actually had that kind of clout, that a bad recommendation from me would kill their chances to work in this field. Finally the woman who had come for me in the trailer slowly raised her hand. She didn't look so red faced now, nor on the verge of a stroke. She was sweaty, but then that's to be expected. I'm a little ashamed to say I noticed that her being sweaty had the effect of plastering her white sleeveless tee shirt to her very attractive chest. Guess it was too hot for a bra--kind of good news and bad news for me.

"Doctor Gabriel, no disrespect meant," she said, "but are you maybe being a little melodramatic? It's just a jar, right?"

"I'm sorry, I can't remember your name." I said.

"Nicki," came the reply.

"Well Nicki, I don't feel disrespected by your question." She looked relieved. Too bad; I wasn't finished. "However, I'm pissed that you think this find is **just a jar**!" At that point, Marty reached over and touched my arm, looking for the volume control I guess. I was too wound up to stop though. "In archeology, we never say that a find of any kind is 'just a' something. Even fossilized crap can tell us an incredible amount about the person or animal that pooped it out, the time in which they lived, what they ate, what the climate may have been like. A small chunk of a jar can tell us when the jar was made, allowing us to date the find we might be working in. They are like precious little calendars just waiting for us to read them."

"Sometimes those little shards have writing on them that shine a light on a distant time: an inventory list, somebody's practice writing, a name. A nearly intact jar may tell us even more. Sometimes we find residue in the bottom telling us what the jar contained--now we know what people were eating or storing. Did you know for example, that we have actually reproduced the ancient Egyptian beer that was the staple drink for those dudes building the pyramids? It was done from scrapings from the bottom of a broken jar? And a whole jar, a sealed jar! My God I can't imagine the potential value of this find!" My voice was getting louder. "Oh there is going to be something of value in it all right or someone 2000 years ago wouldn't have gone to so much trouble to seal it and place it where it was found!"

Marty kind of grabbed my arm this time, but I shook him off. "Nicki, did you happen to notice where the jar was? Even at a glance when I walked up, I could see that it had been in a niche, perhaps a niche that had been sealed too. If it were in a niche in a wall, that would indicate the owner thought it was pretty special. And if the effing niche were sealed, that would indicate that it was more than pretty special, don't you think? Just a jar? Then the Sistine Chapel ceiling is just a big fucking painting!"

I was suddenly aware I was much louder than I needed to be. I kind of stepped out of my body and looked at what was going on. The whole group looked as if somebody had just slapped them. Nicki, of the sweaty tee shirt, looked ill and about to cry. I didn't really like that, but I needed to get through to her--and everybody else. On the other hand, I'm not really a person who rants and raves, so this was pretty out of character for me and overall, I didn't feel really good about it. *Not too late to salvage this,* I thought. I paused and took a deep breath.

In my calm, big boy voice I said, "Look, Nicki, everybody, I'm sorry I went off just now. There's no excuse, really, for raising my voice. I'm just excited and afraid. I'm excited because this jar could be something really, really important, and I'm afraid because if it is, and somebody else gets wind of what we have before it's secure and studied, we might lose control of it. I actually do understand the comment Nicki made. Early in my career, I could easily have said the same thing."

That was a lie, but I wanted to put a little balm on this thing. Looking specifically at her--not her tee shirt, her eyes--I went on, "Nicki, I apologize for jumping you," at which point the group snickered as one; sides were poked with nearby elbows; the tension was lifted a bit. A crooked little smile played across my face. "OK, poor choice of words: I mean I apologize for *criticizing* you in front of everyone for your comment. I was out of line; way out of line."

She appeared to be blushing and she looked again as if she were going to cry but for a different reason. "It's

Okay Doctor Gabriel," she said, "I should have thought before I said anything. I accept your apology, but it's not really necessary. Thank you, though; it's very gracious of you."

I was glad we were all pals again and I could get my attention back on the jar. "Thank **you**, Nicki." I noticed she had more than a sweaty tee shirt as an attribute. She had wonderful eyes--kind of periwinkle in color--and blonde hair in a ponytail pulled through the back of her ball cap. She was a little taller than average and seemed to be in very good shape. Her face was tanned just a touch; just the right amount. But, back to business. "Listen everybody, I really meant what I said, and if you're wondering if I have that kind of clout, any field archeologist with my experience has that kind of influence. I'm not bragging here; we all know I'm an archeological grand poobah with tenure and everything, on the faculty of a major U.S. university, dig director for a few major finds, so yes, I have clout. All of you, make me proud now, keep quiet and you'll all get a great recommendation from me and that will be a career booster. Now let's all get back to work and forget what we've found. Again; I'm sorry for the outburst."

The worker bees dispersed. I noticed that one of the Graduate Assistants was walking beside Nicki as everybody walked off. Josh something--I suck at names and kind of hate it--was gesturing dramatically, leaning in toward her and talking in one of those voices where you're yelling, but at considerably less volume than a real yell. You know, it's the kind of voice our parents used in church to tell us as kids that if we don't stop squirming God is going to send demons to haul us to hell. We're making our point, but only those at whom the comments are aimed get the angry inflection. What the hell was he doing? Was he mad at her and continuing my little tirade or was he telling her she was a dope to accept my apology? Who knows and the truth is, right that minute, I didn't really care.

Josh had been in the doctoral program long enough to complete all the coursework. This was not his first dig with me. He needed field experience and he needed a dissertation topic. Josh was one of those students who seems bright enough but who is always looking for some kind of angle, some shortcut to the ends he's pursuing. He was sloppy in his work, and I had wished a couple of times we had given his slot to someone else when he applied.

Marty and I knelt again in the dirt. He began to scrape more soil from around the jar, exposing more of it. He was going to be right about how tall it was. Soon we were looking at the bottom of the niche in which the jar sat. The sides of the niche were still intact so it was obvious it was a niche set in the wall of the house. At some point the upper wall had been knocked down, which was how the niche filled with dirt and the jar got protected as it got buried. The front of the niche looked as if it had been concealed with some stones and plaster at one time. Later, when we dug down to floor level that would be confirmed by the rubble on the floor. We thought it might have fallen out when the upper wall collapsed. Somebody wanted to preserve this thing and thought it might need to be protected for a long time. Good news for us!

"Marty, I wouldn't be surprised if this jar were placed here as one of the Jewish revolts was heating up. Something important that needed to be hidden away. Then, bam, the Jews lose--as of course we know they did--the owner of the jar is killed or runs away or is arrested. Bingo, we have a time capsule."

We already suspected this was some grand high muckety-muck's private digs. Our location in the Old City was near where the Temple priests had lived so the residences seemed to be larger than elsewhere. Our place was not far from the so-called Burnt House find, which had been destroyed, in the Roman destruction in of Jerusalem in 70 AD. Rome had reached their limit with the sporadic little revolts of the Jews and when, in 66 a major one erupted, Titus, the emperor's son, came in to clean up things. He didn't do it halfway either. The entire city was ravaged and the Temple destroyed. Josephus, an important

Jewish historian of the same time, had indicated in his writing that the area in which we were digging was known for its wealth, and discoveries elsewhere in the area had so far backed that up. We weren't smack in the middle of that area, but we were at least on the fringe.

The radar images indicated that our house was not as big as the Burnt House, which was about 32 feet square. Ours looked to be about 26 feet on a side--still sizable. Sizable meant important. How important? We would be shocked when we learned just how important it was. Like the Burnt House, we discovered what we thought was a courtyard with several rooms off of it and an area that could be a mikvah, or ritual bath. A mikvah in a private home indicated status and some wealth. We had also discovered a layer of ash and debris in two of our test pits, indicating the house was probably burned, which is what happened to the Burnt House, thus it's name.

A couple of our pits showed us that the remnants of the walls were plastered, which was another indicator of some status or standing in the community for the owner. More excavation might reveal frescos, but nothing had turned up. If we did find a fresco, it could be a hint as to whether or not the person who lived here were Jewish. Jewish frescos would not contain images--their interpretation of the Second Commandment forbade graven images of any human or animal. And if what we thought was the mikvah really was one, the deal was sealed. The discovery of the jar in the niche, cinched for me our theory of a wealthy owner. We had something pretty damned important here.

"Good theory," Marty agreed. "But I'll tell you what: right now I'm more interested in what's in the jar than how it got here. I'm not big on speculation with too few facts as you know. I need to get the rest of the soil removed from behind it so we can ease it out. Then, we need to get it out of here. I hope we figure out a way to not lose control of whatever's in it, especially since the IAA called us in on this site."

I removed my glasses and wiped the sweat from my face with the bottom of my tee shirt. "I'm with you. I'd like to protect this find as long as we can. We haven't discovered anything really important for a long time."

"Gabby, you just made an impassioned speech about there being no such thing as an ordinary or unimportant find. Now you're disparaging the contributions we've made with our other work. What the hell?" His trowel scraped away the last of the dirt between the back of the jar and the back of the niche. "You know damn well we're not doing this for glory."

"Yeah, I'm doing it for the pursuit of knowledge--and grant money and to keep my job as Director of the Department of Biblical Archeology at Vanderbilt. Don't forget, I've got alimony to pay. Here, let's see if we can move that thing."

We each grasped a side under the bottom edge and wiggled it a little to loosen it from the substrate. It gave and on three, we lifted. "It ain't empty, that's for sure." It was hard to estimate the weight, but I'd lifted empty jars similar to this. This one had something in it; it wasn't very heavy, but it wasn't empty. We let it settle back where it was. "Let's get some bubble wrap and a crate and get this thing back to the workshop. I want to know what's in it."

"Yeah. We need to do a complete study of the exterior, including high res photos and get them back to Vandy to process. You know we've got to do this thing the right way because it really could have something very important inside."

"I know I'm too eager to open it; I must be having my period." I said.

Marty looked at me with can best be described as the Stink Eye. He was not amused. "Okay, first things first: get it back to the workshop then we can sit up late tonight and plan how we'll process the find. The thing that worries me is I know we can get it back to our workshop without a problem, but I wonder how can we avoid letting the IAA know we've found something significant?"

"Gabby, I don't think we have a lot of time before

we tell them. If we wait too long they're gonna be really pissed. IAA is not as bad as that little asshole tyrant Hawass was in Egypt before he got sacked, but you know like I do, they can get testy. We screw this up with them and we'll probably have trouble working in any country. Let's get this thing back to the workshop, do our due diligence, get it open and see what we have. Maybe if we document everything and release the news to the media as we're telling IAA about it, we can counter their tendency to describe everything as a national treasure and take the important follow up work away from us."

Well, it wasn't a perfect plan, Gabriel thought, *but I don't have a better idea. We'll take it back, do the tedious work we do so well and then, we'll break the seal and see what we have. Who knows, maybe it's just somebody's money and jewels. Not that that would be a bad thing. Until we had done that, we need to keep everybody's lips zipped. Maybe I needed to have another little chat with the team in the morning. Calmer this time, of course.*

CHAPTER 2

At the Dig

We were ready to move the jar. Trevor had been recording every step so we could document everything. Marty had also made sure that still shots had been taken of the process as soon as the top of the jar appeared, but we needed more than that now. Ellie Steinburg, a contract worker who'd been with me on other digs, had a digital camera going. With her fairly short light brown hair and stocky build she was somewhat masculine in demeanor. I'd decided a year or so ago she was probably gay—for a lot of reasons other than her appearance. Ellie had quickly moved up from manual labor to serious archeology; seemed to have a knack for it. In fact, besides Marty, Trevor and me, she was probably the most experienced person on site. Trevor was using the video camera as Marty and I lifted the jar from the niche. We carefully laid it on its side on bubble wrap we had placed in the wooden crate. We then began to stuff more wrap around it, making it as secure as we could. Since we didn't have far to go, we agreed we would not nail on the top of the crate--no unnecessary jarring. We slid it into place and then began to wrap strapping around the crate to keep the top in place.

As we worked, I could see dig members peeking up from their work to watch us. They were trying to look no more interested than usual, but were barely succeeding. I needed everything to look normal because we've already done something that could draw unwelcome attention. We're working in a busy area, lots of people around. Usually the "natives" don't care much about what goes on--they've seen too much to care. But when everybody on the site came racing over to the find area and milled around, that draws the curious. My losing it didn't help either. I could remember seeing people stop on the roadway above us and look down. The spectacle of a raving maniac was news, I guess. I was hoping no cell phone camera was preparing me for my close up on YouTube. This day and age, I'd say it was likely that somebody snapped something, though I hoped not.

The curious won't come into the dig; they know better. But they are, for the most part, Israeli citizens who have pride in their country. So if it seems to them something important is going on, they aren't so jaded they won't stop and watch. The ultra-Orthodox Jews, known as the *haredim,* of which the best known group are the Hasidic Jews, have been known to disrupt digs they felt were engaged in activities not in line with their beliefs, especially where bones were concerned. But not just bones. A recent event occurred at a long excavated fourth century synagogue at Hammath Tiberius. Vandals seriously damaged its mosaic floor, which depicted images of the Torah ark and menorahs. Someone sprayed painted an unflattering comment about the Director-General of the Israeli Antiquities Authority. No one doubted it was the *haredim.* As watchdogs, they were the meanest and would happily run to IAA and raise an alarm even though they were often critical of the IAA's approach overall. IAA was, after all, The Authority. We needed to draw as little attention to ourselves as we could.

Marty and I could have used a little help in manhandling the crate--wasn't that heavy, but was awkward to carry--but we were drawing enough attention all ready. I wasn't calling others over, even if the crate was a bit unwieldy. Saying something about being too old for this crap, Marty and I sort of crab-walked, sort of shuffled over to the pickup truck. The tailgate was down and we slid the crate forward and secured it with some bungees. Then, even though I wanted to leave that minute, I had mentioned to Marty as we struggled with our load that we should work to the normal end of our shift. Maybe by acting as if this wasn't as big a deal as it might have looked earlier, we could defuse some speculation. He grunted his agreement, so having secured the crate, he went back to the dig site to work and I went back to the trailer to do the same.

The next hour or two was hard, but finally, we could head out. The worker bees shoved some equipment into the bed of the truck. Most tools were locked in the trailer overnight, but some things were too valuable to trust to a flimsy lock. You never know in this town. Marty decided to drive the truck and to drive a little more carefully than usual as he headed to the workshop--which we did every night. I had ridden my rented Vespa because it's cheaper and it's easy to get around in. When the season ends, I turn it in and I'm done. I didn't care that the red color is brighter than I might ordinarily choose; next season it would be something else. I hopped on and set out for the workshop. Most everybody else piled into the beat up, and sometime unreliable, fifteen-passenger bus we rented to haul human cargo and headed out to wherever they went at night. Others wandered off to bicycles or scooters of their own. Soon they were all gone.

On my ride to the warehouse, I couldn't help thinking about what might be in that jar. This could be the biggest find we'd made in a long time, a potential life changer. If I had known that was going to be true, and could have seen the changes, I might have immediately turned the jar over to the IAA.

CHAPTER 3

On the Bus

Josh was holding forth as the bus pulled away from the dig. "You know, I have a lot of respect for Saint Gabriel, and I know he's made a lot of contributions to the field, but he shouldn't talk to us like he did back there."

"Josh, let it go." Nicki said. "I was out of line. Maybe I needed a verbal slap like that to remember what we're doing here. I mean, my God, we're digging in a major first century residential area, and from the looks of site, this building is important."

Josh's reply was sharp. "Nicki, you're acting so fucking naive. Sure it's important, but we're adults and we don't deserve to be tongue lashed by some old fart who's having a bad day."

"Josh, please let it go."

"Hey, I can't help but hear you guys and I think Josh is right," piped Ellie, the woman who had been using one of the cameras at the site, and one of the few locals on the dig. Ellie had lived in Israel all her life; most of it in Jerusalem. She had strong opinions about most everything.

"Hell, he's got students, volunteers, and employees, for God's sake, and all of us deserve to be spoken to more civilly. It may not be 'just a jar' but, hey, it's not the frigging Ark of the Covenant either."

"Ellie, Josh, I don't want to listen to any more of this." Nicki pleaded. "He said he was sorry and that's good enough for me. Please, I'm tired and hungry; I'm sweaty and dirty. Be quiet and let's just get to the hostel in peace."

"Good grief, Nicki. Grow a pair!" Ellie growled. Ellie didn't normally bunk at the hostel, but she had moved in the day before. "Just for a few days," she has said, "While the air conditioning in my apartment is repaired."

Josh appeared to cave in to Nicki's request. "Okay. I'll shut up, but I still don't like it and obviously I'm not the only one," gesturing over his shoulder at Ellie. "I bet if we polled the bus, we'd find more who didn't like it too."

Josh sat quietly for a moment looking out the open window, his longish dark hair being mussed by the hot breeze. He wasn't classically handsome, but had a kind of Bad Boy look that many women found appealing. He carefully managed his five o'clock shadow so it was just the right length all the time. Very *au courant.* "I'm just going to say one more thing and then I'll drop it. It's obvious he's being really secretive about this find. It would serve Gabriel right if somebody dropped a dime on him about what we uncovered."

"Oh my God, Josh! You wouldn't!" Nicki said, "That could ruin everything for the project!"

"I'm not saying I'd do it, but I wouldn't shed a tear if someone else did it."

Ellie spoke up, "Me either. We don't have to take that crap!"

Apparently, that was too much for Nicki. She got up from her seat next to Josh and went forward near the front of the bus to stand. Josh watched her lurch and sway as the bus bumped its way through the beat up roads and the heavy Jerusalem traffic. Horns seemed to honk incessantly, almost as much as New York. Small scooters darted through the traffic, daring vehicles to hit them. Diesel exhaust mixed with carbon monoxide from cars. Some parts of the city could be almost deadly just to drive in. Never mind trying to be a pedestrian trying to cross a street somewhere.

As most men would, he turned his thoughts from the find and Gabriel and to her nice ass, still dusty from sitting on the ground at the dig. But his hormone-fueled lust surprisingly was pushed aside as his mind went back to Gabriel's remarks. He still stung a little, even though they weren't directed to him. He didn't like Gabriel's tone--hell, he wasn't that fond of Gabriel, period--and he didn't like Nicki being hurt, especially since he was more attracted to her than was good for him. Or her. Someone watching him could have noticed the sudden shift in his facial expression. It suggested he'd just had an idea or hatched a scheme.

The bus rattled to an abrupt stop in front of the hostel where most of the dig members were staying. People began to get off so the driver could go park. Josh had a nearby apartment, but rode the bus to the hostel as a matter of convenience. As he rose to leave the bus, he grabbed Nicki's backpack from where she had been sitting and pushed his way up to her as she stepped off the bus. "Hey, Nicki, you forgot this." The "thank you" he got could flash freeze food. "Hey look, I'm sorry. I was way off base, especially with that last crack. It just really bothered me that he humiliated you in front of everybody. And you're right, the find is important, and I'd never do anything to jeopardize it. I guess I was trying in my clumsy caveman kind of way to make you feel better," he said smiling, brushing his hair from his forehead. "I'm really, really sorry."

She thawed visibly; anyone could have seen it in her eyes and faint smile. "Okay. Thanks. But please just let it go. I don't want anyone else apologizing to me anymore today. Let's get cleaned up and go for dinner somewhere--my treat, Mr. Caveman; a reward for your efforts." She touched his arm in a gesture of reconciliation.

"Sounds terrific! Meet you out front in thirty minutes?" The invitation was far better than anything he could have hoped for. This would be the perfect time to make a move.

"Make it a hour; I'm pretty dirty and disheveled and there is going to be a line for the showers."

"Sure. One hour. Sounds great. I need to take care of a couple of things anyway." As he walked away, the image of her in the shower flicked across his mind's eye. He willed it to linger.

As Nicki made her way to her bunk, her thoughts turned to Gabriel, but not to the dressing down or the apology. She had found his usually rumpled appearance, the sweat stained hat, the wild hat hair when he removed it, his glasses that seemed perpetually to be sliding down his nose--she had found all that attractive. She had volunteered to call him to the pit just to have an excuse to be with him a minute. She stopped herself, thinking, *Get a grip girl. Nothing can come of this. Think about something else. Just go enjoy dinner with Josh.*

Somewhere in Jerusalem

"Good evening. Rockefeller Museum. How may I direct your call?"

"The IAA please."

"Let me see if someone is still in the office. Just a moment please."

"IAA. How may I help you?"

"I need to speak to the Director-General. I have information he'll want."

"The DG is gone for the day; I can put you through to his voice mail."

"When will he return? I don't want to leave a message."

"I'm sorry, I'm not allowed to give out that information. If you'd like to call later, perhaps tomorrow..."

"I'll call tomorrow. Hey, if he were coming in, what time would he normally arrive?"

"I'm sorry, he has no set time for arrival. He often has meetings away from the building early in the mornings."

"Okay. I'll...I'll just take my chances."

"Thank you for calling IAA. Shalom."

Somewhere in Jerusalem

The phone number and name displayed on the phone was familiar and was answered with, "Hey."

"Hey, yourself. What was going on at the dig today? I could see the commotion and something being put in a crate."

"Yeah. Gabriel went all ape shit over a sealed jar we found in a ruined wall."

"Really? What do you know about it?"

"I heard him or Marty say it had writing on it they couldn't read. They were taking a bunch of pictures to send to Vanderbilt, I think. When he was going ballistic he was saying it had to contain something valuable or whoever left it in the wall wouldn't have gone to so much trouble."

"Interesting. And this is a first century ruin, right?"

"Yeah, I've heard them say some stuff they found

dates to the first century."

"What did they do with the jar?"

"Took it to their warehouse I suspect. Really nowhere else to take it."

"Very good. Keep your eyes open. Take a look at your checking account tomorrow; the balance will have grown--magically."

"Thanks. Always glad to be the eyes and ears of businessmen, especially those with a keen sense of appreciation for loyalty."

"You're welcome. Talk to you later."

"Okey, dokey." They both disconnected.

CHAPTER 4

The Warehouse and Workshop

I was waiting for the pickup, an old Ford imported from the US of A, and something of a clunker, but good enough for their purposes. The team owned the Ford and stored it in the warehouse between seasons. When pressed, I couldn't even remember how we acquired it--or when. It was only driven back and forth from the dig or maybe to the hotel where Marty and I stayed. We expected it to give up the ghost at any time, but it was all we could afford. I had arrived on my little Vespa that had smoked its way down the too narrow streets, fought the traffic and won, beating the truck by fifteen minutes at least.

Our warehouse was in the low rent district along with other dig headquarters and other kinds of normal warehouse businesses in some industrial park. The original use of the building was forgotten by everyone, but it was perfect for the team. On the front of the building, there was one large roll up cargo door and one regular door. There were no windows on the front and no back door on the place. There was a row of windows high up on the two side walls, though. They were dirty but they let in a little natural light and kept nosy people from seeing in. You might expect skylights, like you often see in the movies, but there were none.

Inside, the space was wide open except for three rooms: one large secure workshop, one office and one unisex restroom. All three were across the back wall of the building. The room walls were probably ten feet tall with an open area above the rooms going up another ten or so feet to the steel bar joist roof support. The warehouse had air conditioning, but it was not used much; too costly. There were ceiling fans on long pipes doting the room, which could stir up the hot air and make the place tolerable. Several crude wooden worktables were sprinkled around in the open warehouse; sturdy, wooden shelves built of two by fours and plywood on which were stored finds took up the rest of the space. I had opened the warehouse door as well as the workshop door in anticipation of the truck. The truck backed inside and did its little cough and sputter run on when Marty turned it off. As Marty climbed from the driver's side, Gabriel said,

"Let's get this thing into the workshop. I'm eager to see what we've got."

Marty replied, "I know it's been a long dry spell since we had something 'marketable,' but we have to pace ourselves with this. The crate is safe here till morning. It's not uncommon for you to not come to the dig every day. Ask one of the staff you can trust to come in tomorrow and help you with this." We talked as we off loaded the crate and headed to the workshop.

"Good plan. I'll need somebody who can take pictures. Who else do we have besides Trevor? Damn it! What's his last name? I am drawing a blank!"

"Wiley. His last name is Wiley."

"Right. Damn it. I hate it when I go blank on names like that, especially when I've known someone so long."

"Here's what I suggest," Marty said without commenting on Gabriel's memory. "Let Trevor come here and put some second string photog at the dig, maybe Ellie. Trevor is the pro and we need the first team here. If something else big shows up at the dig, we can always call Trevor in. I'll call him later to set it up and to get him to name his choice to take pictures at the dig. By the way, you need to take a course on how to remember names. Me, I think your lousy memory for names is a charming little professorial quirk. Some of the GA's, however, take it personally when you can't remember—especially their first names. Just a friendly FYI."

"Yeah, I know. I've always had a problem with remembering names. I hate it, but that's just the way it is."

We sat the crate near the worktable on the floor, happy to get it in and safe. Marty went on, "Let me say this too, when you're ready to unseal that mother, you better call me!" Giving me a playful punch on the shoulder, he added, "If you open it without me, I'll never forgive you. Hell maybe **I'll** rat us out."

I got it. He wanted to be here and I wouldn't have it any other way and told him so. I also suggested we get cleaned up and get some rest because I wanted to start very early in the morning. "Tell Mr. Wiley--look I remembered--to be here by 6:00 a.m., clear-headed and camera ready to fire away. Also, I'd like him to e-mail the pix he took of the inscription at the site to Marge at Vandy tonight. I'll e-mail her and tell her to be expecting it and what we need from her and her minions. Can do?"

"Sure. No problem. I know he won't mind, especially if you can remember his name in the morning. Look, I'm dog-tired and the adrenaline is about burned off. I'm out of here."

"Hey Marty, thanks for trying to calm me down earlier today. I don't know why I'm acting so nuts, but it's over. From now on it's the usual patient, meticulous me."

"Good, 'cause I was about to deck that other bastard." He hopped in the truck, gave me a smile and a wave, and cranked it up. I went to the office in the southern corner of the warehouse just to sit for a few minutes and think. We had a little window air conditioner in the office because we kept a few things that needed a little more stable temperature than we could get in the warehouse. It was stuck in a hole in one of the back wall of the warehouse and it rattled away, straining against the outside heat. Still, the little cooling it pumped out felt better than being at the dig. I had to figure out why I was so invested in this find that I would throw my professionalism out the window. Or at least, I needed to quit doing it. After a few minutes, when I realized I wasn't thinking about that at all because I'm not that introspective, I decided to just get a grip and quit doing it.

I had things to do. I needed to get to the hotel to send an e-mail to Marge to be on the look out for the high res pix from Trevor. Then, I decided I really didn't need to do anything more, including thinking about sweaty tee shirts. Although as I decided not to think about them anymore, I noticed I did anyway. Not just the shirt though. Nicki looked pretty good. *Enough*, I reminded myself.

Teachers and students do not make good couples. In fact, it could be a lawsuit just waiting to happen.

I secured the place and hopped on my little Vespa. It cranked on the first try and in fifteen or twenty minutes, with most of the rush hour traffic gone, I was at the hotel. The elevator was on the first floor, and shortly, I was in my apartment. First things first. I went straight to the laptop and fired it up. I jiggled the wireless mouse and entered the hotel Wi-Fi code, got a connection and called up my e-mail program. I read a couple of unimportant ones, deleted one with a joke about a rabbi, a priest and an archeologist--was kind of funny though--and hit New Message. Thirty minutes later I was relishing a tepid shower and thinking about food. At that moment I didn't realize life wasn't going to be this simple and basic again for a very long time. Probably a good thing or I might have bolted and run right then.

CHAPTER 5

Outside the Hostel

The heat of the day was lifting as the sun inched lower. Nighttime in Jerusalem in the summer would seldom feel cool, but the baking heat of the day tended to moderate some. Fewer cars were on the streets pumping out less heat and stink. A light was blinking on here and there, already pushing the impending darkness away. The hostel door opened and Nicki stepped out. Josh was waiting on the walkway.

"Hope you haven't been waiting long," Nicki said.

"Nope. Just got here myself."

"There's a little cafe a short walk from here that I go to on special occasions. That okay with you?" asked

Nicki.

"Sounds great."

"I'm flattered that you think this is a special occasion; I know I sure do," he said. Nicki reached over and tugged at his collar that had twisted a bit and Josh thanked her. He smiled an even bigger smile at this small, intimate act.

Josh had changed into chinos and a blue button down dress shirt with the collar open. His hair was still a bit unruly, but in a more stylish way. His sockless feet were in loafers. Josh was a little under six feet, average build, but a nice flat tummy. His dark hair had a few highlights thanks to his vanity and Clairol for Men. He was tanned, of course, because you didn't work in the Israeli sun and not get a tan. Most women thought him handsome in an indefinable sort of way.

Nicki had chosen her one nice sundress and was wearing her long hair down. Her thong sandals showed off her freshly painted nails. Josh looked pleased. He had noticed Nicki a while back but was a involved with another GA named Melinda. That went south a week or so ago when Melinda said, "no," and he thought she meant "try harder." Nothing happened, but after slapping him and lecturing him about his disrespect for her and for women in general, seeing them as nothing but objects, conquests, just someone to give him pleasure, she stormed off yelling over her shoulder, "You selfish, egotistical bastard!" He let her go; he knew there would be other women; there always were. When looking around for a replacement for Melinda, Nicki stood out from the rest. She was a beautiful woman, maybe a little older than the typical GA. He hadn't made his move; instead he just observed, just chatted casually on the bus, that sort of thing. Today's dust up was the perfect excuse to act. He had apparently decided on the bus to change tactics, to shift away from criticizing Gabriel to being supportive of Nicki.

As they settled into the cafe and after they placed their drink orders, he looked at her more closely as she studied the dessert menu. "No meal was complete without dessert," she explained, "and some take a while to prepare, so we need to decide early."

Her blond hair hung to shoulder length, with a little curl, just enough to avoid the straight look, but not enough to need a straightener when she shampooed. No roots showing suggested she was not a bottle blonde, but rather a natural with some lovely sun-induced highlights. She had the lightest touch of makeup that complimented her blue eyes. There were some crinkles at the edges of her eyes that seemed out of place on a graduate student. Her nails were understandably short--long nails and digging don't mix. No polish; again, no surprise there. But her hands looked a little more veined that one might have expected. In short, she looked older than a typical grad student.

Josh decided he'd have to find out. Then he noticed something he'd missed. On the ring finger of her left hand was what was unmistakably a wedding ring. *What the hell!* he thought. *She's married! How could I have missed that?*

As she laid the menu aside, Josh recomposing himself said, "You know, I don't really know much about you. In fact, as I think about it, I can't remember seeing you around the Department back at Vandy. What's the story? Incoming?"

She laughed an appreciative little laugh. "You haven't seen me there because I'm not enrolled. I'm a volunteer. I've never done anything like this, and when I saw the announcement in the *Biblical Archeology Review* about digs needing volunteers, I looked into it and here I am."

"So you just chucked hearth and home and plunked down big bucks to dig in the dirt?" Josh said with an engaging smile.

"Not exactly. The hearth had grown cold and home seemed to be wherever I wanted it to be."

"A cold hearth. How sad. How'd the fire go out if you don't mind my asking?"

"I don't usually talk about it much. My husband was killed when his private plane was trying to fly around a storm on the way home from a business meeting. He, the co-pilot, and a couple of business associates all died. The FAA thought maybe wind shear slammed into them and they were already too low. Not much left the investigators said."

"Oh my God! I'm so sorry. I didn't mean to pry. Oh my God! I feel so bad for you, Nicki."

"It's okay Josh, I'm not over it, but I'm making progress I guess. He was mostly married to his business--Taylor Capital Management--a venture capital firm, primarily. I wasn't exactly a trophy wife, but certainly felt like arm candy now and then. When I had his attention, he couldn't have been sweeter and more loving. Getting his attention as much as I wanted was the problem."

"He had his priorities misplaced, if you don't mind my saying so."

"That's sweet, Josh. But I kind of knew what I was getting into. I think that's why I'm healing as quickly as I am. I knew the relationship was essentially one-sided and I married him anyway. He was wonderful in the courtship; clearly adored me, but he could only put business on hold so long. The upside is he left me, well comfortable, I guess is the way you'd put it. That's how I can afford to be here. I shuttered the house and hopped on a plane."

"No kids then?" Josh wondered, because this was starting to get very interesting.

"No kids. We didn't marry until I was in my early thirties." She twirled her simple wedding ring around her finger as she talked. "We didn't consider starting a family until we had time together and then I didn't want to start a family in my late thirties which was fine with him. He was a bit older, well a lot older. So here I am, in my late thirties and untethered. Free to roam, so to speak."

"Ah, a roamer! Where do you want to roam? What's on your bucket list?"

"You might be surprised to know that I studied archeology as an undergrad and had begun a master's before I met my husband. I was thinking about returning to finish my degree, so this dig seemed a way to find out if I really wanted that. That's part of the reason I felt so stupid after making my comment today. I know better."

"I've got to say, Nicki, you're full of surprises. I would never have guessed you to be in your late thirties. And, don't take this the wrong way, but you haven't acted rich," as he put air quotes around the word, "since you've been here. You suffer like the rest of us in our cheap hostel when you could probably spring for at least a Holiday Inn Express. I'm impressed!" She laughed.

Josh took the linen napkin from his lap and laid it on the table. "Will you excuse me for a minute. This may be TMI, but nature calls." She nodded her permission, and Josh walked toward the restrooms in the back of the restaurant.

CHAPTER 6

At the Restaurant

When he returned to the table, Nicki was smiling, obviously enjoying her evening. He decided this was all getting better and better: a lonely, intelligent widow who was testing the waters and who, just happened to be...comfortable. Josh wondered how much it would take to be "comfortable." He reasoned if her husband was a private plane flying, international VC dude, that wreck left her with some loot. He decided he needed more information.

"Want to hear something funny," he asked and without waiting said, "I don't even know your last name. By the way, mine's Haffey, Josh Haffey."

"Mr. Haffey, it's nice to meet you. I'm Nicki Taylor." They shook hands across the table as if meeting for the first time both laughing.

The salads arrived. She had suggested the *salat hatzilim*, an eggplant salad served with *tania*--a sesame seed paste--garlic, lemon juice, onions, herbs and spices. The eggplant is grilled over an open flame. This was clearly not the Burger King burger Josh usually ate, but he thought: *what the hell, she treating so I'll just force it down.* A few bites into it and he realized it was quite good.

Josh believed he now had what he needed. Her last name, her husband's occupation, and Google. Soon he'd know more about Ms. Nicki Taylor than she could have imagined. Small talk occupied the rest of the meal that was built around a fish he'd never encountered, gilthead sea bream called locally *dinisse.* The fish was served whole, and in this case grilled, dressed only with freshly squeezed lemon juice. *Very tasty*, he thought, *just like Ms. Taylor.*

"Since we're revealing secrets, so to speak," she said, "I thought you and Melinda were an item, yet here we are."

"Melinda, ah yes. Well, we did hang out a lot, but it wasn't serious. Nothing developed; the relationship just kind of petered out."

Nicki smiled and said, "My good fortune, I guess. You might not have decided 'to go all caveman' today if you were wrapped up with her," flirting with him a little. She quickly changed the subject before Josh could say anything. "Josh, you've been with Dr. Gabriel a while, right?"

"What? Sure. Yeah, I'm closing in on qualifying exams and then I'll be ABD."

"ABD?"

"All but dissertation. The last barrier to the degree and the good life, you know, 'real job' hunting."

"What's his story? I mean I've read his professional bio: Phi Beta Kappa undergraduate at SMU, then study under Carol and Eric Myers at Duke for his Ph.D. A couple of important digs and finds, *etcetera*, but what's the untold story about him?"

Josh wasn't interested in talking about Gabriel, but if Nicki was, so be it. "Well let's see. You know from his bio his first name is Stephen and his middle initial is S. Know what the "S" stands for? You're not going to believe it: Saint. Stephen Saint Gabriel. He won't answer to Stephen, Steve and certainly not to Saint. Said to hate all those names. That's why those close to him call him Gabby or Gabe."

Nicki chuckled, "'Saint' sure doesn't seem to fit him. And I can't see him being a martyr like Stephen. I wonder if there is big angelic announcement he's going to make in keeping with his name?"

"Maybe he did that when he said that he can make or break a career?" Josh cracked.

"Yeah!" She laughed. "Tell me more?"

"He's divorced. Mrs. Saint didn't care for a marriage in which a piece of broken pottery was more important than she was or in which he spent months at a time away. I don't think she ever came with him to a dig, at least not since I've known him. No kids. Was a *wunderkind* in college and graduate school, as you already seem to know. Did a post doc fellowship with the Myers and when a position at Vandy opened up about twenty years ago, their recommendation put him at the top of Vanderbilt's list."

Josh went on, "Up the ladder pretty quickly. Published a lot of good stuff apparently and made some very lucky finds. But to give him credit, he also seems to know where to look. That makes him pretty good at getting grants and strong arming flush alums to cough up some operational bucks."

Nicki took her last bite of fish, laid the fork across the right side of the plate at an angle with her knife beside it and said, "Married to his work too, huh?"

"Yeah, looks that way. He's a good guy, I suppose. I've never seen him act like he did today. Mid-life crisis I guess; he must be 45 or 50. He can be pretty focused and in class, he can be the prototypical absent-minded professor. Can't remember names for shit and sometimes forgets to show up for class."

"Enough about him. Let's get dessert." And with that, she seemed to be finished with Gabby. Josh was relieved. He needed her to focus on him.

As they walked back to the hostel, Nicki said, "I don't usually eat this way over here, but tonight seemed special since you had tried so hard to defend me. Burgers or hummus just wouldn't do." She smiled the biggest smile of the evening as she spoke. He couldn't quite tell if she meant it or if she were making fun of him a little. He decided to take the best meaning possible from it and replied,

"Thank you milady," said with a silly little bow pretending to sweep the ground with an imaginary hat, "I must go to the rescue of any damsel in distress. Can't help myself."

She laughed as they reached the hostel door. "Here we are," Josh allowed. "I've got a little errand to run or I'd walk you to your room and make this a proper date--even if you did pick up the tab. By the way, a considerable tab too, not that I was paying attention. When it's my turn, we'll need to go in a different direction." He hoped he'd have a turn. *Hell*, he thought, *I'll even overspend to have a turn.*

"Sounds fair. Thanks, go run your errand and I'll see you tomorrow." She leaned over and gave him a chaste little peck on the cheek. He got a whiff, just the slightest whiff, of a very nice scent. A scent he'd remember.

Josh's little errand took him to the nearest Internet cafe. He gave the kid behind the desk his Visa card, got his access code, and logged on to Google. In the search box, he typed *Taylor, plane* and even before he typed *crash* he had hits. Near the top of the list was what he was looking for. Her husband had a Wikipedia entry! Josh clicked on the link and found himself looking at a picture of a middle aged, good-looking guy. Scanning the entry, he found gold:

"At his death, Mr. Taylor was rumored to have been worth many hundreds of millions of dollars, perhaps as much as a billion. His only heir was his wife, the former Nicole English. It is known that many of his assets were in trust for her, so the details are not public. It is also known that she continues to own homes on Long Island--her primary residence--a summer retreat on Lake Michigan, and at least one home in England. The company, Taylor Capital Management, a venture capital business, in which he was the majority stockholder, continues under the leadership of his former partners. Ms. Taylor has a financial interest in the company, but just what size interest is unknown since it is a privately held company. It is likely she inherited his interest and that the other partners benefited from a key-man insurance policy on his life."

Holy shit, I've hit the mother lode! He reread the entry again, especially the part about Nicki and logged out. *Here I am thinking I can get a little nookie and I've found the fairy godmother! I have got to play this so cool. It would be so rad to be a kept man!*

CHAPTER 7

The Rockefeller In Jerusalem, The Next Morning

"Good morning. Rockefeller Museum. How may I direct your call?"

"The IAA please."

"One moment."

"IAA. How may I help you?"

"The Director-General please."

"Just a moment."

"Director-General's office."

"May I speak to the DG please? It's important."

"I'm sorry, Mr. Doormann is unavailable. May I take a message or would you like his voicemail?"

"No. No message. When will he be available?"

"He didn't leave word when he'll return. He checks his voicemail when he's out."

"No voicemail, thanks. I'll try later. Shalom."

At Gabriel's Hotel

My night was restless. I wanted to sleep, needed to sleep, but my mind kept playing with the "what ifs" of this find. I had managed to conjure up some pretty radical possibilities, all of them wonderful. Finally, sometime after 1:30 AM I wore myself out and drifted off to sleep. My sleep was punctuated with dreams about the find and all of them were about bad things happening. Of course they were bizarre things, like most dreams. In mine, the jar shattered and demons flew out of it; the jar began to glow and lightening struck out of it; shit like that. When my alarm sounded at 5:00 AM, I wasn't sure I could drag myself out of bed. I did, of course. I turned on the coffee and jumped in the shower, deliberately making it colder than normal. I wasn't human as I walked out of the apartment, but I was better than a zombie.

At the Dig Warehouse

I had called Ellie the night before, to ask her to assist me while Trevor took pictures. She had arrived early on her scooter. With her experience, I thought she would be an asset. Trevor had a lot of experience too, but I needed his photography skills more than his other skills. I hated to think of his graduating.

Ellie and I had snipped the strapping and opened the crate. She already had prepared a foam cradle on the worktable inside the workroom to receive the jar. We removed the bubble wrap and were ready to place the jar in the cradle. We had decided to place it on its side to lessen the danger of it tipping as we worked and to more easily get at the lid. Trevor had arrived about the same time as Ellie and was snapping away; he also had a video camera focused on where we were working. Occasionally, he'd adjust the angle or focus on it. He had set up a couple of lights to improve the high res shots of the jar, especially the inscription. He'd already sent the shots he took yesterday back to Marge. As we did the next steps, he was going to send the better lit images of the writing on the jar shoulder.

We did all the usual tedious measurements with tapes and calipers and recorded them in the field book. A visual examination of the exterior of the jar revealed nothing remarkable. It appeared to have been thrown on a wheel which was common. The clay was consistent in color with other pottery of the period--light mud tan. There were no decorations--only the two words near the lip of the jar. With better light, we were able to make out several more letters, but rather than speculate, we were going to wait to hear from Marge. I had told her in last night's e-mail that this was a high priority and she should text me as soon as she had something.

We examined the lid. As we saw at the dig, pitch had been pressed into the space between the lip and the lid in an attempt perhaps to waterproof it. The pitch was cracked here and there, but generally had held together, making an apparently good seal. Somebody had gone to a lot of trouble. That was good news. I declared that we had done all the outside work that could reasonably be done. We'd been at it since 6:00 AM. It was past time for lunch. We decided to eat and I called Marty and told him to come over. I guessed by the time we were finished with our hummus and pita bread sandwiches I'd brought for us, he'd arrive and off would come the lid. That was the plan. I kind of thought I heard God laughing, but decided it was the creaking of the warehouse as it heated up in another blazing day's sun.

CHAPTER 8

At the Dig, The Present

They were expanding the pit not far from the niche in which the jar had been found the day previously. As Andy Kelly, one of the contract workers at the dig, cleared more dirt from the shallow pit, attempting to deepen it, he found a patch of intact plaster on the walls. That was no surprise. The team was sure the walls had been plastered. But, there was something that was a surprise. Andy noticed a crack in the plaster that ran almost vertically for about two-thirds of a meter and then made a sharp turn to the right. He knew that's not usually how cracks form from settling or building trauma. He slipped his trowel edge into the crack a couple of millimeters and wiggled it slightly. The plaster wiggled. At that point, Andy popped up his head like a prairie dog and scanned for Marty.

Marty was nearby helping another GA decide where to dig next and turned when Andy called out. "Marty, I wonder if you could help me a minute," thinking *I'm not going to be responsible for repeating yesterday's scene. Low key. That's the ticket. Low key.*

"Sure, be right there." Marty dusted himself off a bit, and climbed from the test pit. "We're finished here anyway." A few strides later, he's into the pit with Andy and said, "What's up?"

"I'm not sure, but watch this." He repeated the little wiggle with the trowel. "I think without too much effort, I can pop off the plaster. Ordinarily, I wouldn't bother you, but the shape of the crack makes me wonder what's it's covering. Building cracks don't often occur at ninety degree angles to each other."

Andy had dig experience on other digs, but this was the first time he'd worked for Gabriel and Marty. He seemed bright, eager, and knowledgeable. He was a US citizen, but had moved to Israel because, he said, the opportunity to work in the Holy Land was important to him. He made it apparent, almost to the discomfort of the other dig workers, that he was devout Christian. He was in Jerusalem because Jesus had been here. He claimed being in the Holy Land had strengthened his faith even more. He seemed sincere. On one occasion he had been asked by

Marty to do some work on a Sunday and he explained he couldn't on the Lord's Day. Gabriel and Marty didn't care about Andy's religion one way or another. His experience? Yes, they cared a lot about that and he had good *bona fides* in that area.

Marty leaned in to see the crack more clearly. "Yeah. I see what you're talking about. Got your cell phone with you? Snap a few pictures. I don't want to call over the photographer yet." Andy clicked a few pix and then Marty said, "Do the honors." Andy slipped the trowel edge into the crack and applied a little leverage. A large, roughly rectangular chunk of plaster came loose. Andy eased it onto his hand and slowly pulled it away from the wall. What they saw next changed everybody's plans for the day.

CHAPTER 9

At the Warehouse

My cell rang, or rather played its stupid little tune, and I saw it was Marty. "Hey Marty, I was just about to call you. We're ready. Get your butt over here."

"Gabby, there's been a development at the site. I think you might want to come here instead."

"What the hell? And leave the jar? Are you nuts? We're **ready**! You know: ***ready!***"

"I think we've found another niche not far from the first one. Andy was clearing debris away from the wall and we found a patch. When we removed it, it was clear that flat stones had been inserted into an opening in the wall and plastered over. I suspect this is exactly like the way the other niche was closed in."

I couldn't speak. Another niche! Another jar? Holy Toledo. What was going on? "I'm on my way. You know the drill. Document everything."

Marty interrupted, "Already done, plus nobody else at the site knows about it."

"Okay. Good. Get Andy to piddle in the pit, but don't disturb anything. You wander away; stay close but don't draw any more attention. When I get there, I'm going to the trailer first and spend a few minutes, and then I'll find you. We'll go from there."

"Got it. Act as if nothing's happened. Hurry!"

"Guys," I said to Ellie and Trevor, "I've got to run to the dig. Trevor, I'd like you to bring your high-res camera and come too. Ellie, do you mind staying here and watching things for an hour or so?" She was glad to do it. She said she had some work she could do on an artifact we'd found earlier, so she wouldn't be bored.

Jerusalem traffic has become a nightmare. There is an "unofficial" official attempt to make vehicular traffic so unpopular in Jerusalem's center that people will finally give up and take the bus. The man in charge of traffic and infrastructure has actually said publically, "I shall make you miserable." He's narrowed all approaches to one lane. He created a plaza that further impedes traffic flow. At one point, he's merged two lanes into one, even though there is no good reason to do so. If an emergency occurs and the traffic needs to move out of the way for emergency vehicles, they can't. He's installed concrete posts lining the streets on both sides, "To protect the pedestrians." This is why I ride my scooter.

Even so, if it's not a nightmare, it's at least a bad dream. I find myself squeezing between cars in a way that pisses them off and then jumping to the sidewalk to get by a particularly congested area. Pedestrians seem to take a dim view and make obscene gestures at me, but I can make progress that way. Finally, when I emerged from the worse of it and could see the area of the dig ahead, I slowed down and tried to act normal.

I wheeled into the spot near the trailer under the awning where I usually park and hopped off. Trevor was less than three minute behind me. Casually waving to a few diggers, I unlocked the trailer and went inside. I needed my arrival to look as if nothing important had summoned me back.

It was hot in the trailer. I flicked on the a/c unit and fiddled at my desk for a few minutes. I grabbed the cloth hat I wear on site, wet it in the sink as I usually do, plopped it on my head and walked outside. I didn't go directly to Marty. I stopped at a couple of other pits and chatted with the diggers. I have no idea what we talked about. Finally, after what seems like the amount of time it took the earth to cool, I wandered over to Marty. Trevor was close behind me.

The three of us walked over to the pit, jumped in, and there it was. Clearly flat stones and small pieces of rubble had been placed in a rectangular opening. Bits of plaster still stuck to some of it. “Okay, Marty, let’s start removing the ones at the top so we can look inside.”

He loosened a couple of small stones and shone his small Maglite in the opening. “Hot damn! It looks like another jar with a lid!”

“Let me have a look.” That’s exactly what it was. Even though debris and dirt had dropped into the niche, it wasn’t as full as the other had been. The lid was clearly visible. “Okay. Let’s think a minute. Do we take it out and have two jars to examine at the same time, or do we leave it?” I was thinking out loud. “If we leave it, there’s danger someone will loot it, even if we cover this part of the wall again. If we take it, we’ll never keep these finds quiet. We take it. We can’t risk having some idiot loot it.”

Marty quickly agreed and I told Trevor to document our removal of the rest of the stones and the jar. I called Andy over and sent him back to the trailer to see if we had another crate and bubble wrap. “Andy, if there is no crate, just bring the wrap.” As he started away, I said, “Wait! Just bring the wrap; forget the crate. Maybe that will help us downplay this. And Andy--obviously don't say anything to anybody."

Quickly Marty and I began to scoop away the debris that was up about a quarter of the way on the jar. It was clear the lid had been sealed on this one as well. My heart was pounding and my mouth was dry. We had it free by the time Andy was back with a roll of wrap. "Double a big chunk of that wrap and lay it down. We'll put the jar on it and then mummify this thing with the rest of it. Marty, you and Andy take it to the pickup and put it on the floor of the front seat, please. Marty, take it to the warehouse right now, but go alone. Ellie is there and she can help you if you need it. I'll wander around to the other pits to downplay what we're doing. Oh, one more thing, get started on the processing, pix, drawings, everything we always do. We've got to move fast. Trevor, wait five minutes after Marty leaves and then you go back to take the pictures. I'll be there as soon as I can." As I climbed from the pit and dusted myself off, I wondered what in God's name had we found here? I guessed we'd have a pretty good idea soon enough.

Josh was watching all the action unfold from another pit. "Nicki, look over your shoulder. There goes Marty and Andy with a big bundle heading for the pickup." Josh had managed to get himself assigned to the pit where Nicki was working.

Nicki had her nose buried in whatever she was excavating, but turned around. "What'd you think it is, Josh?"

"Something out of the ordinary. Looks like they're taking it to the warehouse right now rather than waiting till the end of the day. That's unusual. And it's kind of big too, not like a shard or something like that. Hell, do you think it's another jar?" Josh stood up to get a better look. Andy and Marty gently placed the bundle on the floor of the front seat, exchanged a few words and then Marty went around to the driver's side and got in. "As soon as he's off site, I'm heading over to Andy to see what he knows. Oops. Maybe not; here comes the Saint."

Gabriel stopped at another pit, so Josh stretched his back and settled again onto his haunches and started scrapping dirt. "Odd that Gabriel would stay here while Marty drove off with the package. Maybe it's not as big a deal as I thought," he said to Nicki.

"I guess we'll find out when they're ready to tell us," Nicki said. "Oh, look!" she fairly shouted, "This looks like a ring!" She put aside her trowel and picked up a brush and dustpan and began sweeping dirt from the possible ring.

Josh came over and kneeled down. "You're right, it does look like a ring."

Gabriel walked up just then and said, "Hey, how's it going you two?"

"Hey Dr. Gabriel. Going pretty well," Nicki said. "I think I've just found a ring."

"Her first find," Josh volunteered.

"Neat!" Gabby said. "Let me get down there and take a look."

He joined them in the pit. Josh moved a little to give him some room and he quickly was on his knees. He pushed his glasses up on his nose and pushed his hat back a little. Josh noticed that Nicki was looking at Gabriel and not the ring. "Good eye, er, uh, Nicki." Gabriel was obviously proud of himself for remembering her name.

"Thank you, Dr. Gabriel!" She was clearly pleased by the compliment.

"Let me see a pick for a second." Gabriel said. "Hmm, might be an earring. It's at floor level too. Here's my story: lady who lived here, rushes out as the house is being torched. In the scramble, she loses an earring?" Smiling he said, "How's that for going well beyond the facts?"

Josh wondered: *Is the asshole coming on to her?*

"Okay," the teacher coming out in Gabriel, "What do you do next, now that you have it exposed?"

"I brush away more dirt, use the pick to remove as much as I can, then I'll use my trowel to gently lift it, then slide it into the little baggie." She produced one from the pocket of her shorts. "I'll write on the baggie what it is and where I found it and then add my initials."

"Well done! Pretty savvy for a volunteer."

She blushed a little. "I know more than you probably think I do," she said, "I have an undergraduate degree in archeology and most of a master's."

"Do you? I must have missed that when we were screening volunteers. Neat."

"Well, I never met with you. Marty and talked on the phone and I sent my application straight to him. And I came directly to the site rather than coming in with everybody else. I was in England."

"Ah. Well, that explains it. Keep up the good work," as he stood and brushed the dust from his pants. He began to climb from the pit.

"Hey Doc, what was in the bundle I saw them carry to the truck," Josh asked as innocently as he could.

"Uh...It was a piece of plaster with a bit of a fresco on it. We, uh, wanted to get it back to the workshop quickly. Pretty fragile."

"No kidding. A fresco. What'd it look like," *you*

lying bastard "thought Josh.

"Maybe a flower and some leaves. Still had a good bit of dirt on it. We'll need to clean it up before we can be sure. Well, see you guys later," he said and then turned and walked away.

I bet he's thinking he's gotten away with something, Josh thought. It was no piece of plaster, Josh was sure of that much. Josh decided to not tell Nicki of his suspicion. He had decided that as soon as the Saint was in the trailer he was going to the pit from which they took the artifact and see what was left. And it didn't take long to give him the chance. Gabriel made one more stop and then he headed for the trailer.

"Back in a sec, Nicki. Need a potty break."

"Oh. Sure." Nicki was busy with her find.

The more or less shortest way to the Porta-Potty would take him pretty close to the pit he wanted to inspect so he wouldn't look too suspicious. He made a show of mopping his brow on his tee shirt and cut a quick glance to his left. *I'll be damned!* He thought, *It's another niche! And I'd bet my left testicle it's another jar. Hooyah!*

CHAPTER 10
In the Dig Trailer

I sat in the trailer still a bit in shock. What have we stumbled onto, I wondered? What if there are other jars? I needed to get out of here and get back to the workshop. My cell chirped; it was Marge.

"Hey Marge, you're working late, it must be what 10:00 PM. What's up?"

"Hey Gabby. Yeah, it's a little later than I'd like, but once I got started on your photos, I didn't want to quit. Plus, I knew you were eager to hear something and I didn't want to text you."

"You're right. I'm eager. I'm beyond eager. Things are getting pretty interesting here. May have some more pix waiting in the morning."

"Oh? Well, that sounds promising. Look Gabby,

I'm pooped. Let me just tell you what we think we have and I'll email the full report as soon as it's finished."

"Sure, sure. I really appreciate your dedication."

"Oh, you owe me; don't think you don't. But listen; our best guess is the inscription is Greek. Well that's not a guess. We know that for sure. But our best guess of a translation is something like 'Mariamne's Memories.'"

"What?"

"Wait, there's more. Using all our technical shit and some black magic, we found something else was first written where the word 'memories' is written. Looks as if it was partially scratched off and then written over. I'm less sure about this, but we can make out what might be an *epsilon, upsilon, nu* and then some letters we can't read with what we've tried so far. At the end of the word is what looks to be *iota, omicron,* and maybe an another *nu.*"

I was writing down the letters as she called them out. E..u..n..something, something..i..o...n. What the heck? Then it hit me.

"Marge, the word is *euangelion:* 'good news'. Somebody wrote *Mariamne's Good News* and then scratched it to read *memories* instead."

"Gabby, that's what we're thinking; I just didn't want to bias you. That's why I couldn't stop trying different lights, filters and whatever black or white magic I could conjure. I'd really need to be working from the jar itself to be sure, but I'm pretty sure already."

"Wait a minute, Marge. The so-called *Gospel of Mary* has traditionally been dated around 120-180 A.D. We're pretty sure this house was destroyed in the sack of Jerusalem in 70. The time frame doesn't fit."

"I thought about that. Here's my best guess as your chief resident geek and conjurer: This ain't the Gnostic *Gospel of Mary*. This is something earlier by a real Mary. I'm guessing you have a manuscript in your jar; a real Gospel by a real Mary."

CHAPTER 11

In the Dig Trailer

"Gabby, are you there?" Marge asked.

I had to sit down. The strength just went out of my legs. I almost dropped my phone. A real Mary, writing a real account of Jesus, almost contemporaneously with his life! If this is real, I have just become the luckiest sumbitch in the world. But, my God, what a shock this is going to be to Christianity, no matter what the manuscript says.

"Yeah. Yeah. Sorry. Just in shock. Listen Marge, anybody working with you has got to be sworn to secrecy like never before. Threaten their first born or something equally precious. Gonads or..."

Marge interrupted, "Gabby, I get it. Clamp down. Hard."

"Yeah. Yeah, I know you get it. I'm sorry. Listen, I need to get to the workshop and get that jar opened."

"Wait, Gabby. You said interesting things were happening. What's up?"

"We found another jar in the same wall. You'll be getting more photos."

At the Warehouse

My life was frequently in danger, if blasting horns and squealing brakes were any indication, as I pushed the little Vespa through the streets of Jerusalem. In far less time than I'd ever made it, I slid to a halt outside the warehouse door. I didn't bother to remove the helmet local laws forced me to wear; I just burst into the warehouse and practically ran to the workshop. The door was open and Marty, Ellie, and Trevor were startled by my entry.

"You're not going to believe this," I started, a little breathlessly. "I just heard from Marge. The inscription on the first jar apparently says 'Mariamne's Memories,' but that's not the best part. It apparently originally said 'Mariamne's Evangelion,' *Mary's Gospel*!"

"Holy Shit! Gabby, this could be the biggest find since the Dead Sea Scrolls!" Marty bounced up and down on his toes, obviously excited.

Ellie and Trevor looked at each other quizzically,

then Trevor said, "But the *Gospel of Mary* isn't something new is it. I mean we could have a new manuscript of it, but the Gospel's been known a long time. Right?"

I finally realized I had the helmet on and began to unstrap it to remove it. "It's not the same. Let me tell you why. The Gnostic *Gospel of Mary* is a late manuscript, several centuries after Jesus. Ours dates from no later than 70. It's almost certain they're not the same."

Ellie interrupted, "Is the *Gospel of Mary* one that depicts Mary Magdalene as one of the apostles, who Jesus singled out to give some secret teaching to?"

"Exactly. We have another story of her from the *Gospel of Philip*. This is the one Dan Brown used to say that Jesus and she kissed on the mouth and were married. The problem is the actual document has a hole in it where "on the mouth" might have been, so that part is just speculation. Still these finds tell us the Gnostic communities held Mary Magdalene in high regard--that's clear--and believed she and Jesus were close. But again, Philip is written too late to be related to whatever we have in our jar."

"If we have a manuscript in our jar—and I'm certain we do—it was written either by Jesus' mother, Mary or by Mary Magdalene. Either way, we've got a potential eyewitness record! This could blow the lid off Christian thought!"

CHAPTER 12
Jerusalem, 61 AD

Mariamne looked up from her reading and out the open window. She felt sure the city she knew for so long would soon be in turmoil. Jewish rebels were stockpiling armaments, preparing for battle. The Romans were cracking down even more ruthlessly than usual. Almost every week, some Jewish patriot was crucified along the main road into the city. At the same time the tension rose in the city, the original community of followers of her Yeshua were growing old and dying. Mariam, his mother, had died only recently and been laid in the tomb where Yosef, her husband, and Joses, her son, and Salome, her daughter, had lain before her. Their bones had already been placed in ossuaries and pushed in to niches in the walls.

Word had come that brother Saul, who had taken the name Paulus after his encounter with Yeshua, had been arrested in Rome. The Empire was annoyed by his traveling and preaching and needed to put an end. Everyone believed he would not escape death. Peter was also in Rome, but the Jerusalem community had received no word from him and feared his fate might be the same as Paulus. *And,* she thought, *I am old. I will not live much longer no matter what happens between Jerusalem and Rome.*

She looked back down at her work. Idly she turned to somewhere in the middle of the bound stack and read what she had written long ago.

Today as we traveled, a leper was coming toward us. He was shouting "Unclean. Unclean," as is our custom to protect us from being made unclean from their disease. He did not move to the side of the road, but stopped in our path. He said, "Who are you?"

Yeshua replied, "I am Yeshua the Nazarene. Who are you?"

The one who spoke said, "I am Julius from Rome. I was a proud centurion in Caesar's army, but now I wander in shame and sickness, my flesh falling away. Are you the Yeshua who is said to heal the sick?"

"I am."

"Heal me, then!" Julius ordered him.

"I didn't come to heal the evil oppressors. I came to the Jews to call them to establish Yahweh's Kingdom."

"I only did what I was ordered to do; I tried to harm no one who was innocent," Julius replied. "Heal me and I will return home and be a man of peace. I will be a part of your god's kingdom."

"Let us pass, as the law requires."

Julius moved aside and we continued walking, coming very close to him, but looking straight ahead. I asked Yeshua why he didn't heal this poor man.

"Be patient, beloved, and see what happens."

We walked another twenty or thirty paces and heard a shout from behind us. "I'm whole! I'm whole!"

I turned to look and Julius was looking at his arms and legs and I could see even from a distance his skin was no longer pocked and running with pus. As I looked, he came running, fell at Yeshua's feet and asked, "Did you do this? How did you do this? How have I been cured?"

Yeshua said, "You believed I could heal you. You obeyed when I asked you to move aside. You wish to be a man of peace. This was enough. Go home to your family in Rome and leave our land in peace. Tell others what happened when you met Yahweh's messenger."

Again, Mariamne looked up from her reading. She could remember every detail of that day and that encounter with Julius the Roman. She remembered how he wept when he realized his life had been restored. He insisted on following Yeshua, but Yeshua told him again to return to Rome and tell others of his miracle. "If you wish to thank me, then tell others to heed the call to establish Yahweh's Kingdom," Yeshua had said.

She closed the bound stack of pages and began to wrap it in a linen cloth. Rachel was bringing a jar later in which to place the pages. Together they would melt pitch and seal the lid. Elijah was coming to seal the jar in the niche in her wall, to plaster over it so it would not show. One day, when the coming conflict was over, others would be able to come and retrieve it. For now, it needed to be protected. Her work was done. She could join Mariam and the others, if Yahweh willed it.

CHAPTER 13

At the Workshop

Ellie still seemed puzzled. "I mean, this would be neat if it were an eyewitness account, but aren't the other Gospels eyewitness accounts?"

"Actually, they're not. The earliest Gospel, Mark, was written around 70 AD, but Mark isn't listed as an apostle or even a follower. Some New Testament scholars believe he was John Mark, the son of another woman named Mary. This Mary was a well to do lady in Jerusalem and early Christians apparently frequented her house. There is some evidence that John Mark met Peter this way and began to make notes of stories Peter told and sermons he preached. Eventually, he turned them into a narrative. Without boring you, just trust me when I say it's very unlikely the other Gospel authors were eyewitnesses."

"I'll be damned. I thought they were," Ellie offered.

"Nope. If the story of John Mark is true, that's as close to an eyewitness as we've got. Soooo, you see why this find could set everything we think we know about Jesus on its ear?"

Marty spoke up, "We're a little ahead of ourselves. We're only assuming the jar has a manuscript. I'll admit it seems likely, but we need to open the jar and actually see what we've got. Gabby, we've got to keep a lid on this until we know more. By the way, I checked the new jar we found. No writing on it, so we have no clue about it. I can hear something moving in it as we move the jar, but it kind of clunks when it moves, as if it's something hard."

"Here's what I think," Marty continued, "After we open it, let's say it's a codex. Trevor does high res shots of every page. If he needs more lights or shit, we buy it for him. Once we've got that done and safely emailed to Marge, we call in IAA and go public."

"That's exactly what I was thinking on the ride over here," Gabriel said. "They are going to take the find from us, but they can't keep the images we send back home. We assemble a team back there and do a detailed study. We'd be way ahead of them." Marty and Gabriel kind of high-fived. They aren't that good at it.

"Trevor, we're going to make you famous because we're going to let you in on the biggest secret the world has ever seen." I told him the plan and finished with, "So whatever equipment you need to do the highest and best professional photography you've ever done, you've got to get. ASAP. What'd you say?"

Trevor said it wouldn't take much. He had most of what he needed in his personal stash back in a locker he had rented. I told him to take the truck, get the stuff from the locker, and buy whatever else he needed. I fished out my personal AMEX card and gave it to him. "If you have a problem when you try to use it, have them call me." He told me he didn't think there'd be a problem because the people at the store he was off too knew him very well and knew he worked for me.

"Great," I said, "Get going. We're going to open the jar. Ellie, sit tight, we've got work for you too."

Marty and I needed to move the second jar to the secure office. We laid it, rewrapped, on the floor and tossed a tarp over it. We returned to the warehouse and I said to Ellie, "You know how to use this video camera?" pointing to Trevor's camera. She did.

"Good. Trevor's got to run an errand, so we need you to document what we're doing. We're going in the workroom and start on the first jar. Shoot away."

Marty and I looked at the pitch seal. We used picks to see if it would snap away cleanly or if we were going to have to try cutting it with a Dremel tool. We were eager, but we forced ourselves to work slowly and carefully. Not much of the pitch came loose. Using the drill meant we were risking damage to the jar and the lid. On the other hand, we were in agreement that whatever was inside was more important than either. Still, we kept picking away hoping we could avoid the drill or use it sparingly. We were at this long enough that Trevor returned. It didn't seem like several hours, but clearly it was. At that point, Ellie switched to stills and Trevor took over the video duties.

Trevor rigged a couple of more lights to give us an even better image quality. After picking, and picking and getting ready to get the cutting tool, I decided to try something else. I remember how Howard Carter had cut Tut's mummy out of his sarcophagus. The linen wrappings were coated with an excessive amount of resins that had stuck the mummy to the bottom of the sarcophagus. Carter heated a spatula like knife with a flame and then cleanly sliced away at the resin. I got a small tank of propane and had Marty hold it while I heated a flat bladed dental tool. It sliced easily through the pitch. I worked quickly so the pitch wouldn't harden and soon I was ready to try to remove the lid. I reached for the handle that was part of the lid, a three-quarter inch high tab kind of thing and tried turning the lid. It moved. We shouted. I turned it some more to whispers of "careful," "easy now," and similar unnecessary cautions. I felt it come loose in my hand. We were ready to remove it. No more assuming or guessing. We were about to *know*.

CHAPTER 14

In the Workshop

I pulled the lid away and set it down. Trevor shone a light into the jar for me. The inside seemed unusually black and there was the faint smell of pitch. I could see the top of something that looked like cloth. "Okay. I need gloves," and quickly snapped on the pair Ellie handed me. While I was gloving up, Marty looked inside and agreed that it looked like cloth. Then he gloved up too. I thought I could reach inside with my fingers and maybe get a grip on the cloth, which now seemed to be wrapping something. The cloth was a deep dingy brownish black color and was stiff to the touch. I slipped the gloved fingers of my right hand on the right side and my left hand on the left side of the cloth covered object and pulled toward me.

Nothing happened. It was stuck. I tried to wiggle it loose. It didn't move. "Marty, please get me the endoscope," I said, wiggling it again. Marty went to the office where we kept it locked up and was back in a minute or two. In the meantime, I had let go and was trying to peer inside. With the endoscope in hand, I snaked it into the space above the bundle. Trevor shone a light in to help. I knew why I smelled pitch. Not only was the jar sealed with pitch, the inside of it was covered in pitch and the bundle was stuck in it. Marty was watching the screen of the endoscope with me.

"Well that's going to be a bitch to get out," he murmured. "I don't think you can use the hot knife trick again. Not enough room."

"Yeah. I think we have three choices. We can pull the bundle out with brute force or we can cut the cloth and try to slide out whatever is inside it. Or, we can smash the jar."

"Oh, I don't like those options," Marty said. "I'd really like to preserve the jar too. Brute force carries too many unknowns. And cutting the wrapping; that's got to be a last resort. Getting it out whole can give us so much more information."

"True." I agreed, "I don't like them either, but I'm

at a loss." Then Trevor spoke up.

"Uh, docs, I have an idea if you want to hear it." We did. "Let try an experiment on the lid. Some of these lights can get pretty warm. Let's see if the light will soften the pitch on the lid like you did with the hot knife. If it does, we can try to do the same to the jar."

"Trevor, I'll never forget your name again! Great idea! Set it up. Plus, let me springboard off that. What if we take a couple of hair dryers and slowly heat the outside of the jar while shining one of your hot lights inside it. Maybe the lights and the jar getting warmed will do it." We agreed it was worth a try.

I sent Ellie to buy four hair dryers while Trevor worked on the lid. Before she got back, it was clear the light would soften the pitch, even as old as it was. We got four dryers because we had decided we needed to heat the jar evenly. We were going to make a cradle to set in it--Marty was already working on that--then station the four dryers around the jar, keeping them set at the same temperature, moving them up and down and slowly increasing the heat. There was risk, no question. But we had decided the bundle was more important than the jar. If we couldn't save the mother, as it were, we were going to save the baby.

After what seemed like hours, I finally looked up from the jar. From the looks of the dim windows, it was dark out. I checked my watch. We'd been at this jar opening for three hours. I was hungry and needed to pee, plus my legs hurt from standing and my arms from holding the dryer. I'm sure I wasn't the only one in bad shape. We had been sticking our fingers in the jar periodically to feel the pitch. It was softening, slowly, but softening. I announced, "I'm going for it." I slipped on the gloves again and climbed up on a stool so I could get above the jar. I reached in and grasping it as before and tried to wiggle it. It wiggled. "It's loose!"

I pulled with a little more force, it moved. "I've got it; it's coming." And it was. It kind of popped loose from the bottom and the side at the same time and I lifted it out.

"Quick, get a tray for me to put this on!" A tray appeared, and I lowered the bundle to its side. As Trevor continued to shoot videos and Ellie stills, Marty and I did some preliminary examination on the bundle. The cloth seemed to be coated or dipped in an oily material--olive oil, petroleum?--couldn't tell. It was stiff and where it folded back in on itself, stuck together. So we have something wrapped in oiled cloth and placed in a pitch lined jar. Clearly, protecting that something from moisture was important.

The bundle measured about ten inches by nine inches and was about four or so inches thick. Assuming it was wrapped in a couple of layers, what lay beneath was about double the size of some of the Nag Hammadi documents, which were also in codex form. Looking good. I got a flat-ended dental tool from the set of picks we kept handy and worried away at the edge of the cloth that was on the side of the bundle. Before I could make any headway, Marty who was looking on said,

"You know Gabby, we should get a textile expert in here. Maybe even have them remove it."

I love Marty and I have lots of respect for him. We've worked together most of our careers. He is careful and professional in everything he does. I value that. But he was starting to get on my last nerve. "Marty, I'm not waiting. The textile is important, sure. But what it wraps is the prize. Want a textile expert? Sure. Right after I get this damn cloth off my book!" Thank goodness I wasn't as loud as I had been at the dig, but I didn't like it that I had turned up the volume at all. More calmly I said, "I'll be very careful. You can get it off if you'd prefer, I don't mind. But it's coming off tonight."

"Gabby, let's stop for a few minutes. We need to get some food. We need to talk. We can work on this thing in a little bit. We're on the same side, buddy, but let's just slow down a minute."

Food. That sounded good and then suddenly, I knew I couldn't wait much longer to pee. I caved, but I was gracious. "Sounds good. An hour won't matter. Hell, we might really need to lock this thing away and come back tomorrow--no really; I'm not being sarcastic. It's waited 2000 years, I can wait over night. We'll all be sharper and rested. Let's order food and talk." As I snapped off the gloves and started to the restroom, I said, "Trevor. Make backup copies of everything you and Ellie have done while we wait for a pizza. Use thumb drives. I've got some in the office if you need them. Also, email everything back to Marge. We'll have enough backups that nobody can screw with our find."

And that's what we did. I peed. We ate. Trevor did his thing. And we talked. I realized Marty was right; one more night wouldn't kill us. But no textile expert. The fewer people who knew, the better. I sent Trevor and Ellie home, again sworn to secrecy. Marty and I cleaned up a little. I locked the workshop door and we were ready to leave. "Marty, go on. I'm going to check something in the office. I'll see you tomorrow."

"Gabby, you're not going to do unwrap that without me are you?"

"No. I swear on Commodore Vanderbilt's statue, I won't."

"Okay. Tomorrow."

I went to the office and unlock it and flopped

down at the desk. Something was gnawing at me. I needed a minute or two to deal with it. I figured out what was troubling me as I sat at the makeshift desk in the office. I had one more thing to take care of before I left. As it turns out, that 'one more thing' was a very smart move.

CHAPTER 15

Somewhere in Jerusalem, 9:00 PM

"Yes?" he said as he answered his phone.

"It's an important find and you'll want it."

"Is that so?"

"It is. The jar was opened today and there was a bundle inside that Gabriel is convinced is a first century codex."

"Where is this codex now?"

"A place I know. I can acquire this codex for you, but given its potential value, it will cost more than usual."

"Oh, really. Perhaps you can tell me where this

place you know is located and I'll get it myself."

"No."

"How much? I think a reasonable fee is $10,000 US up front, plus forty percent of whatever you get for it when you sell it."

"The hell you say?"

"You want it? I can find other buyers."

"Okay, deal. When?"

"Get the money ready. I'll have it soon and will call you."

"Be careful with it. It could mean a lot of money to us both."

"Of course." The conversation ended with that.

CHAPTER 16

The Warehouse, 1:15 AM

The part of town in which the warehouse was located was a kind of industrial park consisting of multiple buildings, all looking pretty much the same--nondescript. Each was separated from the other along the streets on which they were located by a ten foot alley. Each building had a large lamp over the freight door. Most were left on at night, but not all. Apparently, those units that were rented were illuminated; the others were not. The effect was one of intermittent pools of light that punched little holes in the darkness on the stained and cracked concrete ramps in front of each building. Clouds scuttled across the small crescent moon that was only occasionally visible and offered no real light even then. The streets in the industrial park were laid out in a grid pattern and were wide enough to allow eighteen-wheelers to back up to the freight doors, but most businesses took their deliveries from smaller vans these days. The industrial park had long since been vacated by the last of the tenants as they left for the day.

A solitary figure dressed in dark clothes and carrying a backpack draped over one shoulder walked very close to the buildings, moving quickly when reaching a pool of light, head on a swivel, looking for curious eyes. There were none. The person was apparently alone in the unfenced park, free to roam over its acres of buildings. But there was no roaming; there was obviously a destination. Coming to an alley between the dig warehouse and its neighbor, the figure disappeared down the alley, paused a minute or so to adjust to the reduced light.

The front door had a deadbolt lock in the steel door and the light over the door ruled that out any way. The freight door had a padlock; one of those you can shoot with a gun and it won't spring. That was not the way in. The exterior walls were concrete block, which were likely eight inches thick. Each block is essentially hollow and held together with the others by mortar. The backpack held a hammer and a chisel among other tools. The intruder was going to attempt to go through the block wall. Uncertain about how much noise it would make to hammer at the blocks, a few test blows were required. Even if it made some noise, the intruder reasoned there was nobody in the area this time of night.

The figure in dark clothes found the darkest spot available in the alley that was about halfway from front to rear. The hammer and chisel were removed from the backpack. There was also a small Maglite which was could be held in the mouth, pointing a small beam at the wall; *very Macgyver like,* the figure thought. Concrete blocks are two hollow cells, separated by a one-inch concrete web. Attacking the blocks rather than the joints seemed to be the best idea. The hammer was drawn back and a block was stuck. It broke. Moving to the right, the blows were repeated. Same result. Next, the web from between the two cells in the block was knocked out. Surprisingly little noise was being made. *Good*, the intruder thought.

The chisel was placed inside the block with the point against the far wall of the block. There was just enough sticking out to allow the hammer one good solid blow. The other side of the block shattered allowing a look into the darkened warehouse. These blocks were laid so the end of the block above was centered over the block below in a pattern called a running bond. For a hole at least twenty-four inches or so square, six or seven more blocks needed to be removed. If the rest went as quickly as the first, the hole would be big enough to be inside in ten minutes.

As the figure was getting ready to break another

block, there was a noise on the street running in front of the buildings. The figure froze. Looking down the alley toward the road revealed light on the street. There was a moment of panic as the intruder thought, *I'm trapped*! The flashlight went off and the figure lay on the ground to become a smaller target. In a few seconds, a pickup truck moved slowly across the opening of the alley where it intersected the street. The driver was raking a beam of light across the face of the buildings. It was security. The light shone down the alley, passed overhead for only a second and the truck was gone, leaving behind only the sound of music coming from the truck radio; then that faded too. *I should have planned better. Case the joint, as it were instead of Ramboing it. Too close,* the figure thought. *Too close.* The intruder lay there motionless for five minutes to calm the heart rate and to be sure the truck was gone far enough to be unable to hear the hammer at work. Then cautiously the hammering resumed.

With the hole finished, the tools were returned to the backpack that was pushed into the warehouse. The figure wiggled in after the backpack, stood up and instinctively brushed off. The first order of business was to slip on vinyl gloves. *Can't leave fingerprints behind.* With the flashlight on, the beam did a slow pan of the space. Ahead to the right was what was probably the main workshop. As quietly as possible the intruder walked to the workshop. The door was half glass with octagon shaped security wire embedded in the glass. There was a window to each side of the door with the same kind of glass. The flashlight beam pierced through the glass illuminating a large worktable in the center of the room. Nearby was an open crate and the whole table seemed ringed with lights set on tripods. The jar was easy to spot sitting where all the lights would have converged when they were on.

The door was steel, except for the glass, as was the door frame. There was a prominent deadbolt. *I couldn't pick a lock if I had to, so if I'm was going to get in, some glass has to shatter. I don't like it, but what choice do I have.* The intruder dropped the backpack and removed the hammer. The wire in the glass is supposed to make it harder to break and it did. It took several blows and punches at the wire until there was a hole big enough for a hand to reach in and turn the deadbolt. The door was open, the intruder stepped into the workshop and all hell broke loose.

CHAPTER 17

3:01 A.M. At the Agripas Hotel

I'm not charming in the middle of the night when a phone goes off near my ear. "What?" I managed to croak out with my eyes still closed.

"Dr. Stephen Gabriel?"

"Yes."

" This is Prath Security. We have an alarm at your warehouse. Our truck is on the scene and has reported the two exterior doors are secure, but a hole has been knocked in a side wall. Our guy did not enter the building, but looking in he can see an open door to an inside room. We have called the police and they are sending a car."

"I'll be right there. Thank you. Shalom."

I punched "end" and hit speed dial for Marty. As I pulled on some clothes, I filled him in. As quickly as we could, we drove to the warehouse. The police were there as well as the security truck. I showed them my credentials and we walked to the front door. My heart was pounding as I opened it, reached in and flicked on the light, keyed in the alarm to stop the intermittent noise, and, at their instruction, stepped back. The two officers walked in, guns ready. Marty and I looked in and could see the workshop door standing open, the glass broken in one corner near the deadbolt. The security guard was also armed and had followed the police. The three of them made a sweep of the space and in a few minutes, called us to come in.

We headed straight for the workshop. One of the cops asked, "Anything seem to be missing?"

Earlier In the Warehouse

The intruder was startled. The place had motion detectors and they had just been set off. That wouldn't provide much time to take care of business. Moving quickly to the jar the intruder turned it around so the inside could be inspected. Empty. *What the hell?* There was a quick examination of the rest of the room. The crate was empty. There was a metal tray on the table, but it was empty too except for bits of black material and a couple of threads on the tray. *Could be locked in that other room, but no time to find out.* A quick exit was required and the intruder headed for the hole in the wall, backpack in hand. *Damn! So close! So close,* was the last thought as two feet disappeared through the breached wall.

3:35 AM, The Warehouse

I turned on the lights in the workshop. Marty and I did a quick sweep and didn't see anything obvious missing. "Let me check the office." I left the workshop and walked the few feet to my office. The door was locked. The glasse in it and in the two sidelights were intact. Still, I got my keys and opened the door. Flicking on the light showed everything to be as I remembered leaving it. Over in the corner was the bundle from the second niche still covered in a tarp the way it had been left. I turned out the light, walked out and locked the door. "Nothing missing there," I said as I reentered the workshop.

One of the officers said, "I guess when the intruder opened the door and the alarm sounded, he didn't have much time to load up, so he left with nothing. Let me ask you something doctor. You apparently store artifacts from digs here. Is that what they were after, you suppose?"

"I'd say so. Going straight to the workshop makes me think they would know or guess that anything of special importance is locked in there rather than stored on the shelves in the big room. Most everything we have here could be sold on the antiquities market legally or illegally. Probably thought he'd steal something and then sell it to a collector."

"But nothing's gone?" the officer asked.

"The most important thing in the room right now is that jar. It looks moved, but it's still here; so is the lid."

"What's special about the jar," the younger of the two officers asked.

Marty answered before I could, "It's just our latest find. Not many intact jars like this from the Old City where we're digging. Otherwise, nothing special."

"Oh. Okay. We could get our crime scene out here to dust for prints and such, but since nothing's missing..."

"Sure. No need for that." I didn't want extra people snooping around here.

"We'll fill out our report and a copy will be sent to you as soon as it's done. You want us to use this address or some other?"

"This address is fine. Thank you all for coming. Especially, you," gesturing toward the security guard, "I'm sorry I didn't get your name."

"Jacob Horowitz, sir. I'm just glad I got here so quickly. Couldn't have been three minutes from the time the office called me that was as soon as the signal was received at the office? Four minutes from alarm to my arrival tops. I'd just made a pass by not fifteen minutes before. I called myself checking the alley, you know, shining a light down there. Must not have looked very carefully or he was already inside."

"Still, getting here that quickly probably saved us from some real damage. Thank you again. And you too officers. Shalom." They nodded an acknowledgment and headed for the main door.

When we heard the engines of their vehicles kick to life, Marty said, "I'm still pissed off that you took the package back to the hotel last night and put it in your room safe. I'm mostly pissed off you didn't discuss it with me before you did it."

I had told him about it on the drive over. I had tried to explain it was a vague uneasy feeling that prompted me to do it and he had responded that I could have called him before I did it, on the drive to the hotel, even after I got to the hotel. He was right. I could have and I should have. I really couldn't explain why I didn't. I'd hurt him and I didn't like that. But if I hadn't taken it...I didn't want to think about it.

"As lucky as we were that I did it, we've got a

problem. This wasn't random. Somebody knew we had something important in here and they want it. We've got to be really careful from here on out or something bad is going to happen." I had no idea how bad.

CHAPTER 18

At the Warehouse

Marty and I had gone back to the hotel, showered, changed and eaten breakfast. The so-called "Israeli breakfast" we had isn't listed like that on any menu, but every place that serves breakfast tends to have about the same thing. You begin with juice, coffee or tea, and a salad. Yep, a salad. Typically the salad is finely chopped tomatoes, cucumbers and peppers, drizzled with lemon juice and a touch of olive oil, and salt and pepper to taste. *Salat katzutz* it's known as locally because it was developed on the *kibbutzim* in the early days of the state of Israel when everyone was poor. But, there's more: next comes eggs, both hard and soft cheese, freshly baked bread, olives, jam and butter. If this isn't like home, not much here is. But, you can always ask for cereal or walk to a ubiquitous Mickey D's.

As we ate, we talked about our next step. We agreed that with the break-in we didn't need more people to know what we had, so no textile experts. They could have the cloth once we had it off the codex we were sure was inside. We were sticking with our plan to photograph each page, but we didn't think the workshop was the place to do it. Not only did we have a hole in the wall, but it just didn't feel safe anymore. Our hotel was a three star, fairly new one, the Agripas Hotel in the center of Jerusalem. Agripas, wasn't cheap, but it wasn't too pricy given what you got. Marty and I each had what was called an apartment--a large room with bed and separate sitting area, a bath, and a small kitchenette. There was video security, Wi-Fi, VOIP, and an armored entrance door to the building. Our room doors were steel with a peephole and a deadbolt instead of the now standard card key. Jerusalem could be dangerous. Better to be prepared. Oh, and down the hall were a washer and dryer, but we tended to use a nearby laundry, Zohar Cleaners. Yaniv always took good care of us and, if we asked, he'd drop off our clean things at the hotel.

We decided we could set up on the small dining table in my apartment. Trevor would need to bring his lights and stuff from the warehouse and we'd get going. I made a list on a napkin of the kinds of instruments I thought I'd need. Marty would go to the warehouse and get them, along with two trays--one for the cloth once we had it off and one to put the codex in. After calling the warehouse owner so we could get the repairs started there, I'd head to the site to talk with the troops. By midday we would meet back here and get started unwrapping. We drank the last of our coffee and headed out.

At the Dig

The worker bees were wandering off the bus at the site when I arrived. I saw Josh, Nicki and Ellie standing together and asked them to pass the word to everyone to gather under the large awning in front of the trailer before they got cranked up for the day. I asked them to let me know when everybody was present and I went to the trailer. Before I could do any useful work, Nicki knocked at the door. "Doc," she said, sticking her head in, "I think we're all here except Marty and Trevor. Do you want to wait for them?"

"They're going to be taking care of something at the warehouse, so we won't wait." I got up from behind my piled high "desk" made from some crates and a flush panel door and headed toward her.

"Is everything okay?" she asked, "Forgive me for being so forward, but you look like crap."

"Perfect; looking like crap matches how I feel. Very early rising today. You'll hear all about it in a minute.

But thanks for noticing and asking."

She wasn't sweaty. Too soon for that. She had on a light blue tee shirt, no bra again, and some stone colored shorts with tennis shoes. She was tanned, of course, from working in the sun, her blonde ponytail bleached from sticking out the back of her ball cap. She looked good and I asked myself why I should notice that. I mean, I know I'm a man and all, but the sky could fall any moment and I needed my mind on our work. I literally shook my head, as if to clear the thoughts of her away, and stepped out under the awning. This was very odd for me. I'm usually blind when it comes to female dig team members.

"Ladies and gents, there is the proverbial good news and bad news this morning: the bad news is somebody broke into the warehouse last night and then broke into the workshop. The good news is nothing was taken, especially the jar we found two days ago." Just like the movies, they all began to speak to each other, look shocked and shift from foot to foot. I was watching pretty carefully because I thought it had to be one of them, but nobody looked or acted especially guilty. Like I would know, right?

Andy spoke up, "Doc, any idea who did it; any leads? I guess why is obvious, but who?"

"Yeah, the why seems obvious; somebody was planning to steal some of our artifacts probably to sell on the black market. The who? We literally have no clue. The person or persons, knocked a hole in a side wall big enough to crawl through, then broke into the workshop. The big room has sensors on the cargo and front doors, but the warehouse itself isn't alarmed. However, the workshop and the office have motion detectors. So coming in through the wall didn't trigger an alarm. When they opened the workshop door, that did it."

"When the sensor is armed and detects movement, it does two things. It begins to make a pretty unpleasant and loud noise and second, it automatically dials the security company. We're assuming that when the alarm sounded, the creep knew he didn't have long, so all he could have done was snatch and grab. But he didn't. Marty and I had opened the jar and it was left on the table. It had been moved, but nothing else was disturbed. We think the guy who broke in knew the jar was there and assumed it contained something and went straight to the workshop."

"What was in it?" somebody asked.

"Nothing. Well, not exactly nothing. There were some coins and a necklace, but not the haul we'd hoped for, so 'nothing' only by comparison to what we'd hoped." Ellie's eyebrows went up at this lie, but like a good trooper, she stayed quiet. "Those things had been removed and placed in a safe off premises. We'll begin paper work to allow us to take them back to Vandy for more study before we give them to the IAA." I thought I pulled that lie off pretty well, given I hadn't anticipated the question.

Josh spoke next. "What about the fresco from yesterday? Is it okay?"

"Yes, it was elsewhere and is safe. Once the dust of this break-in settles, we'll be taking a closer look at it." I was getting good at this lying game.

"Any more questions?" I waited a count or two. "Okay then. Remember the little speech I made a few days ago when I was being an ass?" They chuckled and nodded; a few said something else I didn't quite hear about being an ass. "Then you'll remember my saying we have to zip our lips about this find. By the way, that should be the general rule when working on a dig site, but more to the point: here are our working hypotheses. One: one of you did the break-in." The movie crowd thing again. You could almost hear them say, "Is it I Lord?" "I'm not saying any of you did it; hear me out. Two: one of you talked." They were quieter this time, but didn't like what I said anymore than number one. "Maybe not on purpose or to cause us harm, but talked. Or, three: our leading hypothesis: a bystander was drawn to the action and decided to investigate. There were people on the walkway watching as we assembled and as I exploded. Who we are is no secret. Finding out our warehouse location, no big mystery. So, we think that's what happened. You're all aware that there are plenty of people in the country and in this city who don't like it being dug up."

Well this was kind of lie number three. Yeah, those were our options, but I didn't really believe it was number three. I thought it was one or two, probably two. Graduate students, are for the most part, poor. We don't pay them shit because they have to have field experience. We don't pay volunteers anything but room and board. Slip a little info to some backstreet dealer about an important find and make a few bucks. Contract workers can make decent money, but not nearly enough; it's seasonal work. My money was on a graduate student, but I had no clue who it could be. Sadly, I'm not very close to many of them and couldn't tell you much about their moral fiber.

"Look, Marty and I are going to be tied up all day off site dealing with this break-in thing. Knock off. Come back tomorrow and we'll pick up where we were."

Like most students, the idea of a cancelled class is a good thing and a bad thing, mostly a good thing. You get to goof off, but you also don't learn anything. Mixed blessing I guess. However, they didn't argue. They headed to the bus, chatting and, I guess, swapping theories. Except for Nicki, Josh and Ellie. I heard Nicki tell them to go ahead. She'd see them later; she needed to talk to me for a few minutes. Josh offered to stay, but she insisted. He didn't much like it, but wasn't going to make a scene. She called to me,

"Dr. Gabriel, may I speak with you a few minutes. I know this might not be a good time, but I might be able to help a little."

I assured her I had a few minutes and welcomed her into the office. The little air conditioner rattled away in its hole in the wall. I offered her a Coke from our little fridge, but she declined.

"I don't want to take much of your time, but there's something I want you to know."

Oh crap! I thought. I hoped to God she wasn't about to come on to me. I wasn't entirely sure I wouldn't like it. "What I wanted to tell you was that if you need to beef up security at the warehouse or here at the site or take some other measures, and need some money to do it, I can help." Before she could go on, I mumbled something about that being nice or sweet; sweet is what I think I said, but wished I hadn't. Then I told her she should hang on to her money.

"Dr. G, I don't really need to hang on to it. I have enough to help. I don't want to seem presumptuous by offering, but you don't really know anything about me, but I'm fortunate enough to have some money...well a lot of money. So, really I can afford to help. Plus, I have a lot of influence with a foundation back in the states...."

I'm pretty sure my mouth fell open. One, because she was a rich chick and two that she had enough interest in what we were doing to help financially. "Nicki, I don't really know what to say. You've caught me off guard. Well, certainly: thank you for the offer, but I'd feel odd taking your money. If you want to put in a good word to the foundation for next season, that would be wonderful. I'd be happy to fill out the paper work and meet with them if that's necessary. By the way, what's the name of the foundation?" She had the grace to blush a little before she said:

"It's the Nicole and Roger Taylor Charitable Foundation."

"What? You have a foundation? I mean you and whoever Roger is have your own foundation?"

"Roger was my husband, but he died in an accident. He had the foundation before we married and changed the name afterwards. He thought I could help run it. I've been involved, but I just chair the quarterly board meetings now that he's gone."

"Quarterly board meetings? How big exactly is this foundation, forgive me for asking?"

"Our endowment is about $40 million I think. We

usually make grants of about $2.5 million to $3 million a year. We don't have to rely on market growth to replenish our endowment; my husband's company, in which I'm a majority stockholder, makes a large gift to it each year as a part of its tax strategy."

"Nicki, I'm speechless." We're always scrambling for grant money. Having someone with some influence on a board is an incredible break for our department and program. Still, I was having a little trouble processing what I'd just heard. All I was able to say was, "Thank you for even offering."

"Dr. Gabriel, we don't have to rely on them if you need money right now. I'm a bit embarrassed to tell you this, but I have access to...well to as much as you'll likely need and can cover any costs you might have during this crisis. I think the expression most people would use is that I'm 'filthy rich' or maybe, 'she has more money than she knows what to do with.' I really do. Look, Dr. Gabriel, I'm having the time of my life here. I've already decided to go back to school and finish my academic work. I think archeology is what I want to do with my life, so being able to show my appreciation to you for helping me discover that is such a small gesture."

"Nicki, now I really am in shock. I had no idea. Well, hey, if you want to help who am I to say no. We might want to hire some more security; I just hadn't even thought about that since I didn't think we could afford it. We're always on kind of a shoestring. I mean, look at that bus you guys have to ride in." I decided to take her a little bit into my confidence. "Nicki, since you've been so open with me, let me share something with you. Absolutely can't tell a soul. We've think we've made a bigger discovery than anybody can imagine. I lied about the contents of the jar. It's something big, but we're not sure exactly what yet. And we found a second jar. I lied yesterday about the plaster chunk with the painting on it. We haven't even had time to open it yet, so we don't know what we have. I know I can trust you to keep this to yourself." She nodded vigorously and gave me assurances I didn't really need.

"We've think we have a manuscript wrapped in oiled cloth from the first jar. Because of a premonition, I took it to my hotel for the night for safekeeping, or the break-in could have been truly catastrophic. We're going to find out what we have today and I think you've earned the right to be there. Want to ride back to the hotel on my scooter and watch the unwrapping?"

She did.

CHAPTER 19
At the Agripas Hotel

Nicki and I rolled to a stop in the garage and headed to the elevator. I was still feeling a little befuddled. Here was this girl, well obviously a woman, who'd been digging in the dirt, living in the hostel with the rest of the grunts, who now was Miss GotRocks. Lots of rocks, apparently. As we rode the elevator up to my apartment, I suggested to her that the extent of her wealth was something we should understate with the others. We'd just say she had a trust fund that was going to lend us whatever money we needed with no interest and generous payback terms. She agreed.

I opened the door to find Trevor and Marty setting up some equipment I didn't recognize immediately, but obviously a camera was involved. "Hey, Doc. Uh, your AMEX card and receipt are on the cabinet near the TV. I might have spent a little more than you wanted me too, but when I got to the store..."

I interrupted him, "It doesn't matter. You got what you thought we needed. That's what I wanted you to do. Plus, I have some other news. Guys," gesturing to Nicki, "Nicki's joined our little party because she is going to help finance our venture. It's a long story and we'll talk as we work. Ready to go?"

"Gabby, can I see you alone for a minute. I have something to tell you," said Marty. Gesturing to the bathroom he said, "Step into my office for a minute." I did and he followed me in and shut the door. "What's going on? Why didn't we talk about this first? Damn it, if you take the codex without telling me and now you've invited her in. Why somebody else and especially why her? God! Don't tell me you've got the hots for her!" I told him. Only I didn't tell him the trust fund story; I told him what she'd told me.

"That's why." He was stunned too.

"Well..uh..okay then. I just wanted to know. Sounds good." All the steam was gone out of his anger. "Damn! Filthy rich, huh? Damn." Marty opened the door and I closed it behind him. I needed to pee.

When I was finished, I looked at myself in the mirror as I washed my hands. I looked haggard. I had helmet hair, which I tried to finger comb, while noticing the pepper color seemed to have more salt color than usual in it. My eyes were bloodshot and I had dark circles under them. My golf shirt was wrinkled. My pants were faded. And wrinkled. I hadn't shaved, and I don't really look good with stubble. Right that minute I felt much older than my 44 years. I sighed, dried my hands and joined the team.

I took a flat bladed pick and began trying to tease away the cloth. It was slow going, because unfortunately, the layers were stuck together like an Egyptian mummy's linen wrapping. The oil seemed to have bound the layers together much like the rosin on a mummy's wrapping. Also, pitch was soaked into the wrapping along the short edge on which the codex sat in the jar and on a long edge too. I'm guessing the codex was placed in the jar like an upright book, then slipped over to one side as the jar was moved around and before it was placed in the niche. Also it's likely it was hot in that niche, both from the fire that consumed the building and from the heat of weather before the ruins were finally covered over. That could soften the pitch and pitch could drip down on the wrapping as well as causing the wrapping to stick to the side and bottom. The pitch must have still been tacky and the wrapping stuck to it. I just wanted to be careful so I worked slowly. Getting it all off required periodically stopping to turn the bundle ninety degrees and then turning it end over end and ninety degree again. Marty or

Trevor took turns holding it in place while I worked. It seemed as if I had been working for hours before we had unwrapped first layer.

I was hoping and even considered praying that the next layer would come off more easily. Finally, we had enough off to expose the top sheet of writing and then the wrapping just kind of peeled away. First glance at the codex seemed to confirm that it was parchment or vellum rather than papyrus. "Looks likes animal skin rather than papyrus," I said.

"What's the difference," Trevor asked?

"Papyrus sheets are made from the pith of the papyrus plant that are cut about 40 cm wide, wet and then laid in several layers, each ninety degrees to the other. The layers are then hammered together, mashing it into a single sheet. It's dried under pressure and then polished with a stick or rock. It's an ancient, cheap material on which to write. However, it degrades easily in a variety of conditions. Parchment, on the other hand, is usually made from cow or goatskin. Vellum is a finer, more finished and more expensive grade of parchment."

My initial quick look suggested this was vellum. Under the top page were other pages of what was almost certainly vellum too. Whoever wrote this codex wanted the finest material available. A codex of vellum pages suggested money and importance. I was getting really excited. Adding to the excitement was the realization that we could snip off a piece of the vellum and have it carbon dated.

"Vellum is a superior writing surface, but does have one important drawback--it is easily affected by humidity. In the Middle Ages, books made from parchment or vellum had heavy covers that contained a couple of straps and buckles, like little belts. They allowed the books to be tightly closed to keep the pages from being distorted by the humidity. Even when books switched to paper, the habit of the buckles remained for important books for a couple of centuries."

It was good we were opening the codex in the hotel because the air conditioner sucked moisture from the air as it cooled it. That would help with preservation for the short time we were going to be photographing it. The pages of the codex were held together along one long edge with strips of leather-- like leather shoelaces--threaded through three holes. This would allow the pages to be turned, much like a modern day book. The top page was dark and the writing was almost completely obliterated. My guess was the oiled cloth and pitch had stained it. I was afraid it might have seeped even farther into the codex. We'd know soon.

Even without turning the codex over I could see some of the bottom pages looked much like the top page.

I could also see that the bottom edges of all the pages were dark where the pitch had mixed with the oil and penetrated. The top of the pages were only stained with the oil--no pitch. I lifted the top page that was kind of stuck to the second one. I was able to separate them without too much trouble. I tried turning another few pages. They were a bit brittle; the thin leather had dried out, maybe even some dry rot involved. With my gloved hand, I tested the leather strips; they were hard and very brittle; dry rot for certain. Untying them wasn't going to work unless we tried to introduce moisture of some kind. I decided not to take the time and reached for a small pair of surgical scissors. Before Marty could object, I'd cut through one.

"Gabby! What the fuck!"

"Marty I know you don't like that move," as I snipped the other one, "but we can't invest the time in trying to salvage them. I want to be able to lay each page flat so Trevor won't be hampered and I want to get the record made."

I stepped away to let Trevor work. Then it hit me: we wouldn't need to snip the vellum for dating; the leather strips that held it together--that's what we'd date. The vellum had been processed way more than the strips would have been. The strips would likely get us a better date.

"Marty, we need to bag the strips. We're going to

try to get a C14 date from them."

"Great idea!" He grabbed a glass tube from our stash from the warehouse and, using tweezers, slipped them in the tube, then sealed it with a rubber stopper. "We need to get these to a lab and get going on the tests."

"Yeah, but not here in Jerusalem. If we turn up with something with a first century date, somebody's going to be asking questions. We need to get it back to the lab at Vandy." We discussed this a few minutes and decided we could FedEx it. The hotel had a pickup at 6:00. "Marty, please e-mail Marge and alert her. This goes without saying: put a rush on it."

"All right Trevor, it's all yours." I said, "I'll turn each page after you do what you need to do." Trevor stepped up and began to explain how he was going to take pictures of each page in several different light conditions and with several filters, even infrared. The device he brought in was going to make this semi-automatic, but it was still going to take a lot of time per sheet to give us the widest range of options for study on the computer.

"Doc, I'm probably being overly carefully, but I'm going to go on the assumption that we won't get to study the actual manuscript itself. Something could happen and it's out of our hands. We've lost control of finds before. I'm going to stop every few pages and email what I've got to Marge back at Vandy."

"I'm with you, Trevor. It takes as long as it takes. But we just need to keep at it to get it down ASAP," I said. "Do your magic."

"As I take them," he said, "they'll be automatically stored on my laptop and on a flash drive," he went on. "I spent some of your money on a twenty-two inch monitor which I've plugged into the computer. You can see them larger than life as I take them and you can try to read what you see on the monitor." I was pleased. I wanted to get the photos taken, but I also wanted to know what we had. But then Nicki spoke up.

"Is there any danger of the pages deteriorating as they are exposed to air? I read where some documents like the U.S. Constitution are kept in a special oxygen free case."

She surprised me because she was right, of course. There was some danger. I thought it to not be very immanent though and said, "We should be able to get them photographed without a problem, but you're right. The sooner we can reduce their oxygen exposure the better. Maybe we'll make that the IAA's problem."

Trevor had photographed the first couple of degraded page with different light and different filters and was getting ready for the next one when I said, "Guys. Wait. We've got the codex oriented wrong. Semitic languages are from right to left and, therefore, back to front. We need to turn this thing over."

Marty, slapped his forehead. "Of course! What are we thinking? My money is on Aramaic which is Semitic." He grabbed a pair of gloves and gently reoriented the codex. However, the images already taken gave us the end of the story, as it were, as a start. That could be exciting. If we could read the damned thing.

Our new first page was very degraded too. Same problem, it appears. The back of it was badly degraded as well. The oil had apparently soaked through and perhaps some pitch as well. The third page was dark, but not as bad. Its reverse was dark, but getting lighter. It seemed as if hours had passed while Trevor meticulously "did his magic." I was still pumped and it made waiting very hard. Finally, we came to a page that was nearly pristine, except for stains at the bottom and cracks. That was the one I wanted to take some time with. "Listen everybody, this page is almost perfect. Trevor can you snap away, while I stop and take a look at this one?"

"Actually Doc, it helps if I can see the monitor. It lets me know for sure what we're getting and if I need to take more shots." I waited impatiently for Trevor to get the page documented which took a while. He had to change lights then changes filters, and click. Then do it again. He was trying for as many angles and filters and lights as reasonable. It seemed to take forever to get a page done. Finally, he had this one finished.

"Dr. Gabriel," Nicki said, "if your laptop is here, you can download what Trevor's taken so far to a thumb drive, and you can study it all you want while he keeps working."

So, I thought, *rich, pretty, smart and computer savvy. Nice package.* But I didn't linger with those thoughts. I wanted to know what we had. I did as Nicki suggested and took my laptop over to the desk. Marty could turn pages for a while. I opened the file and tried manipulating one of the worst pages. Nothing I could be sure of. My heart was pumping and I didn't have the patience to keep trying. I clicked open the file of the best page and watched it load. Nicki was at my shoulder. "Drag up a chair," I said.

Office of the Roman Catholic Patriarch of Jerusalem

"The office of the Patriarch of Jerusalem. How may I help you?"

"May I speak to his Excellency, the Archbishop please?"

"May I ask who's calling?"

"It's a rather sensitive matter I'm calling about and I'd rather give my name only to him."

"I'll connect you to his assistant. Just a moment."

"Father Newhouse speaking."

"Father are you the Archbishop's assistant?"

"I am. May I ask your name?"

"Father, I must speak to you or to the Archbishop at once. I have a matter of some importance touching on the faith of the Church I must tell you."

Newhouse rolled his eyes. *Great. Another nutcase,* he thought.

"Have you spoken to your parish priest, my son? Perhaps that would be the place to begin." *I need to shuffle this guy off to some priest somewhere.*

"Father, I can imagine you think my concerns would just be a waste of your time. What if I told you a manuscript has been found in a current dig that could alter Christian faith? Would you talk to me then?"

CHAPTER 20
At The Agripas Hotel

My Aramaic was passable, but I had an Aramaic dictionary on my laptop. If I was uncertain about a word, I could try to look it up. I turned to Nicki, "You don't happen to read Aramaic do you?" She laughed a nice robust laugh.

"No, sorry. Not one of my accomplishments."

I didn't think so, but what the hell, a little flirting wasn't going to hurt. I focused on the screen and began to read from right to left:

"*and then we came to Tiberius on the Lake of Gennesaret, sometimes called the Sea of Tiberius. We went immediately to the seaside where fishermen were cleaning and repairing their nets. He called out to Simon bar Yohanan, whom he later named Cephas, and to his brother. We knew them because they had come several times to places where Yeshua proclaimed the news of the coming Kingdom. Afterwards, they would linger and ask him questions while others wandered away.*

He said to them, 'Leave your nets. Mariamne and I are going to fish for people and we need you.' Immediately, they left their nets and began to go with us.

'Master, we must go home first and tell our families. How long will we be gone?'

His answer surprised me. 'We are your family. Come with us.'

They talked to each other as we walked away. Then Simon ran to us with his brother behind. 'We will go with you.'"

I fairly shouted, "It's what we thought it was. It's the Magdalene's account of Jesus' ministry! My God in heaven! We've got the calling of the first apostles! Simon is Peter! Lake Gennesaret is what we call the Sea of Galilee. It's not exactly the Markan story, but there's no question: this is independent evidence of the calling of Peter and Andrew!" I started reading again, "*We walked a little more and he saw Yaakov and Yohanan,* ["That's James and John!"] *his brother with their father Zebedee. He called out to them and they left their father to the nets with his men and they too*" The page ended there.

"This is Mary Magdalene's memoir of her time with Jesus! We've got an independent source of his life!"

We were all excited, but Nicki was also a little confused. She was asking the kinds of questions many people ask: Don't we already have four sources for his life--the Gospels--and don't they tell us all we need to know? She had missed the little history lesson I gave at the warehouse. I tried to quickly summarize a few facts for her beginning with, "We've tended to think so." My professorial nature kicked in and I started teaching. As Trevor continued to take pictures of the codex, I started talking.

"There was some unknown Christian, who lived some time before AD 180, who didn't think we had all we needed to know about Jesus. He--or she--wrote a fanciful account of Jesus as a little boy, a somewhat mean spirited and mischievous little boy who could do miracles. One of which was to bring back to life a little boy he killed as they played!"

"Hey," Trevor injected, "I've heard that, but I didn't know where it came from."

" Yeah," I said, "Lots of people over the centuries have heard some of these things. They're contain in a manuscript titled the *Infancy Gospel of Thomas* and were apparently to help the curious with some questions they had. This writer wasn't the only one who felt a need to help out. There is another manuscript called the *Protoevangelium of James* apparently written around the same time as *Thomas,* that tells us of the birth and upbringing of Mary, Jesus' mother, as well as providing some infancy stories of Jesus. In this version, Jesus is born in a cave on the way to Bethlehem."

Nicki injected a question: "So people just started making stuff up about Jesus?"

"No, they weren't necessarily just making up stuff," I explained. "They were trying to assist the faithful by fleshing out incomplete stories. After Jesus' resurrection he had 'competition,' as it were, in the form of other messiahs. Some had more complete biographies and apparently some Christians thought they needed to assist Jesus' rep by filling in the blanks. Also, there were early doctrinal issues that needed attention, for example Mary being a virgin, perhaps even a perpetual virgin."

"But," Nicki said, "Matthew's Gospel says she's a virgin. Doesn't it?" She sounded a little unsure, given what she'd been learning.

"I'll give you the whole story later," I said, "but the short version is when the Hebrew word used to describe Mary was translated into Greek, it took a word that in Hebrew meant 'woman of marriageable age' and made it 'virgin,' which is a possible translation, but a questionable one in this context for a lot of reasons." Nicki looked shocked. I get it. I was too when I first heard about a mistranslation. "Hey, there's more," I offered.

"The *Protoevanbelium of James* is the first known writing that describes Joseph as a widower with children when he marries Mary. The writer claims that references to "brothers and sisters" in the texts really mean "step" siblings. This idea led to the development of that notion in the Church in later centuries and paved the way for Mary's perpetual virginity as a dogma of the Catholic Church."

"So," I continued, "with all this writing out there, and with the Christian movement spreading, someone needed to figure out what should be believed and what was a heresy. There was a bishop in Lugdunum in Gaul, modern Lyons, France, named Irenaeus who was born around AD 125. He was one of the first great theologians of the Christian movement and had lots of influence around the Church. He stepped up. One of the things that spurred him on was the work of a misguided Christian named Marcion. He was the son of a bishop in Sinope, Turkey around AD 130 or so. The guy was filthy rich because he was a ship owner. Marcion went to Rome around 142 and insinuated himself into that Christian community by making a donation of 200,000 sesterces to the church there."

Trevor asked, "How much would that be today?"

"It's hard to know for certain, but I happen to know Roman soldiers of the time made less than 3.5 sestertii per day or about 1300 per year so it was whopper of a gift."

Trevor spoke up, "So he was trying to buy his way into the church in Rome?"

"Essentially. Maybe for the best of motives though. He thought he had a truth they needed. See, Marcion rejected the God of the Hebrew Scripture, viewing that God as inferior to the God depicted in Christian writings. That's not all he did though. Marcion did a little editing of the written works the Church was using in their worship and teaching, kind of a proto-Bible. In his collection he kept most of Paul's letters, but he also edited out references to the Hebrew God or to Hebrew Scriptures. He rejected Acts, 1 and 2 Timothy and Titus. The only Gospel he recognized was Luke, but again, an edited version with the biggest edit slicing out the chapters describing Jesus' birth. So historians credit Marcion with creating the first Christian canon or standard from all the writings out there. He wasn't just a nut case; he was pretty convincing. He attracted a lot of followers and established a number of churches after the Roman church kicked him out. By the way, to their credit, they returned his money."

"So he just decided he knew what Christians should base their faith on and started hacking away at religious works? Is that what you're saying," asked Trevor.

"Yep. And even though he had a lot of followers, most Christians believed him to be heretical, Irenaeus among them. He felt compelled to do something about this travesty of a canon produced by Marcion. Believing that Marcion was on the right track about there needing to be an official canon set by the Church, Irenaeus created the first list the larger Church supported. It's a list that is remarkably similar to the books we have today. It would take another couple of hundred years or so to finalize it, but the basic shape was there. As a matter of fact, it is to his reasoning that we owe the existence of today's four Gospels as the only ones. Through the force of his arguments, which are fascinating, he convinced the Church that only four belong among the revered works of the Church. He wrote a book called *Against Heresies,* and on the matter of the Gospels he said something like, there couldn't possibly be more or fewer than four. Why? Because there are four corners of the earth and four principal wind directions."

Nicki said, "You're not kidding are you?"

"Nope. That's what he said. Look it up. Given the age in which he lived, the argument had a certain logic to it that was compelling. Okay, that's the story of why four. Names had been attached to the writings, the names we use now. But how that happened and when is a big question. An overwhelming majority of mainstream scholars agree: we don't really know who wrote them. Sometime before Irenaeus, the current names were affixed to copies of the Gospels, but most mainstream scholars think it was primarily to give them the weight of apostolic authority, rather to identify the actual persons who wrote them. Could men with these names have written them? Sure. Could they have been followers of Jesus, eyewitnesses? Maybe."

"So these Gospels could have been written by people who didn't even know Jesus personally?" Nicki asked.

I repeated my earlier comments about John Mark and added, "If a man named Luke wrote Luke he isn't listed among Jesus' immediate followers. He's a person we know from Paul's writings, a gentile convert and physician. He doesn't even claim to be an eyewitness. According to his Gospel, he did a lot of research including reviewing others' writings, to create his Gospel for someone named Theophilus, whoever he is. Remember these words from the opening chapter of Luke?" I grabbed up a Bible from the nightstand drawer and turned to Luke and began to read:

"Since many have undertaken to set down an orderly account of the events that have been fulfilled among us, just as they were handed on to us by those who from the beginning were eyewitnesses and servants of the word, I too decided, after investigating everything carefully from the very first, to write an orderly account for you, most excellent Theophilus, so that you may know the truth

concerning the things about which you have been instructed."

As he continued to take photos, Trevor said, "So his research is why people call him a historian. Hmmm. How about that?"

I went on, "In *The Gospel According to John,* there is a disciple identified five times as "the beloved disciple," a description not used in the other Gospels. In Chapter 20 or 21, 21 I think," as I flipped pages in the Bible, "yeah, 21," finding what I was looking for. "The claim is made that this Gospel is based on the written testimony of the beloved disciple who was an eyewitness. Listen.

'This is the disciple who is testifying to these things and has written them, and we know that his testimony is true. But there are also many other things that Jesus did; if every one of them were written down, I suppose that the world itself could not contain the books that would be written."

"Very early in the life of the Christian community, that disciple was identified with John the apostle. Modern scholars are mixed in their willingness to accept this identification as a fact because while a strong case can be made, it's not compelling. As for Matthew, for whom the *Gospel of Matthew* is named, he *could* be Matthias, who had traveled with Jesus' group 'from the beginning' and was chosen to take Judas' place. That could make him an eyewitness, but because he *could* be, doesn't mean he was. So see, we may not really have any eyewitness accounts.

You probably know the Gospels don't always agree with each other and maybe it's because the oral traditions each was relying on was different."

"Maybe now you can see then what makes this find so potentially explosive. No one doubts that Mary Magdalene was there for almost everything. She followed him, and according to Luke, she along with other women, even helped finance Jesus' ministry." I kind of smiled at Nicki. "Plus, all four Gospels put her at the empty tomb, one as the first eyewitness, as it were, to the resurrection. So to read from her own hand her account of events, to hear her version of what Jesus said in his teaching and preaching, to perhaps finally lay to rest the actual relationship she had with Jesus--these things are of incalculable importance."

Trevor and Nicki were suitably awed. Marty simply said I had done a good job of not boring them to death. After all, it's not like he didn't know this stuff already. What I didn't say in my little lecture was this: as important as this codex may be in a search for the truth of the story, depending on what's in it, the excreta could hit the oscillator big time. What if her versions of teaching or miracle working are dramatically different from the accepted view? What if she writes that she and Jesus were sexually involved or married? What if her Resurrection story differs significantly from any of the Gospel accounts?

This little codex was potentially a bomb that could shatter a lot of accepted ideas. Of course it could confirm important things as well and end up being wonderful instead of controversial. But what's the likelihood of that--that's too simple and life is never simple.

What would we find? What is on those first few pages that we may never be able to read? When they are read, what will we learn?

CHAPTER 21

The Rockefeller Museum, Jerusalem

"Rockefeller Museum. How may I direct your call?"

"The IAA, please."

"I'll connect you."

"IAA. How may I help you?"

"The Director-General's office please."

"May I say who's calling?

"Please tell him it's a matter of some importance and I'd rather not identify myself to anyone but him."

"Very well. Just a moment." The receptionist got the DG on the phone and relayed the message. Skeptical as he was, the DG decided to take the call. It was a slow day."

"Shalom. This is DG Doormann."

"Ah, Mr. Doormann. Thank you for taking my call. I have some information for you which I believe to be of the highest important. Since I may have obtained that information in, may I say, an unusual way, before sharing it with you I would need certain...uh, assurances."

"I'm afraid I need a little more to go on before I can offer any, uh, assurances."

"Fair enough. Let us speak about hypothetical matters. Suppose a person believed he was sending an e-mail on a secure Wi-Fi connection, and suppose he even thought his e-mail was encrypted. But, even with those constraints, let's say someone were to, let's say, accidentally intercept such a message."

"In other words, someone was hacked?" asked the DG.

"I didn't use that word. Let's just say one was able to read such a message and it contained information about a significant find here in Jerusalem."

"If there were, to use your words, 'a significant find' anywhere in Israel, I'd already know about it unless it happened this morning."

"Well, sir, that's the thing. This hypothetical e-mail contains, among other things, wording which can only be interpreted to mean the true nature of the find is being hidden from the IAA."

"Hidden?"

"Yes. Hidden."

"Okay, suppose someone had such an e-mail. Yes, it might be of interest to us."

"Suppose the find was described in this e-mail as so rare as to be without equal and could shake up the Christian and maybe the Jewish world. Would the IAA be interested in offering a gratuity for such information, very detailed information? Perhaps even a photo or two included in the information?"

"Before I answer that, I want more information from you. How did you, or perhaps I should say, someone happen on such information?"

"I make it my business to frequent dig sites, especially those directed by certain people. I observe. I pay attention. Maybe I know someone who works on the dig site who enjoys sharing information with me. Maybe that person suggests something important is happening. My curiosity is piqued and I want to learn more. Sometimes in my quest to learn more, I find a way to be nearby when someone is sending or receiving e-mail or making a phone call. Sometimes being nearby means I learn useful information. But this time, the information isn't something I can use in my business because it is too big."

"So, let me see if I follow you," the DG said. "

You are familiar with important dig sites, visiting them to observe what is happening?"

The caller interrupted, "Yes, perhaps I see people at the site get especially excited. Or perhaps I see someone taking an unusual number of photographs."

"I see." The DG went on, "You have a friend at the site. You ask the friend about the excitement and the friend passes along useful information. And then, in various ways you follow up on that information? Do I have this right?"

"Exactly so. The reason I need the 'certain assurances' I mentioned is because sometimes an artifact may disappear from a dig and be exchanged with a business associate."

The DG, grimaced a little. "In other words, you sell a stolen artifact on the antiquities market?"

"I'm not saying I've done it, but I know it has happened. And if I had done such an illegal thing, that would need to be overlooked when you learn what I know."

"I'm afraid," said the DG, "I can't quite give you a blanket Get Out of Jail Free card without knowing more. However, it's possible, given the information you say you can provide to arrange for, let's call it, leniency."

"Oh, Mr. Doormann, leniency is just the beginning. I think the information I have is worth perhaps a million US dollars."

"The hell you say! We don't have that kind of money, and even if we did, we wouldn't use it to purchase this kind of information. I'm afraid you've overestimated us."

The caller remained calm. "Mr. Doormann, trust me when I say it's worth every penny. I'll tell you what I'll do. I'll have a courier come by in a bit with a little taste of what I can provide. I'll call back this afternoon after you've perused it." Without waiting for a response, the phone was dead.

Doormann hung up and leaned back in his black leather office chair. He looked at the ceiling for a moment, then swung his chair to face the single window in his office. He looked out on the grassy front lawn of the museum. *Could there be something in Jerusalem worth a million dollars to the IAA*, he wondered? *Of course there could be. He just didn't want to pay the asking price for it. But by God, he thought, if an artifact worth a million dollars to a "wholesaler" was out there for the taking, IAA would take it. Perhaps without paying the scoundrel a 'gratuity.'*

Doormann swung his chair ninety degrees, stood, and headed for his office door. As he opened it, his assistant turned to face him. "Use our Caller ID and get me the phone number of the person who just called." The assistant pushed a button on the phone, looked at the read out and said, "It's a blocked number. I would suspect it is from a disposable prepaid phone."

"Oh well. It was worth a try," said the DG as he strode back to his office to await the courier.

CHAPTER 22
At The Agripas Hotel

"Doc," said Trevor, "I've been thinking. I don't think it's going to work very well for me to try to e-mail several of the page files as I do them. For one thing, they are kinda large files, especially because they're encrypted. The group I sent took more than five minutes to be finished. For a second thing, even though our Wi-Fi connection is protected, it's not foolproof. Third, even though our files are encrypted, I'm uneasy about someone being able to intercept and decrypt them. I'd like to stop and back them up to a second flash drive every few pages. We'd keep one here for our study and FedEx the other to Marge overnight every day"

"Every day?"

"Yeah. At the rate this is going, we've got at least another day, maybe two of photos to go. I don't want to speed it up by shorting some technique I'm trying on each page 'cause you never know what we'll need."

I sat there for a minute mulling over what I was hearing. Trevor couldn't work through the night to speed up the process; or at least it was unrealistic to expect him to. This was tedious work. I didn't want to bring in backup to do it because we needed to keep the number who knows about this find low. "Marty, if you have no objection, I think we'll go with Trevor's last option."

"I trust FedEx," Marty says, "If we get the last pickup of the day, they'll have it in the air in about two or three hours later. Eight or nine hour flight gets it to the Memphis hub at around the time to send it to Nashville that night. It's in Marge's hands by 10:30 the next day. Not as fast as e-mail, but if we're looking for security, this is the way to go."

Nicki looked kind of sheepish and, like a first year student, slowly raised her hand. "May I say something," she asked tentatively? Everybody nodded. "What if we got it to the airport tonight at say 10:00 o'clock and there was a private jet waiting to fly it straight to Nashville and a car waiting at the airport to take it to Vanderbilt? Trevor could get a lot of work done today and we get it off to Marge, plus we have more to review tomorrow. Trevor works tomorrow and we use FedEx for the second batch."

"Nicki, do you have any idea how much that

would cost?" I asked with some little exasperation in my voice. "We don't have that kind of money. Hell, Trevor's extra equipment is on my personal credit card, the dig is so poor."

"To use an expression I've heard before, I believe it would cost a butt load. But Doc, remember what I told you about my...uh...trust? I can, I mean, it can cover it."

I was in shock again. Nicki had just offered, I'm guessing, many thousands of bucks like it was nothing. I flashed back to the expression she used when she told me of her situation, "more money than I know what to do with." Okay, then. I can help her spend it. "Nicki, splendid idea. Thank you from the bottom of my heart. We'll take you up on your offer. Trevor, keep shooting."

Marty and Trevor are speechless. Trevor turns to his cameras and Marty, shaking his head, lends a hand. "Nicki, do whatever you need to do to set this up. Anything I can do to help, just let me know. And, please, 'thank you' is so inadequate, but that's all I can say."

"Dr. Gabriel, I'm so pleased to be able to help. I'm going to step into the bathroom and make a phone call and I'll be right back."

"That's all it's going to take? One phone call?"

"Yeah. I just need to let my administrative assistant back in the States know what I need. She'll set it all up."

"You have an assistant," I said kind of dumbfounded.

She leaned over and whispered in my ear, "When you're 'filthy rich' you need help keeping up with stuff, especially if you're off in a foreign country playing Indiana Jones," and headed off to the bathroom.

The IAA Director-General's Office

The door to the DG's office opened after a soft knock. "Sir, here's the delivery you were expecting. The receptionist handed over a sealed envelope. After thanking her, the DG took his silver letter opener, given to him by a former Prime Minister in appreciation for his work in antiquities, and slit the envelope. Inside was a copy of an e-mail with the identifying information at the top redacted; other portions were redacted as well. Attached to it was a picture of a clay jar. He begin reading:

As I said when we talked on the phone, we have agreed back here that the inscription on the jar is two words. The first word is Mariamne. No doubt. The second word is almost certainly the Greek word for "memories," so it reads, Mariamne's Memories." However, we were able to detect parts of some letters that appear to have been partially scraped off before the second word was written. Based on what we can read, about six, maybe five letters, some at the start of the word, others at the end, we conclude, as you suggested on the phone, that the word removed is likely, but not certainly, to have been the word for "good news," i.e. Evangelion in Greek. We are trying other techniques to see if we can raise the other letters to be certain. Really need to be examining the jar rather than photos--as good as they are. Kudos to Trevor. Superior work as usual.

The rest of the material was redacted too. The DG held the page up to the light to see if he could read through the black lines drawn through the redacted material and discovered this was not a magic marker. The original document had been altered and printed out--no doubt to thwart attempts like the one just made.

So, he mused, *someone thinks they have a jar with an inscription Mariamne's Memories or Gospel or in English, Mary's Gospel. Clearly the jar isn't the gospel, so the inscription must refer to the contents. The jar in the picture has a scale beside it and it could be large enough to hold a scroll or codex. But if it were a manuscript, when was it written? Scholarship already knows of the Gnostic Gospel of Mary; could this be another copy of that?*

The DG laid down the documents, took off his stylish glasses and rubbed his eyes. He resumed his musing: *Was this find made in Jerusalem or somewhere else? Too many unknowns to make sweeping assumptions about. Interesting though. Even intriguing. We are a long way from a million dollar payout though.*

The DG slipped his glasses back on and reached for his keyboard. He logged on and called up a file called "Current Digs" and opened it. It was just what the title suggested, a list of all the digs currently active in Israel. The DG began to speak aloud, only for his benefit. It was one of his little quirks and helped him concentrate. "Let's see. Let's suppose this is another Gnostic *Gospel of Mary*. The last one dated from the fifth century. Do we have any digs that are poking around in sites where fifth century documents might be found?" His eyes scanned down the page and he called up page two. Nothing on either. Page three. *Nope*, he thought.

Again, out loud, "Okay. Let's say it's not Gnostic. Let's say it's late first or second century." He started backwards from page three, then page two and was about to click on page one when something caught his eye. "Hmmm. Gabriel is digging in the Old City. He's already told me they found a large residence, but I haven't heard anything more from him except about the Roman coin. Could this be it?"

He picked up his phone. "Sarah, I believe we routinely request a list of all dig personnel from each dig director, right?" She replied in the affirmative. "Please check Dr. S. S. Gabriel's list for the name 'Trevor.' A first name." Sarah replied it would only take a moment or two. "I'll hold, then." *Could Gabriel be hiding something from me?*

Seems unlikely given our history, but then you never know, he thought.

"DG," said Sarah, "There is a Trevor Wiley on the list."

Frowning, the DG thanked her and hung up. Out loud again, "I don't like this."

The DG turned back to his computer, opened up his address book and called up Gabriel's name. A cell phone number was listed. He was reaching for his phone to check in with Gabriel when it rang. "Yes?" Sarah informed him that the caller from earlier in the day was again on the line. "I'll take it. Thank you." He punched the flashing button and said, "DG here. Shalom."

"What did you think of the material?"

"It was interesting, but far from being enough to excite me. Still too many unknowns. Want a short list?" Without waiting for an answer he went on to share the concerns he had raised as he read the material for himself. "And so much redacted. So many questions raised by what you chose to omit. So, you see, it could be important; it could be extraordinary; it could be nothing but a jar. And, please forgive me for saying so, it could be a fantasy or a fake you've created. Now if you have something more conclusive, perhaps we can talk, but based on what you've shown me, I don't see anything that piques my interest--

certainly not a million US worth of interest."

"I completely understand, DG. My goal was to show you what I am able to retrieve. You'd like more. A day or two perhaps and I will confirm that the 'more' I have is worth sharing with you--or someone."

"Do you have a name? It's awkward talking to someone without a name," the DG asked politely.

"Sure. Call me Judas."

"Well, Judas, that's certainly a dramatic name with sinister overtones."

"Yes. But Judas is apt. And since you're not being very cordial to my overtures, I may just take my information to someone else. I happen to think the Roman Catholics would love to know what I know."

"Judas, don't be hasty. This is Israel. We are not as compassionate and forgiving when betrayed as some nations. I didn't tell you to go away; I told you I'd need much more. Is that so wrong of me? After all, a million US is a lot of money."

"Forgive me for my impatience. Of course, you shall have first choice. Only if you reject me will I consider another buyer. As I said earlier, give me a few days and expect another delivery. We can talk after that. Fair enough?"

"Absolutely."

"Good." The phone went dead. The DG replaced the receiver. *What a prick*, he thought. Out loud he said to himself, "Now what was I doing before he called? Oh yes, calling Gabby." As he reached for the phone, it rang again.

"Sorry to bother you Dr. Doormann, but I've just remembered something that's an interesting coincidence. Recently we received a report that one of the dig warehouses had been broken into. I wouldn't even bother you with it, except it's Dr. Gabriel's warehouse. Since you asked me about his dig personnel, I thought it might be important."

"Thank you, Sarah. You were right to alert me. This is why I pay you the big bucks as they say in the US. What do we know of the break-in?"

"We didn't get a detailed report; the security company only alerted us that there had been an incident."

"Very well. Please contact them and have them fax over or e-mail over a complete report. I want to know what happened. Oh, and Sarah, I want to know ASAP; make certain they understand."

"I'm looking up their number as we speak DG. I'll be back to you as quickly as possible."

Doormann replaced the receiver. "What the hell?"

he said to himself. "Too many coincidences here."

CHAPTER 23
At the Agripas Hotel

Now that we had our plan to transport our findings to the US, I had another idea I wanted to bounce off Marty and the others. "Guys, I have a suggestion. Since most of the pages appear to be in pretty good shape, let's flip the codex back over and photograph the degraded last pages. Those could be the most time consuming and the end of the story, as it were, could be the most important part of this find. Then we'll flip it back and resume the pages that are less degraded. But, Trevor, if they appear in pretty good condition, cut back on the number of images with different filters and stuff. We'll get as much done as we can tonight and get it on the plane to Marge. We'll have our two sets of thumb drives, then erase the hard drive images. We'll send one set of drives out on the plane tonight and secure the other here for our use."

"Doc that would speed up things. If you or Marty will take a look at each page and tell me if it needs the full treatment or not, we can probably cut the time in half. We won't finish, but we'll make more progress."

"Okay. One more thing. As soon as the degraded pages are done, we're all taking a break. We're leaving here and getting something to eat. An hour won't cost us many pages and, besides, if we have the first and last done, I think that may matter most." Trevor and Marty both started to protest at the same time. "No guys. We need the break. I'm pulling rank. And Trevor, to be on the safe side, wipe the hard drive and make the thumb drive copies before we leave." They grumbled but knew it was probably useless to argue. I seldom acted like a dictator, but when I did, people close to me knew I was unmovable.

I sat back down at the computer and called up the image of the first page we'd photographed that looked undecipherable to me. I decided to take another look to see if anything was readable. Nicki said if we were going out to eat, she wanted to run to the hostel and change out of her dig clothes. I offered the Vespa and she took me up on it. As the door closed behind her, my cell phone rang that ring I hate. Maybe, I thought, she could help me replace it since she was techno-savvy. I pulled the phone from my pocket and saw who was calling.

"DG Doormann! What a pleasant surprise. I was about to call you to make an appointment."

"Shalom, Gabby," he said. *Did I detect some coolness*, I wondered? "I would be most happy to make an appointment with you. Did you have a particular purpose?"

"I wanted to personally update you on the Old City dig. We've had an interesting discovery there of a sealed jar in a ruined niche in one of the walls. The jar has some writing on it which I'm having my person at Vanderbilt try to read for us. It's pretty degraded, but we photographed it and e-mailed it for study. We decided to not open the jar until we get her report which I expect any time."

"That is very interesting, Gabby. Perhaps you can bring some photos when you see me. Here, let me look at my calendar. Would tomorrow morning at 9:30 work for you; it's really all I have tomorrow and I'm eager to talk with you."

"Absolutely. That would be perfect. Uh...DG, did you call about anything in particular?"

"Just wanted to check in with you, perhaps get an update."

"I'm terribly sorry I haven't briefed you sooner. I've just let some administrative matters get in the way. Vanderbilt politics, you know."

"Yes. Yes. We must all answer to others. Very well, Gabby, until tomorrow. Shalom."

"Shalom, Director."

The line went dead and a part of me did too.

The Director-General's Office

As he replaced the receiver, a soft knock at his door was followed by Sarah stepping in. "Sir, I've just gotten a fax from the security company. The break-in was accomplished at night by some person or persons knocking a person sized hole in a side wall and entering. When the intruder or intruders broke a workroom door and opened it, an alarm sounded. A few minutes later the security guard arrived, followed quickly by the police. They did not enter, but shone a light inside and could see the workshop door standing open."

"A few minutes later," Sarah continued, "Dr. Gabriel, who had been alerted by the security company arrived and let the police and guard in. No one was present, the intruder apparently having fled at the sound of the alarm. Nothing was taken, according to Dr. Gabriel's examination, but he reported a large jar on the worktable in the workroom had been disturbed."

"This jar," said the DG, "Any other information about it."

"No sir. Just that it had been moved."

"A police report filed?"

"Probably only a notation of the call. The guard said when the police asked Dr. Gabriel if he wanted an investigative team on site, he said since nothing was missing, no."

"That's it?"

"Yes sir."

"Thank you, Sarah. Most interesting. Most interesting." Sarah closed the door behind her. *Oh*, the DG thought, *Gabby, Gabby, Gabby.*

CHAPTER 24

At the Agripas Hotel

I punched End on the phone and said, "Shit! This can't be good. Marty, that was the DG. He's calling, he says, just to get an update on our project. When has he ever done that before? When? I'll tell you when: never! He's heard something. Shit!"

"You're meeting with him tomorrow morning?"

"Yeah. I've got to download some images to my iPad to show him. Trevor, create a little file for me that I can show him without giving too much away. I need some photos of the jar as a whole and a couple of the writing. Make it the worse ones we have. Maybe a couple of the niche with the jar in it, too. That will give us a little time."

My adrenaline was pumping, but I knew we had to stick with the plan to eat. I needed to be as clear-headed as I could be while I was thinking up how to bullshit Doormann. There was a knock on the door and we all jumped a little. I went to answer it, peeped through the security peephole in the door and saw Nicki standing there. I barely registered that she was in a sundress. I slid the chain back and turned the deadbolt and let her in.

"You're back just in time; we've got to go eat now and get back here and get cracking with the time we have. Something's happened." Without waiting for her to speak, I turned to Trevor. I could see he was finishing up the material for my iPad. "Trevor, do you have everything we've done so far on thumb drives?"

"Yes sir," he replied. "I'm copying it to another so we'll be current. In fact, it's done."

"Great! After you've done that, pull them both and you take one and give me one." I paused. "You know, one of us needs to stay here while the others go eat and then we can swap out. I'm uneasy about leaving the codex and don't want to put it back in the safe because that just adds time we don't have. You know, getting it ready to go in and then getting it out and setting up again."

Marty spoke up. "You three go ahead; I'll stay and watch things. Make it snappy though; I'm getting hungry."

"I know I said we all needed to get out of here for an hour, but things have changed. Want us to bring you something? We're not going to be gone for a whole hour."

"Sure. Anything. I don't care."

I spoke to Nicki as we were leaving the room and walking down the hall, "We've got the degraded pages photographed and another several as well and they're on the flash drives Trevor and I were talking about. We'll shoot whatever else we can tonight and get a drive to the plane. But how are we physically going to get the drive to Vandy?"

"I'll give it to one of the crew members," she said.

"But we don't know them," I retorted.

"I do. It's our company plane and it's flying in from Paris; in fact they're on their way. They have a second crew with them too, so other than stopping somewhere *en route* for fuel, they can fly through the night."

"We can trust them?"

"Absolutely."

As Trevor, Nicki and I walked to a nearby place to eat, I filled her in on the phone call. I concluded with, "Goes without saying, we've got a problem. I'm almost certain somebody dimed us out to the IAA."

CHAPTER 25

At the Agripas Hotel

Marty was looking out the window of the apartment at nothing in particular. The view from the window was of a crowded city with buildings seemingly jammed together in no particular order. He could see the rooftops with their satellite dishes or old-fashioned TV antennae. Taller, newer buildings seemed to be springing up like mushrooms. Traffic sounds from the streets below were muted, but audible. A knock on the door interrupted his reverie. *That didn't take long,* he thought and headed toward the door.

He hadn't put the chain on when Gabby and the others left, and he saw now the deadbolt wasn't set either--just the regular lock when the door closes. He checked the peephole kind of automatically and recognized the person standing there. *What the heck?* He thought as he opened the door. The punch in his face from the butt of a pistol in a gloved hand sent him reeling backward, blood already streaming down from his nose. The intruder didn't wait for him to regain his balance before his face was hit again with the gun, this time sending Marty to the floor. A quick kick to Marty's side was followed by another powerful kick to the side of his head. And then a second brutal kick to his head. Marty stopped moving.

The intruder turned from Marty, slipped the gun into a pocket, pulled a small plastic garbage bag from another pocket, and picked up the codex. Carefully the codex was slipped into the bag all the way to the bottom, and then the bag folded over it, making a neat little black bundle. Next, Gabriel's laptop was shut, USB cords pulled from it and then placed in backpack. Looking at the laptop that Trevor was using, a decision was made to leave it. But not intact. The screen was smashed with the butt of the pistol that had reappeared. A glass was filled with water from the bathroom and poured onto the keyboard. Tilting the laptop on its side, the rest of the water was poured into the ports there. The glass was replaced on the little tray that had held it. Glancing around the room, nothing else of value seemed handy.

A quick look at Marty showed the blood from his nose, face and the side of his head was oozing onto the carpet. He wasn't moving. Standing over Marty with the gun in hand, the decision made was another kick to the head rather than a shot. Satisfied, the intruder moved toward the apartment door, stopping off in the bathroom only long enough to towel off the blood from the shoes. The gloves that had been slipped on were stuffed in a pocket, the backpack put back on. There was a finger comb through the short light brown hair, a deep breath and then the door was opened.

Someone was in the hall about to the enter the room across the hall and one door down. A half turn made it hard to see the intruder clearly from that vantage point. Hearing Gabriel's door open, the man in the hall turned to speak, to just be friendly. He could only see the person coming from Gabriel's place in a profile view. As he continued to look and while he fumbled with his key, the person coming out of the apartment looked back into the room and said, "Thanks, Doctor G. I really appreciate it. I'll see you in the morning." The door closed and the visitor turned away from the man in the hall, and started toward the stairs at the far end of the hall. *Just a student*, thought the tenant of the other room and slipped into his apartment without another thought.

On the Street Coming From the Restaurant

We headed back to the apartment, feeling a lot better, even a little rested. The short walk was pleasant since all the day's heat was gone and the temperature was comfortable. I told Trevor and Nicki that the situation we were in was even more complicated than they knew. We had another jar. Unopened because we hadn't had time to investigate it. We had talked a bit about my strategy with the DG including whether or not I would tell him about the second jar and decided I would not. "Bet you guys didn't expect this much excitement when you signed up, did you?"

"Doc, I have to tell you. Honestly, the three seasons I've been with you have been basically boring, except for the after work experiences, so hell no, I didn't expect anything like this," laughed Trevor. "Not much glamor and excitement in photographing pottery or ashes from a hearth."

Nicki chimed in, "Well I've seen all the Indiana Jones movies so I was sure we had something exciting in store." She laughed, pushing her hair behind her ears as she went on, showing some small gold hoop earrings. "Seriously, I thought maybe I'd find some little something that would be the highpoint of the season for me. Or more likely, I'd be carrying buckets of dirt to a sifter so, no I didn't expect anything like this."

I chuckled. "Well, guys, me either. No matter how this turns out, this has been the wildest ride I've ever been on. In the old days, we would have called this an E ticket."

"Hey, I've heard of that," volunteered Trevor.

"That's how Disneyland and Disneyworld used to 'charge' for their rides. The more exciting the ride the higher the alphabet letter on the ticket."

We turned into the hotel with Marty's dinner in a sack and a six pack of Cokes in hand. These light-hearted moments would be the last for a while. When I pushed the button for the elevator, I couldn't have known that, of course.

CHAPTER 26

The Roman Catholic's Patriarch's Assistant's Office in the Chancery

Earlier In the Day

"You're claiming you have a document of some kind critical to the faith of the Church. Is that correct?"

"Yes, Father. I have reason to believe such a document has been discovered in Jerusalem and is being kept from authorities and from the Church. As a good Catholic, I can't stand quietly and allow this to happen."

"What do you mean when you say 'reason to believe' such a document has been discovered?"

"I can't give you my sources for their protection. But, I'm given to understand certain correspondence has been read that divulges the existence of a document that purports to be from the hand of a very important eyewitness to the events surrounding Jesus."

"What may I call you? It's so awkward talking to a person without a name."

"You may call me Matthias."

The priest was silent for a count. "Matthias? Like the disciple who was chosen to replace Judas as an apostle after his betrayal of our Lord?"

"Yes, Father."

"Very well...Matthias...what more can you tell me? Or would you like to meet and speak face to face?"

"Father Newhouse, I think a meeting might be too risky for me. This correspondence I mentioned...it might have been...uh..."

"Stolen, Matthias?"

"I would prefer the word 'intercepted,' Father. It is the case the person who sent it and the person who received it, are unaware it was read by someone else."

"Illegally obtained, then?"

"I am not a person who can make such judgments with certainty. I only know the contents seem to be more important than some legal distinctions."

"Matthias, do you know if the IAA is aware of this document or, perhaps even in possession of the document?"

"I have reason to believe they know of the document, but do not yet possess it."

"I see. Well then. What is it you want from the Church...Matthias?"

"I am ashamed to even mention this, Father, but I am a poor person. I would gladly turn over the information I have just to please the Church, but I would hope the Church might wish to compensate me in some way for my risk."

"Certainly. I understand that. The Church has often aided those who have its best interest and the interest of our Lord foremost in their minds but who are struggling. Did you have something in mind?"

"For a copy of the letter that describes the find and for some related photographs, a small gift of $50,000 US would be wonderful."

"What?"

"Please Father, let me finish. Once you see what I offer, that money will be like the widow's mite, next to nothing. When I deliver what it describes to you, you will want to offer me considerably more."

"Matthias, $50,000 US is a great deal of money for the Church, especially, forgive me my child, for a--what do they say in America--a pig in a poke? How about this: I can arrange $1000 for a look at the correspondence. If it seems legitimate and as important as you say, then we can discuss again the larger sum."

"Father, I've have gone to great expense already to obtain this material. Let's say $5000, ten percent, with the balance on delivery, after you've read it and checked it out."

"Because you are obviously so much in need and have taken great risks for the Church, I agree. How shall we make this exchange?"

"There is a coffeeshop near the Chancery Office you sometimes frequent, no? Go there in two hours in your collar. A young woman will greet you warmly. Sit with her. You will hand her an envelope with $5000 cash in it. She will hand you an envelope with the information I believe will change your world. When you leave the table to order coffee, she will disappear. She doesn't know you; she doesn't know what is in either envelope."

"Very simple. I can do that."

"Oh Father, one thing I didn't mention. In case you're considering shafting me in some way, I have recorded this conversation and won't hesitate to post it on the web."

"Matthias, perhaps as a replacement for Judas, you have done honor to his name. I regret you have put me in such jeopardy, but in these kinds of things, I suppose one can never be too careful. Who knows, perhaps, I myself recorded this conversation to protect myself if false accusations are made. Goodbye Matthias." The priest, a bishop actually, because an archbishop who was one of the few metropolitans in the entire Western Church, warranted no less, replaced the phone. He then clicked off the digital recorder he had attached to the phone early in the conversation and slipped it into his pocket. *You see, you little shit,* he thought *the Church has dealt with people such as you for centuries. Who do you think you're fucking with?* Because bishops have assistants, Newhouse buzzed his and asked him to come to his office. *The Church has many ways, my friend Matthias, of dealing with those who would harm her and so do I.*

At The Agripas Hotel

Feeling refreshed and even a little light-hearted, the trio approached the apartment door. Gabriel knocked the familiar rat tat a-tat tat tat rat rat rhythm and waited. No sound came from inside. He knocked again, this time in a more conventional way. Still no sound. He reached for his key, stuck it in the deadbolt and turned it. The deadbolt wasn't engaged. He put the key in the knob and turned it, the click of an unlocking door was the only sound. "Damn it!" Gabriel said out loud as he opened the door, "Marty, you didn't have the..." And then he saw Marty on the floor, blood pooling around his head. He rushed forward.

As he knelt, he said to no one in particular "Call 101 for an ambulance. Then call 100 for the cops." He put his fingers on Marty neck.

"Is he alive," Nicki asked, shocked and panicked?

"I'm calling them Doc," Trevor said.

"I think I feel a pulse," Gabriel said. Putting his ear on Marty's chest, he said, "I feel a heartbeat, faint but there. Nicki, get a towel please! I want to put some pressure on these gashes on the side of his head."

"The ambulance and the cops are on the way, Doc." Trevor looked around. "Oh my God! The codex is gone! My computer's been trashed! Your computer's gone!"

"Here's the towel, Gabby," Nicki said. "I have a damp one too for his nose." She began to dab gently at this face, his nose, his bruised and cut lips. "I propped the door open for the medics," she said.

Just then, Trevor's words registered with me. "What? The codex is gone! Oh shit! Oh shit!"

Marty moaned. "Marty, it's Gabby! What happened? Who did this to you?" But Marty wasn't answering. He moaned again, stirred slightly, sighed and then was quiet.

Emergency services in Jerusalem are truly rapid

responders. The ratio of ambulance coverage to population is 1:10,000 which makes the average response time something under six minutes. That seems very quick, unless you are the one waiting for the responders. Your friend, your mentor, even your surrogate older brother, may be dying and time distorts, twists, lengthens. Seconds seem to take forever to slip by. Ticking clocks slow down. A sense of urgency is almost overwhelming; yet trying to rush time is completely futile. The shock of Marty's injuries and the lost of the codex felt overwhelming. My heart was pounding. I felt light-headed. Anger, fear, and panic swirled around in my head. My mouth was suddenly dry. I couldn't truly begin to assess what it all meant or what we would do now. I was conscious of Nicki nearby and I could hear Trevor talking, apparently to the desk clerk. It dimly registered that Nicki had called me by my first name rather than Doc as she usually did. But that was pushed aside by my certain belief that Marty had just died.

CHAPTER 27

The Director-General's Office

The DG again turned to his computer and opened his address book. He quickly found the name and number he was seeking and reached for his phone. He punched in the number he retrieved and listened to the ringing.

"CTS Universal Services. May I help you?"

"Avi Hoffman please. This is the DG of the IAA calling."

"Certainly. I'll put you right through. One moment." Music played softly as he waited. In the promised moment the phone rang once and he heard "DG Doormann, Shalom. How may I help you?"

"Avi, I have a sensitive matter I need looked in to. I'd prefer to not discuss the particulars on the phone. When can you get here?"

"For you, I'll cancel my next appointment and be

there within the hour; much less in fact. Say thirty minutes."

"Excellent Avi. I knew I could count on you. Shalom."

"Shalom, DG. Though when you call me, peace is usually hard to come by."

"Sadly so my friend. Sadly so."

They both hung up and the DG turned back to his computer and began to make some notes for Avi. Avi was, beyond doubt, the best investigator, private detective, snoop, whatever you might want to call him, in the business. He had contacts, some called them tentacles, everywhere in Israeli controlled lands and in certain other areas as well. If he wanted to know something, he would find it out. No matter how difficult or how sensitive, or how deeply someone believed they had buried the information. Formidable. Of course, these skills were not inexpensive; there was a premium attached to most work and well worth it. Because, not only was he good, but most important, he could keep his mouth shut.

At the Agripas Hotel

I was about to start CPR when the medics rushed into the room. "Step back please," ordered one of them. They immediately knelt next to him and began to assess him. "What happened to him," one asked as he worked.

I told him we had been gone and had found him this way. "There was a robbery as well. Whoever stole our things must have subdued him first," I tried to explain. "Is he alive?"

One of them said to the other, "Get the gurney." It had been left in the hall. The one who remained behind was affixing an oxygen mask to his face. "Yes. Barely," he finally replied. The gurney rolled up and they lowered it as far as it would go. Looking up to us, one of them said, "Give us a hand. You, slip your hands under his back; you, get on this side and slip your hands under his legs. When I say now, lift him and slip him on the gurney. Okay. Now!" They lifted him and lowered him to the white sheet of the gurney. Marty's head rolled to one side. "Benny, get the neck brace. We've got to stabilize his head." Blood leaked from Marty's nose under the mask. "Shit!" The medic lifted the mask and rolled some gauze into a cylinder and gently pushed it into Marty's nostril, then slipped the mask back in place. Benny was putting on the neck brace. The gurney sheet was already turning red where the side of Marty's head was bleeding.

"All right everybody, stand back a little while we lift the gurney. With one of them on each end, they lifted it to its full height and locked the legs in place for transport. "Which of you wants to come with us? Someone will need to go to the hospital with him to help admit him."

"I will," I said. "He's like a brother." We three and the gurney started for the door. We were met by two officers of the Israeli Police, the *Mishteret Yisrael*. In Israel, there is no municipal police department such as we have in the States. The Israeli Police force operates wherever Israel has civilian control. Each carries a handgun and they each have access to some version of the M1 Carbine or a 5.56mm submachine gun in their cars. One of them spoke to me. "What's happened?" he asked in very accented English.

"My friend has been terribly beaten by a robber who took some of our things. I'm on the way to hospital with him. Can these two fill you in so I can leave? He's very bad off." The gurney wasn't waiting for me. I shouted after them, "Where are you talking him?" Over his shoulder one of them said, "Shaare Zedek Medical Center. It's the closest." I knew it. It was right in the center of the city where we were.

I yelled back, "I'll be there as quickly as I can." The elevator door opened and they were gone. "Please," I said to the police. Let me give you my card," which I fumbled for in my wallet. "You can call my cell for anything these two can't tell you." The older of the officers, in his fifties with mostly grey buzz cut hair and tired eyes, looked at the card. "An archeologist, huh? Did they take archeological material?"

Suddenly, I wasn't sure what to say. While Buzz Cut was questioning me, his partner, a thirties-something, non-descript man was looking at the equipment we used for photographing the codex. "What's all this stuff," he asked.

To Buzz Cut I said, "We are photographing a codex, a kind of ancient book we discovered in order to preserve it. It was taken. My laptop was taken. The other laptop was vandalized. As far as we know, nothing else was taken."

"Why are you photographing the book in a hotel," Buzz Cut asked?

"Our warehouse workshop was broken into recently and it hasn't been repaired yet. We came here because we had nowhere else to go."

Non-descript Man asked, "Does the IAA know about all this? Do we have a report on file of the break-in at your warehouse?" Clearly this guy is not taking things at face value.

"I'm meeting with the Director-General in the morning to brief him. We'll call him as soon as things are under control and tell him about today's robbery. Look, these two know all about what we're doing. May I please go to my friend?"

"Yes, go on. We'll talk to them and fill out a

report. I think we should call our crime scene people and see what we they can find. In fact, Eli give 'em a call right now. Okay?"

As I was running out the door, I heard Eli speaking Hebrew on his radio that was strapped to his shoulder. I didn't wait for the elevator; I ran for the stairs taking them two or three at a time. As I dashed through the lobby and out the front door, I saw the ambulance doors being closed. "Wait! Let me back there with him!" Benny obliged, I climbed in and we were away. Benny had removed the oxygen mask and had replaced it with one of those masks with a big black bulb on it. I learned later it has a name: ambu bag.

"Here, pump this. He's bleeding through his nose too much to inhale. This will force air into his mouth." I pumped. He inserted a needle with a little valve on it and attached a line from an IV bag. I glanced at it: Ringer's Solution. It looked like water. He moved quickly in everything he did. He cut Marty's shirt to expose his chest.

"What's that for?" I asked.

"In case he codes so I can zap him," he answered. With the shirt cut away, the large bruise from the kick in the side was visible. I was betting on broken ribs. Benny probed gently at the bruise. "Broken rib or ribs. May have punctured a lung. Maybe that's why the oxygen wasn't getting to him." Marty did not look good.

It did not comfort me that the ambulance was using the siren; *bad sign* I thought. However, I felt better, when in a minute or two we swung into the hospital drive and slammed to a stop. Quickly the driver reversed the ambulance and backed to the ER doors. Medical staff were waiting for us. I stopped bagging Marty and climbed out. They grabbed the gurney and whisked him inside. I followed and was shunted off to a person with a clipboard while Marty disappeared through double doors into a hall and behind curtains. I stood there and watched, still in disbelief.

Then I thought, *That could have been me. Or Nicki.* And, without any warning, I fainted.

CHAPTER 28

A Coffee Shop Near the Chancery

Earlier in the Day

Bishop Newhouse had gone to the coffee shop as instructed. He was pleased that Matthias had chosen this shop; it was a local, family owned place rather than those ubiquitous brand name places. He liked the ambience. He liked being recognized and greeted by name. He liked that the owner, Angelo, and he argued over money each time. This good Catholic man never wanted a bishop to pay for his coffee, or anything else for that matter. Newhouse always protested and always lost. To his credit, he slipped a few bills into the tip jar and said, "I'll light a candle for you when I return to the Chancery." Sometimes he actually did.

As he took a few steps into the shop, an attractive young woman of perhaps thirty, fairly leaped from her chair and rushed to him. "Father," she said, "So kind of you to meet me here. Please, sit." Her complexion was clear, her eyes bright, her light blond hair tousled, her smile genuine. More quietly she said, "Here's what you came for." With that she slid a letter-sized envelope toward him from under the newspaper in front of her. He noticed she didn't completely remove her hand from it.

The bishop reached into his inner coat pocket and removed a similar sized envelope, plain, no diocesan return address on it. He laid it on the table and slid it toward her. "And here's what you came for." He smiled as he left his hand on his envelope just as she had. She laughed lightly, lifted her hand and looked at his hand. He lifted his and each took possession of their new envelope.

"Thank you so much," she said. "Would you want your coffee now?"

Newhouse slid his chair back and rose, "Yes," he said, "I do want my coffee." He nodded a slight nod to her and moved toward the counter. When Angelo saw him, he beamed, "Bishop, I didn't see you come in. Welcome! Welcome! The usual *padre*?"

The girl picked up her book bag, took one final sip of her drink and, leaving the newspaper, walked out through the shop door. She looked both ways at the curb and risked her life by dashing into traffic. She made it safely to the other side where she quickly entered a bookshop. When Newhouse heard the coffee shop door open, he turned to watch her leave. Unlike so many women her age, she was not in pants. She wore a simple, but very short skirt and the currently popular ballerina flats. Her legs were shapely and tanned. He watched as she darted across the street and was still watching as she entered the bookstore. *I wonder,* he thought, *if I followed her right now, would she lead me to Matthias? Probably. But then what would I do?*

'Here you are, Your Grace! Enjoy!" Angelo said beaming, as he slid the steaming cup toward Newhouse. "Please, take this cinnamon roll too! Fresh from the oven!" They began their ritual about paying. Angelo vigorously shaking his head and holding up both hands. The bishop offering the bills, pleading, then stuffing them into the tip jar.

"I'll light a candle for you my dear friend." *Perhaps for you and for me and God's Holy Church,* he thought as he walked out the door.

The Chancery

Newhouse sipped his coffee as he walked back to the Chancery and still had some left as he entered his office. He tossed the remainder into the wastebasket under his desk and sat down in his black leather swivel chair. He took the envelope from his inside jacket pocket and reached for his silver, ivory tipped letter opener. Slicing the envelope neatly, he removed the contents: a heavily redacted e-mail and two inkjet printed photos and a Post-It note with a URL handwritten on it.

He read through the material twice, looked again at the photos and turned toward his computer. Newhouse called up his browser and typed in the URL and clicked Return. In a moment there appeared a YouTube screen. He clicked the button to start and was watching a shaky video of something at a dig. It looked as if two men were pulling something from a niche in a wall. He reached for his phone and punched in a three digit number. After a few rings, he heard, "Yes?"

"Your Excellency. May I step into your office? I have a matter of some consequence to discuss."

"Yes. Come."

We walked swiftly the few steps from his office to the Patriarch's, knocked softly and entered. He handed the archbishop the materials for which he'd paid $5000. "Please, your Grace. Read this."

The aging priest took the offered document, picked up his reading glasses and slipped them on. After reading the first few lines, he looked up at his assistant, then returned to his reading. "*Mater Dei!* How did you come by this? This can't be real."

"Your Excellency, I'm very much afraid it may be real. At any rate, we must investigate this further. If it is real, the Church, of course, must have it--no matter what it says."

The archbishop slowly stood, began wringing his hands and said, "Yes. Yes. Absolutely. Do whatever it takes to investigate this and, if it is genuine, to obtain it."

"Don't worry, Excellency. I shall do all in the Church's power. I will keep you informed at every turn, but I recommend we tell no one about our quest. If, for example, someone in the Curia were to learn what we are doing--prematurely--we might be making our work harder than it need be."

"Yes. Yes. The Red Hats want always to control everything. We will tell no one. Start immediately."

"As you wish, Excellency. God bless our endeavor."

"Yes. God bless our endeavor."

The bishop turned and left, walking the few steps back to his office, his heels clicking on the black and white checkerboard patterned marble floor. He opened the heavy walnut door and headed to his desk. He swiveled his chair to face his computer, moved his wireless mouse, opened his address book, and found the name and number he sought. He punched in the number on his personal cell phone and in a few moments was talking to his favorite religious, a man who would gladly die for the Church. Or perhaps even kill for it, if the stakes were right.

CHAPTER 29

Shaare Zedek Medical Center

I wasn't out long. A gruff looking nurse was holding an ammonia ampule under my nose. Reflexively I pushed it away. "I'm all right. Just a little light headed." She helped me to my feet and tried to steer me toward a wheelchair. I demurred in the strongest way possible. "Was I out long?" Learning it was only a minute or so, I knew I hadn't missed any news about Marty. "That man the EMTs just brought in--he's my friend. We're Americans and I'm the closest thing to family. We work together--well technically he works for me." Assuring me there was paperwork to be done, the amazon nurse steered me to the admissions desk located in the ER lobby.

I answered questions for an interminable length of time. I signed my name at least a dozen times and had my personal AMEX card swiped. Just as we were winding up, Nicki and Trevor burst through the door and scanned the room. Seeing me, they rushed over and asked the only question that mattered, "Is Marty Okay?" I told them I hadn't heard anything since they took him back. I discreetly left out my bout with the vinyl tiled floor. "We may as well find a place to sit. I've got to call the DG and come clean."

I called. I called his cell phone, a number I'd had for a long time, but never used. He was surprisingly kind to me, given I'd kept a major discovery secret from him and was only just telling him. He didn't ask for an excuse and I didn't offer one. What could I have said? You people at IAA are way too proprietary; you never like to share credit; I needed this find for personal reasons? None of those began to justify what I'd done. I suspect he was kind to me because of what happened to Marty. If that were the case, when Marty was out of danger, the DG would likely rip me a new one. I guess I deserved it.

When I ended that call, I made another to Marge's home number in the States. Guess what? She doesn't like being awakened in the middle of the night. I quickly filled her in on Marty. Of course she was shocked and cried as we talked. We'd all been friends and worked together for a couple of decades so it was understandable. Then I told her about the robbery. She was stunned and cried some more. Once she had a grip, I gave her a little job to do. "You'll get a delivery from me in the morning. It's a flash drive with everything we got done tonight before the robbery. Copy it and lock it in our safe. The original drive can't be out of your sight. If you leave the room where it's stuck in a computer, take it with you. Got it?"

"Yes. I'll guard it like I guarded my virginity until...well never mind when. No! Better even than that." She chuckled.

"Good. After you've looked over all the material, make a phone call." I gave her the name of a somewhat controversial magazine editor. He had been instrumental in getting the Dead Sea Scrolls made available to the wider academic community, breaking the decades long monopoly a few select scholars had. I told her to call him and drop my name. "Then," I said, "tell him what we found including your findings on the jar." I also told her to tell him she was flying to Washington with the information for him to review. "Take the drive with you. Our goal is to publish as soon as possible, wherever we can. Let any press releases come from him. Make sure," I told her, "that our Department gets the credit, though. And tell him to call me with his plan before he pulls the trigger. Nothing goes out until I approve it. Got it?"

She did.

Now that I had taken action to get the word of our find to the world at large, I turned to Nicki. "Here's my copy of the thumb drive; we've still got Trevor's. Go ahead and get it to the airport. Getting this to Marge is more critical than ever." She took it with a look of grave concern on her face.

"I don't want to leave you here," she said, her eyes softening as she laid her hand on my arm.

"I'll be okay. Take it and call me when you start back to see if we're still here or gone to the hotel."

"Okay," she said. "Watch over him, Trevor." She leaned over and kissed me softly on my stubbly cheek and then headed for the door. I liked it. Even with all the shit swirling around us, I liked that kiss.

After she left, I asked Trevor to fill me in on what had happened at the hotel after I left. It was pretty much what you'd expect. He wasn't allowed to touch his computer until the crime scene people had gone over everything including pictures of everything in the room. He had continued answering questions about what we were doing and thought maybe, just maybe, he'd finally convinced the officers on the scene that we were legit. As he and Nicki were about to leave, a couple of detectives showed up and wanted to start all over with the questions. He'd told them we could answer them in the morning, but they were heading to the hospital. There were a few words back and forth, with Trevor insisting they were leaving, and they left. In the process, he'd slipped my iPad into his backpack.

Again, I had no real sense of time. Looking at the clock in the waiting area didn't help because it was obviously not working. Or if it was, it was running very, very slowly. Trevor and I sat quietly for the most part. My thoughts turned to Marty and our life together. It began when I arrived at Vanderbilt with a freshly minted doctorate, some post-doc work, and very little field experience. I was brought in as an Assistant Professor, one rung up from the bottom, but on a tenure track.

Marty had been there for a number of years before I arrived. He was tenured, taught one undergraduate class, and spent all the rest of his time in the field or studying finds in the lab. He loved what he did; it was his life. He had been promoted to Associate Professor and it looked as if he would be stuck there forever. He mentioned one time over a beer that he'd almost been married once. He'd lived with a woman for a couple of years and he said, "She just didn't like dirt under my fingernails or my bags never really being unpacked. I decided then," he said, "not only is this not going to work, I don't have time for a wife." When it was obvious my wife and I were going to divorce, he was sympathetic, but said, "It is a mother fucker of a thing to make work when you love discovery the way we do." Not elegant, but seemed true in this case.

Marty took me under his wing pretty quickly,

seeing potential in me for good field work, I suppose. He mentored me and he helped with Departmental politics. I got tenure because of a favor he called in--at least that's what he's always said. As I moved up the ladder, he couldn't have been prouder. When my name was put forward as chair he said, "If you sit behind that desk all the time, you're going to hate being chair. You've got to negotiate plenty of time to work in the field to survive in that job. Otherwise, my boy, tell them to get fucked." I got the job and I got plenty of time in the field, too.

My phone sang in my pocket, but I didn't recognize the number. I answered it anyway. It was Nicki. She said, "The package is on the plane and I just watched it do a rollout to take its place for departure. Where are you?" I let her know we were still at the hospital and she said she was on her way. So clearly, a fair amount of time had passed since we arrived. Just then a man in soiled scrubs, with his mask pulled down below his chin came through the double doors of the ER and walked straight toward me.

"You are with the man who came in earlier, yes? I am one of the surgeons who worked on your friend, Dr. Joseph Belz."

"I'm Gabby Gabriel. Please, how is Marty?"

"We have done surgery and now have taken him to the ICU. He is gravely injured. His nose was broken.

Slightly more force and the bones would have been driven well into his brain with catastrophic results. The bone under his left eye socket was shattered; we can't assess the damage to his eye yet. We have done surgery to repair both of those areas, but the eye socket will need more work later. He had two broken ribs, with one rib puncturing a lung. As bad as all this is, it is under control. The worst is that his skull is cracked in several places with a few fragments of his skull driven into his brain. We have removed, we think, all of them. However, he has sustained a severe concussion and insult from the bone fragments and his brain is swelling. We may still need to remove a piece of his skull if we can't control the swelling. He's still feeling the anesthesia effects and won't be coming around any time soon. I'm sorry to have to give you such bad news."

"Is he going to be all right? Eventually?"

"His age is working against him, of course, but these injuries would be severe for anyone. We will know more in a few days. But even if he survives, we can't be sure what brain damage has been done or how he might be affected. We surmise he took two hard blows to the face and then two or three powerful blows to the side of his head. The kick in the side was the least of his problems, but still, all of that together is a tremendous amount of trauma."

"So he could live and be okay or he could live and have memory loss or worse, or he could even die. Is that what you're saying."

"Yes. All those outcomes are possible. However, in fairness I must say being unaffected if he recovers is not very likely. But who knows? Medicine is an art as much as it is a science. We must trust God, yes? You will notify his family?"

"There is no one to notify. Thank you Doctor Belz. I appreciate your candor."

"Ah. Well, then. You may wish to go to the ICU waiting room. The staff can direct you. You can be kept up to date there. Shalom." He turned and headed back to the ER.

My head was swirling. We had the robbery to contend with, the IAA and God knows what else and overshadowing all those was Marty. What would we do next, I wondered? How to carry on without Marty and how could we honor what Marty had endured simply because he stayed behind to "watch over everything?" I had questions, but no answers. I looked at the waiting room clock that had finally begun to keep real time: it was 2:20 AM. And suddenly, all the starch went out of me and I felt ready to collapse.

"Trevor, I'm going to the ICU waiting room for a

bit. Can you get to our two dig sites in the morning and tell everybody what has happened to Marty, but nothing about our find? Tell them it was a room break-in, an apparent robbery. Tell them to keep working; Marty would want that. And tell them I'll see them sometime during the day with an update."

"Sure, Boss, I can do that. Hey, you could just tweet us and then you wouldn't have to leave if you didn't want to." Like I had a Twitter account along with a clue as to how to use it. Before he left, he set one up for me on my cell phone and while he was at it, changed my ringtone. While he was taking care of that and showing me to use Twitter, Nicki returned. She asked about Marty and I told her all we knew and added I was about to head up to the ICU waiting area. She insisted on coming too so we said our goodbyes to Trevor and headed to the elevator. I pushed the button for our floor and the doors opened immediately. As we moved to enter, Nicki took my hand.

"I know you're worried sick," she said as the doors closed. "I just thought you needed to not be alone while you wait."

Making no move to let go of her hand, I said, "Thanks Nicki. Marty and I go way back. He's been mentor, friend, big brother to me my entire career and I've tried to be a good friend to him, one worthy of his efforts. I'm having a little trouble imagining life without him."

"Oh, Gabe! Don't try to imagine that! Imagine he'll be back with you soon. "The doors slid open, we walked to the nearest chairs in the almost vacant ICU, and still holding hands, began our vigil. Eventually fatigue overtook us and we both slipped into a dreamless sleep.

CHAPTER 30

The Intensive Care Waiting Room

I awoke to someone's phone ringing. No one was answering it and I finally realized it was mine; I didn't recognize my new ringtone. I pulled it from my pocket, almost dropped it from still being half asleep, and answered it. "Gabriel." Nicki stirred beside me and signaled she would return in a moment and moved off to the hallway.

"Gabby, I'm sure I have awakened you. Forgive me. This is DG Doormann."

"No problem. The chair I was dozing in is killing me."

"You are at the hospital then?" he asked. "How is Marty?"

I filled him in with all we knew. "Gabby, I'm so

sorry to hear the bad news. I will pray for him and shake my fist at God a little for permitting things such as this."

"Thank you DG. I'm afraid I'm not much of a praying man. Maybe I should be."

"God listens to our thoughts, Gabby, whether we use formal prayer or not. God knows your concern for Marty."

The DG's comments were a surprise to me. I'd really only experienced him as a hard-nosed protector of Israel's history and artifacts. Here he was showing a facet I would never have expected. "Sir, if God can know what's in my thoughts, his ears may have been burning. And not in a good way."

The DG laughed and said, "God can take it, Gabby. God can take it. Listen," he said, "I wanted to know about Marty, but I also have another reason for calling. You came clean with me; after reflection, I want to come clean with you. I knew about your find before you told me you had found something, a jar, to be specific. I knew it had writing. I knew what the writing said. How did I know these things? Someone provided me with a snippet of an e-mail you received from someone, apparently someone at Vanderbilt. They also provided two photos of the jar. I then surmised the jar had a document of some sort which you were not telling me about."

I was fully awake now. Nicki was making her way back from what I guessed was a potty break, but she was also carrying two cups of nasty vending machine coffee. As she sat down, I put my phone on speaker and gave her the universal sign for silence then mouthed "DG". "Sir, I'm...I'm...stunned and chagrined all at the same time."

"Later we will talk about why you felt you needed to keep this all secret from me. Now we have a much bigger problem. Here are my hypotheses at the moment: someone besides you was copied on that email and forwarded the redacted version to me."

I interrupted, "No one was copied. I was the only recipient."

"Unless they were sent a blind copy, then you'd have no way to know. But on to my next possibility: someone had access to your computer, saw the e-mail and sent it to himself or herself. But I reject this one too. My third and favorite one is you were hacked in some way."

"Yes. Yes I can see how any of those things could have happened. I am not at my computer all the time. There are times when it's in the trailer at the site or in my room when I suppose someone could have accessed it. But that person would need my password and the encryption password. Hacking I hear about, but why pick me to hack?"

The DG went on, "Gabby, I have had an investigator looking into this matter, a process I began as soon as I received the e-mail. A courier presented the e-mail to me after an anonymous phone call from what my man called a 'burner phone.' It is his belief that someone is reading your e-mail remotely, that is, intercepting them in some fashion and then using a fairly simple decryption program on them. I suspect you do not use the highest encryption technology available, yes? So this would be simple."

I got it. I then added to the scenario. "That would mean someone would be aware of what we were doing at the dig and then tracking us to someplace they could capture our Wi-Fi transmissions. Shit. Shit. Shit."

"Yes. My investigator, who is tireless and has many helping hands, has a theory. Someone knew you were at the hotel, rented the apartment next to yours, and set up shop. In his investigation, he has already learned, that in fact, the apartment was rented only a few days ago, shortly after the discovery. It could be a coincidence. Except that person moved out during the night last night."

"Do we know who?"

"We have a name, but since the apartment was paid for in cash, we have no way to be sure the name is legitimate. My source is checking databases, but with no luck so far. We'll have to find this person some other way.

I think the plan today is to review video footage from security cameras both at the check in time and last night."

"Perhaps I can assist with that. Maybe I'll recognize someone." I offered.

"I will pass along your offer. My investigator had thought this was the person who assaulted Marty. But in speaking with tenants on your floor, who were not happy to be awakened in the middle of the night, we learned that your neighbor from across the hall reported someone leaving your apartment at about the time of the assault, appearing to be speaking to you, and then walking down the hall toward the stairs. He thought it might be a student of yours since the person, a male with a tenor voice, said, 'Thank you Doctor G.' Either that was a clever ploy, says my investigator, or a second person with access to the same information. A confederate perhaps or a freelancer, is what my man called that person."

I didn't know how to respond. I felt invaded, almost raped. "DG, I doubt that person was a student of mine. None of them call me Doctor G, because of the Doctor G medical examiner that is on TV in the US. We're very clear that is not OK. It was a ruse."

"Excellent information. I will pass that along," he told me.

I thanked the DG for sharing all this with me and

then said, "I have a bit more information that may prove useful. I'll let your 'man' decide." I then told him about my ranting scene at the dig the day of the discovery and my noticing one or more people on the walkway above the dig who could have been taking photos or videos. "If that happened, it could be anybody." I don't know why, but I kept back the information about the second jar. Yet I knew that if someone were intercepting e-mails, that person could know about that jar and that the DG might find out about it too.

"Thank you, Gabby. I will pass this along. Oh, I didn't mention, I knew about the break-in at your warehouse too. That was important information. And you see, the e-mail had a person's name embedded, a Trevor. I guessed there might be a connection, checked our records and discovered you have a Trevor on your site. Then I called you and you began trying to cover your tracks with me. No. No. Don't interrupt. We shall talk of all that later. We must first find the codex."

"I'm sorry, sir. As lame as that sounds, that's all I can say."

"I think I understand your motives, as much as I'm not happy with your behavior. For now, we are allies working toward the goal of recovering the codex. Just one more thing Gabby. Do you have any other information that will be useful?"

I froze. I wasn't telling him about the second jar; now I was faced with whether to tell him about the photos of the few pages we were able to make. I hedged my bets. "I will know more about whether or not I have more when I have been in touch with the lab at Vanderbilt. Some work is going on there that may shed some light. Perhaps I'll hear today."

"What would we do without our laboratories? Yes, if you hear from them, you must call me Gabby. No more games. We are allies, remember?"

"Yes. Allies. I will call."

"Then update me on Marty if there is any change and we will talk later. Shalom."

"Shalom, DG. Shalom."

Nicki had heard it all and the expression on her face fairly screamed that I'd lost my mind. Then she said, "Let's see if we can get a report on Marty. Then we probably need to figure out how to protect the second jar."

In the Director-General's Office

Sarah was not yet at work; she had taken her child to the doctor for something. When the phone rang, the DG answered it. "IAA. Director-General Doormann."

"I'm surprised to hear you answer directly. Were you expecting a call from me? It's Judas."

"Yes, Judas, I recognized your voice. No, I was not expecting a call. My assistant is out this morning."

"I have new information as I promised. I have photos of several pages of the codex I can share with you. But, DG, this will cost you."

"Judas, you must forgive me for being cautious. The original million dollars you had mentioned--remember how I told you we were not rich. Before I could obtain that much or more, I must have something more substantial than your say so. I'm not suggesting this is a ruse, but I must have facts, evidence. I'm afraid I would need electronic copies of the photo and not inkjet printer copies. We must be able to study them to see if they are truly worth what you ask."

"Yes, of course. You must be prudent. I understand. But, I'm pissed off now. So I'm not feeling all that cooperative. I'll have to think about your need for the electronic copies. I'll call you later."

Judas hung up and Doormann hit Caller ID. Blocked Number. He spun in his chair and called his investigator. "Avi. I need to see you. I have talked again to Gabriel and have some information. Also, Judas called just now and I want you to listen to the recording I made.

First, let me tell you what I've learned: the codex is stolen and from what Judas said, I don't think he has it. Still I want you to listen to the recording and we can decide how to proceed. Even what he offers, if he can deliver, is valuable."

"Let me wrap up the little task I'm working on and I will be right over. You checked the Caller ID?"

"Yes. Nothing."

"Okay. Give me an hour or so. Shalom."

The two men hung up and the DG leaned back in his chair. "Gabby's not telling me everything; I can sense it," he said out loud. "Avi needs to do a little more digging into him."

CHAPTER 31

The Intensive Care Unit

Nicki was right. We needed a plan for the second jar. I said, "We need to get it open and see what's inside. If it's nothing, we can forget it and focus on the stolen codex--not that I know what to do about it. If there is something in the second jar, we can protect it more easily than the jar."

"We should document it as before, right?

"I can get Trevor to take some pictures, but--fuck it--let's just get it opened."

"Okay," she said. "Let's check on Marty. Call Trevor. Get breakfast. Head to the warehouse."

"Apparently, in your other life, you are pretty decisive, maybe a little bit bossy," I said and smiled.

"Yes, I am. But in a nice way. I always smile as I get my way."

"That's good information. I won't forget it." Then she kissed me.

"I probably shouldn't have done that, but you've caught so much shit in the last twelve hours, I thought you needed something good to happen." I kissed her.

"I did. And it did. Let's see about Marty." After all, she wasn't a student, so technically, I wasn't crossing any inappropriate boundaries was what I told myself. I conveniently ignored the fact she was an employee. Oh well.

There was no change in Marty according to the nurse at the nurses' station.

"Can we at least see him?" Gabriel asked.

"I'll take you. But you can only stay a minute or two. He's heavily sedated and won't know you're there anyway."

She took the pair to Marty's small room. Marty was lying in bed with his head slightly elevated. His face and head were bandaged, and what flesh they could see was discolored from bruising and betadyne. A tube snaked from the monitor to an oxygen mask placed over his nose and mouth. A Foley bag hung low at the side of the bed to catch his urine output. A line began at a bag of clear liquid hanging on a pole and ended in Marty's arm. A pressure cuff was on his arm and a clip was on his finger. Both had lines leading back to the monitor. It traced a methodical pulsing line as his vital signs were displayed. Other than his heart rate, the numbers meant nothing to Gabriel and Nicki.

Nicki held Gabriel's hand as they looked at this man who meant so much to him. A tear from each eye made a rivulet down each of Gabriel's cheeks. "He's got to pull through, Nicki. He's got to."

Nicki squeezed his hand more tightly. She too was beginning to feel a little overwhelmed by the moment. She understood death far more than she wished to. And she also knew from experience that words at moments like this seldom help. They stood a moment longer and went back to the nurse's station.

Learning that it could be hours, maybe days, before Marty would would regain consciousness, Gabriel made sure they had his cell number and Nicki and he started to the elevator. "You know what?" she asked, and then proceeded to tell Gabriel what.

"Let's go back to the hotel. You take the time to get cleaned up and change into working clothes. I'll take your scooter and run to the hostel and do the same. I'll come back, we'll take the truck or rent a car and after we eat, go to the warehouse. We need some time to shake off yesterday. A hour won't matter. Okay," she asked as she smiled. "Isn't that a good idea?"

Gabriel was pretty sure that arguing with her about it wouldn't accomplish anything. Besides, he had some of Marty's blood on his clothes and he was scruffy looking--didn't smell great either. That was the plan agreed to. They got a cab and headed to the hotel. Gabriel called Trevor on the way and told him that a little later, they would swing by the dig site and pick him up and to bring his camera.

Trevor said, "Doc, I've had some time to process everything that happened. Look, we've lost the codex, but not the pictures. The thumb drive you have has everything we captured, just like the one we sent to Marge. We have some stuff on your iPad. Granted we didn't get the whole thing, but we got some. I took my computer apart last night when I got back--couldn't sleep. I pulled the hard drive and can take whatever was on it and put it on a new hard drive. Anything there that's not on our thumb drives can be saved. Electronically, we've been inconvenienced, but not crippled. So, while we need the codex for obvious reasons, we still can prove we made a hell of a discovery."

"Thanks, that's good news, Trevor. We'll swing by a computer store and replace both our laptops later today." I glanced at Nicki and she nodded a 'yes' so the bank was still open. "We've got to protect the second jar and its contents so that's our ultimate destination this morning. We also need to be careful how we use Wi-Fi." Gabriel told him the working hypothesis on how they were hacked.

"Holy crap! They used the hotel Wi-Fi to fuck us," he pointed out unnecessarily.

"Not elegantly put, but yes. Give the troops some guidelines for the rest of the day and we'll see you shortly."

Gabriel pressed End. As he did so, he thought, *"End" is such an ominous word; especially right now.* He truly hoped they hadn't reached theirs.

CHAPTER 32
The Chancery Office

Newhouse turned on the small flat screen TV in his office and tuned to the English language news station, IBA Channel 1.

"...the local news, Dr. Martino Fratini, assistant dig director of an Old City dig staffed by US archeologists and crew, was brutally attacked last night in an Agripas Hotel apartment. The motive seems to have been robbery with several items taken including dig director Dr. Stephen Gabriel's computer and an unspecified book. Police think Dr. Fratini may have known his attacker since there was no sign of a break-in. He remains in critical condition at an area hospital. Now let's go to Rebecca for a look at local weather for today. Rebecca?

The bishop clicked off the TV. He thought, *a book at an archeologist's apartment valuable enough to be taken and to have severely injured someone in the process. Is there a connection with Matthias?* He turned to his morning tasks, checking e-mail; opening mail he didn't get to yesterday. Fully and hour passed since the newscast when his work was interrupted by interoffice line, which he answered.

"Bishop, there is a phone call for you on line 2," said his assistant.

"Thank you," he said, I'll take it." He lifted the receiver, punched two and said, "Bishop Newhouse."

"Bishop, so glad to have found you in."

"This is Matthias, yes?"

"Indeed. Bishop I know you're busy, but I wonder if you ever have time to watch the news on television?"

"Should I? Is there something important I should see?"

"There was a report on the early news that has probably been running all morning on the news stations. A sad story, really. A man was brutally beaten and robbed in a hotel. Is nowhere in our city safe?"

"I have seen the story." The bishop was feeling wary, tense, eager to see where this line of conversation was going.

"I heard a book was taken. Bishop, what kind of book is so valuable that a person would beat and rob someone for it, I wonder?"

"I could only speculate and with so little

information, that seems unproductive," Newhouse replied coolly.

"By the strangest set of circumstances, I happen to know what kind of book," Matthias said with a bit of a hostile tone to his voice.

"Is this why you have called me, to tell me of this book?"

"Your Grace, when we spoke last, I mentioned information which I thought you would find valuable--very valuable. I asked for a few days to make my case. I'm sure you remember."

"Yes, I remember."

All the light-hearted teasing tone vanished from the caller's voice. "I have the book in my possession. I will describe it to you. It is, I believe, what is called a codex. Its pages are leather. Some are soiled very badly, but most of the codex is in very good condition. Sadly, I can't read it. It looks to be in old Hebrew or something--not Greek, I read Greek--but what do I know of such things? I thought perhaps if I sent you a photocopy of one of the pages you would be convinced of my abilities--and my worth. What do you say?"

"I am, of course, very interested in seeing what you have. But, since we both know you obtained this codex illegally, I must consult with others in the Church before I can promise anything."

The cloying, teasing tone returned to the caller's voice. "But of course, Your Grace. I understand. Even bishops report to others do they not? I will give you twenty-four hours. I will call at this same time in the morning. Oh...one other thing...the one million US was for information. The price of the book is ten million US. I will expect half of that money in cash after you view my proof of possession. The balance will be wired to an account number I will provide when I turn over the codex."

"Matthias, I know you do not want to haggle, nor do I, but we have a problem. First, I think it prudent to give you a down payment of only one million US. Five is such a lot of money. There are scoundrels in the world who would take the money and keep the book to peddle to others. I'm not saying you would do such a thing, but surely you understand my caution. Second, I can more easily obtain the smaller sum quickly. Third, I must have experts view what you provide to be assured of its authenticity. You understand all this, yes?"

"Bishop. Bishop. Bishop. Where is the trust and compassion I hear about when people speak of Catholics? You are a hard man. I'm very disappointed. So, here's what I will do. For two million you can have an actual page from the codex. You can have twenty-four hours from the time you receive it until you must wire the balance."

"Matthias, my child, here is what I can do. At noon today, you will go to the Cathedral of the Holy Name of Jesus in the Old City. To the right of the main entrance after you enter the nave, you will see a confessional on the right and left. You will go into the right most one. You will see a package that will contain one million dollars on the floor under the seat. You will take the package and you will leave behind a legible page of the codex. You will be watched, but not approached unless our watcher thinks you are conducting...funny business?...I believe they say."

"Newhouse," all pretense of civility was gone from the caller's voice. "You're an asshole and probably a bastard as well. We will make it 3:00 o'clock rather than noon. I will call you at noon tomorrow--not the twenty-four hours as I first offered--and you will tell me that you will pay me another ten million on top of the one million down payment. You have pissed me off so the price has gone up. I can easily have other buyers if this is anything approaching what we both think it is. Hell, I may just sell off one page at a time. Or, if you fuck with me again. You will be left with nothing. So are we clear?"

"Yes. Three o'clock. You will call at noon tomorrow. The price has gone up. We are clear." Newhouse disconnected and then quickly punched in the number of his paid muscle. Speaking out loud to himself while punching in the number, he said, "You will pay for this insult you little shit. I'll have the codex and then hunt you down and take the money back. You shouldn't piss me off like this."

At The Warehouse

Nicki had done as we had planned, including picking up Trevor. He asked if we could go ahead with the computer purchases now. In addition, he needed more flash drives and SD memory cards for his cameras. We stopped at an Apple store and when greeted, Trevor asked if they had reconditioned laptops for sale. Before the sales associate could answer, Nicki said to the clerk,

"No. Not reconditioned. We want two of the best, newest generation laptops you have and whatever else my friend thinks he needs."

The clerk began a sales pitch for the hottest laptop when Nicki interrupted, "We don't care. Get two of them, please. Now. We're on a short tether here."

The clerk looked a little put off and then asked, "Certainly Miss. Umm, may I ask how you plan to pay for the things you need."

Nicki flushed, with what I can only imagine was anger, but said, softly, as she rummaged in her wallet,

"How about we use my Platinum AMEX Card? Would you like to see some ID to prove I'm the person whose name is on the card, and piss me off a little more? Maybe entice me to ask for the manager?"

"No, Miss. I'm terribly sorry. I didn't mean to offend you. Let me get the laptops from the back," and he scurried off thinking of his commission, no doubt, or perhaps an unhappy manager. Trevor wandered over to where SD cards and thumb drives were on racks and began to pick out what he needed.

"A little testy are we?" I asked.

"Not really, but it sometimes helps to act that way to move things along. He was just doing his job, but I don't have time for that today." She smiled a sweet, radiant smile and gave me a little wink. Before long we were pulling up in front of the warehouse. The roll up door was open and it shouldn't have been. My first thought was the second jar had been stolen.

CHAPTER 33

In the Intensive Care Unit

Marty slowed opened his unbandaged eye. He began to move around on the bed and moan. Very quickly an ICU nurse rushed in. "Dr. Fratini, please don't move around; you'll accidentally dislodge a line." As she tried to calm him, she also looked at the monitor to which he was connected. His heart rate was elevated, and his blood pressure and oxygen sat were marginal. He tried to speak and tried to pull off the oxygen mask that they were using because of the damage to his nose. A nasal cannula would cause too much discomfort and they were trying not to have to intubate him. The nurse helped him remove it, "Here," she said, "let me help you. We can't leave it off long Dr. Fratini, okay?" Marty's lips were parched and he began to moisten them with his tongue. Then he spoke to her, "I want a priest," he said, and closed his eye as if the effort had been exhausting.

"Any particular priest, Dr. Fratini?"

Marty's eyes flickered as if to open them, but they remained closed. "Catholic priest. Any. Confession," he said.

"I will begin immediately to try to summon one. We don't have one on staff, but I will call a nearby church to see if they can send someone. But, Dr. Fratini, even though you're in the ICU, we don't think you're in grave danger of death." She tried to comfort him. His pulse began to quicken. He tried again to open his eye. He managed to raise his voice a little this time. "Need to confess. Get priest, please!" The pleading in his voice was unmistakable.

"Right away, Dr. Fratini. We'll call one right away." Marty relaxed a little and his pulse rate began to return to normal.

At the Warehouse

Gabby jumped from the car Nicki had rented followed by Nicki and Trevor. He ran for the roll up door, certain he'd be met with another catastrophe. He yelled as loud as he could, "Police!" The second jar would be gone; he knew it. But like many things we are sure we know, he was wrong. He found two very startled workmen. One was replacing concrete blocks in the hole the intruder had made. Another was installing new safety glass in the workshop door. Both jumped when they heard him. Nicki came up beside him, "Police?" she asked slightly befuddled. "It was all I could think of," Gabby said, a bit sheepishly.

"I'm sorry gentlemen. I thought you were breaking in. Please, go on with what you were doing." Gabby had a better thought. "Wait. Can you take a break; perhaps have coffee or lunch. We need to be alone for a bit," and he winked at them. The two looked at each other, shrugged their shoulders and nodded in the affirmative. While Gabby, Nicki and Trevor stood around, the workmen brushed themselves off and headed for the door.

"Thank you. Thank you both. Again, I'm sorry I startled you. Please can you give us, say an hour?" Yes, they nodded an hour; two if he wanted it. They were both smiling and one nudged the other as they gave each other knowing glances. As soon as they were out, Gabby pulled the roll up door down, went out the entrance door, and locked the roll up door with a padlock. He came back inside and threw the deadbolt on the entrance door.

"Okay," he said, "let's see what we've got." The trio walked to the office and Gabby unlocked the door. Everything looked the same. He went straight to the second jar and removed the tarp. He grabbed the bubble wrapped jar and carried it out to a worktable in the warehouse. "Trevor, start shooting. I'm going to remove the bubble wrap and take a closer look." Trevor did as he was told while Nicki looked on and asked if she could help. She couldn't.

With the wrap off, Gabby started his inspection. The jar was almost identical to the first except there was no inscription. The lid was secured with pitch like the first one, but otherwise, the jar was unremarkable. Gabby said, "I noticed when I was moving it, something inside shifted. I didn't hear any rattling, just something shifting of position. I'm guessing the inside of this jar isn't pitch lined. All right, let get to work on the lid." They decided to use the hot spatula again and were getting the propane ready. They were all startled by the loud sounds they heard coming from the front of the building.

In the Intensive Care Unit

"Excuse me," the priest said to the nursing station clerk, "I believe someone called for a priest? My name is Father Donlin."

"Father, our patient Dr. Marino Fratini, is in critical condition, but we think he will survive. How well he'll be able to function is an open question, but we don't think he's in mortal danger. Still he asked for a priest and we wanted to get him one."

"May I ask what happened to him?" he asked as he slipped on his *viaticum*, a small purple stole he removed from his pocket.

"He was severely beaten in a robbery at a hotel."

"Oh," exclaimed the priest, "He's the one on the news this morning!" making the connection.

"Perhaps father, I didn't see the news. You may have come for nothing. He comes and goes. Here's his room." They entered and the nurse and priest walked over to Marty's bed. "Dr. Fratini," the nurse said softly, giving him a slight nudge, "The priest you requested is here....Dr. Fratini?" as she nudged him again. "The priest is here." His eye fluttered and he reached for the mask, groaning loudly this time. He had reached with the arm on the same side he had broken ribs. The nurse again helped him remove the mask and he tried again to open his eyes, this time succeeding. He licked his lips.

"Father," he said, "bless me. I've sinned." The priest looked at the nurse and she nodded and excused herself. He slipped on the *viaticum* he had folded in his pocket and kissing the cross sewn into it, slipped the small purple stole around his neck.

"My son, how long since your last confession."

"I don't know. A long time. Please Father, I need you to write something for me. I must confess to someone besides God. Please. Do this for me."

"My son, a nurse could have written something for you. Why did you send for me?"

"I need God's forgiveness, Father, but I also need a friend's forgiveness." A tear began at the outer corner of his eye and slowly slid down his wrinkled cheeks, tracing its own path through the contours of his face. He continued speaking, haltingly, "You must write what I confess to you and you must give it to my friend if I should not recover."

"May I call you Martino?"

"Everyone calls me Marty, Father."

"Marty, let me suggest this. Confess your sins to me. I will absolve you. Then we can talk of writing."

"You must give the message to my friend Gabby! Even if you only hear my confession, you must tell him what I said!" The monitor began to beep as his blood pressure and pulse began to rise.

"As you wish, Marty. As you wish. Now what is your sin?"

"Betrayal, Father. I have been like Judas." Marty went on with his confession. Pausing when he was short of breath. Tears again streaking his cheek and wetting his pillow. He didn't have the strength to keep his eye open but he continued to talk, even though still haltingly. Finally, he said, "That's the story, Father. Please write it down so you don't forget. Read it back to me and if I die, give it to Gabby. He'll understand."

The priest promised. "But first Marty, let me absolve you. He began to intone one of the most comforting of Catholic prayers: "God the Father of mercies, through the death and resurrection of your son, you have reconciled the world to yourself and sent the Holy Spirit among us for the forgiveness of sins. Through the ministry of the church, may God grant you pardon and peace. And I absolve you of your sins, in the name of the Father, and of the Son and of the Holy Spirit. Amen." As he said the words, he traced the sign of the cross on Marty's forehead.

"Thank you, Father. Now, please write."

"Let me step out to the nurse's station to get some paper. I'll be right back." He stepped out and walked the few steps to the nurse's station. From the corner of his eye, he noticed a figure dressed in scrubs with a white coat enter Marty's room. *The doctor*, he thought. To the clerk at the desk, the priest said, "May I have some paper; perhaps a tablet. Dr. Fratini wants me to write something for him."

"Sure. Let's see, what do we have. Oh, we don't have anything with lines on it except Nurses' Notes. Will that do?"

"I'm sure it will. Thank you."

"Need a pen?" she asked.

"No thank you. I always carry one. By the way, do you know who a 'Gabby' might be; someone close to Dr. Fratini?"

"Let me check his chart. His emergency contact is a Dr. Gabriel. Could be him."

"Thank you. May I have Dr. Gabriel's phone number?"

"I'm really not supposed to give out that kind of information, but since you're a priest, I guess it's all right." She read him the number and he jotted it down on the tablet he held.

After thanking her, the priest turned back toward Marty's room just as a doctor was leaving. He nodded and asked, "How is he doctor?" The doctor replied with just one word. "Resting. Peacefully." The doctor continued walking away from the room.

CHAPTER 34

At the Warehouse

The banging was coming from both the cargo door and the warehouse entrance door. And with the banging was yelling, "IAA! Open up immediately. IAA! Open up or we will batter down the door."

"Shit!" Gabriel grabbed up a nearby hammer and smashed the lid. He reached inside and pulled out a leather pouch with a drawstring. The leather was old and cracked from what looked like dry rot, but it was intact. He handed the pouch to Nicki.

"Put it on one of the farthest shelves so it looks like any other find and get back here." As she ran to the shelves, Gabriel ran to the door yelling,

"I'm coming! I'm coming. Hold your horses." That was greeted with more banging and yelling. He glanced over his shoulder to see that Nicki was breathlessly back at the table, as he fumbled at the deadbolt on the front door. As it opened, four or five men rushed in, each with a weapon. The leader asked brusquely, "Who are you?" The other men fanned out but didn't come in and farther.

"I'm Dr. Gabriel, the dig director whose warehouse you're in. Who the hell are you?"

"We are associated with the IAA. We're here to retrieve from you artifacts you have failed to inform the IAA that you found. Specifically, we are looking for a codex and a jar. And we intend to arrest you as well." As he said this, his eyes fell on the open jar on the worktable. "What is this? This is the jar we have come for. What have you done with it? It looks broken."

"I'll answer your questions in a minute. First, who the hell in the IAA sent you? DG Doormann and I have an understanding and it doesn't include arrest. I want to call him."

"Fuck you!" the leader said. "After you've been arrested you can talk to him personally. Now tell me what happened to the jar and where is the stolen codex!"

"Fuck you!" I yelled back. I was about to say more when he hit me on the side of my head with his pistol. I staggered back. Nicki screamed and Trevor froze. Nicki quickly recovered and ran to my side. She yelled something at him, but I didn't catch it. My ear was still ringing from the blow.

"You will answer my questions, now!" He pulled Nicki away and kind of pushed her toward one of the others with him. To another he said, "Go guard the guy with the camera. And bring the camera to me."

"Now, what happened to the jar?" he said, more of a snarl that a question.

"As we were opening it, the lid fractured."

"Really? And what did you find inside the jar?"

"Nothing. See for yourself. We only just opened it. You can ask the workmen who were here when we arrived. They were repairing damage from a break-in and went for coffee. They can tell you we've only been here a few minutes."

"We will ask them. When will they return?"

"I don't know."

Speaking to the other men in Hebrew, he seemed to tell them to gather up the pieces of the lid, put them in the jar and take the jar to their truck. One was dispatched to the workroom with similar instructions. I said, "Please be careful with those. They are quite valuable."

"Shut up," he replied. "Turn around." He began to zip tie our hands behind our backs. "You are under arrest for failing to register historical artifacts. I suggest you say nothing, not because it can be used against you, but because it will piss me off and I'll be forced to hit you again--this time hard enough to silence you."

"I need my purse," Nicki pleaded, to which the leader said to the man holding her, something that must have been equivalent to "take her to get it," because they walked toward the office where she had left it.

The leader turned Trevor's camera over and began to look at the shots that had been taken. I sincerely hoped he had not taken one of me smashing the lid. I looked at him. He looked as if he were about to pass out. I don't think I've ever seen him that pale. To his credit, he didn't. And from the look on the leader's face, Trevor hadn't snapped a pix of me smashing the lid.

"One other thing before we leave here. Where is the codex?"

"We have no idea. It was stolen from our hotel. DG Doormann knows this. We didn't steal it from ourselves. Our friend who was alone with it was badly beaten in the process. Why would we do that?"

"Obviously, to cover up your theft."

"Oh, good God! You can't believe that!"

"Oh, but I can. And I think I do. Now shut up. I have a phone call to make."

Turning me over to one of his henchmen, the leader stepped away and pulled out his cellphone. He didn't step far enough away; I could still overhear what he was saying. My Hebrew left something to be desired, but I got the gist of it.

"I have a report for you. Our investigation has led us to believe that Gabriel was involved in the missing codex and we have arrested him and two others in their warehouse." He was silent while the other person spoke to him.

"No. No. It's true. Please. Listen." He was interrupted by the voice on the other end. Then he spoke again. "But sir, we also discovered he has a second jar and he opened it just a few minutes ago. He claims nothing was in it." He paused again.

"Yes. A second jar. The lid was broken; he says it was an accident as they were trying to take it off. I reviewed several pictures of the jar, including a blurry shot of the inside. It looked empty." He paused again.

"Sir? Very well. You, Gabriel. He wants to talk to you."

While the leader held the phone, I said, "Hello?"

"Gabby, I am sorry beyond words." It was the DG. "You will be released immediately. This man, this rogue, is an investigator I hired before we talked and became allies. He has no authority to arrest you and hold you. I am mortified by all this. Please, Gabby, say you forgive me." He sounded genuine.

"Mr. Doormann, of course. We can't always be on top of what our inferiors do." I looked at the leader. "I understand. A complete mistake. He went well beyond his mandate. Striking me with his gun was just another example of being out of control. What? Certainly." I said to the leader, "Guess what? He wants to talk to you again."

I couldn't make out the words, but I could clearly hear the volume. Several times the leader tried to interrupt, but was obviously told to shut up. The leader turned back to me, "He wants you again."

I said, "Perhaps you can cut my zip ties and those of my friends." He barked something in Hebrew to one of the others who pulled a nasty looking knife and set us free, starting with me.

"Yes, DG, did you wish to speak to me?"

"Gabby. Please come with these men to my office. I want to make this right for you. You will hear my wrath toward them and feel my compassion for you." A little over the top, I thought, but what the hell, "We'll be happy to come," I replied.

"Splendid. May I speak with Avi one more time?"

"Here...Avi...he wants to speak to you again." I handed him the phone and he turned away, listening. In a moment, he hit End, put the phone away and turned back to me. "My apologizes gentlemen and madam. I have made a grave mistake. The DG has asked that you accompany me to his office."

"We'll take our car and meet you there. Oh, by the way," I said to him, "I have something you need." With that, I did something I've never done in my life. I cold-cocked the sumbitch. Hurt my hand like hell, but it was worth it. I'll never forget the look on his face. I really shouldn't have done it, though; he still had his gun. I'll give him this; he was gracious.

"I deserved that," he said as he rubbed his jaw. "Please, though, for both our sakes," a menacing tone came to his voice that didn't match the smile on his lips, "don't ever do it again." With that, he told his men to move out and they all headed for the door. Over his shoulder, he said, "We will escort you to the DG's office. We are ready when you are."

Clearly, we weren't going to have time to look at the pouch. No matter. It was safe. When Ari and his muscle were out the door, I asked Nicki, "What did it feel like? Is it another codex?" Her answer surprised me.

"No. It was kind of lumpy."

CHAPTER 35
In Avi's Car

Avi pulled out his cell and punched in a number. Receiving an answer, he said, "Jeremy, get three men to help you. You have the address of Gabriel's warehouse. Go there quickly. There is a hole in the wall on the southern side of the building. Check out the alley, climb through that hole and see if anything looks out of place." Avi ended the call and quickly placed another, this time to the DG. Doormann answered almost immediately. "We are on the way. They are right behind us in their car. That shit Gabriel hit me! Little prick."

"Avi, I'm sorry I had to make such a big show of dressing you down. I'm afraid I will need to do it again when you arrive here. Think nothing of it. You have done what I wanted. I will want to know how you discovered Gabriel was involved and what leads you have on the codex. And how you learned of a second jar.

"One of our agents was at the dig site the day after the first jar was found. He didn't see anything as suspicious as the day they found the first jar, but he noticed something strange in one of the pits. Bottom line, he saw them remove some plaster from a wall, then remove stones and expose a niche. In the niche sat what appeared to be a jar. He watched further and the jar was removed, wrapped in bubble wrap and placed in the truck they use for hauling tools. He didn't think much of it, until I contacted him in the course of our investigation. When he asked if a second jar had been reported recovered and learned it had not, he told me the story."

"Excellent work. I suppose he was waiting to see if Gabriel and the others would report the find. I think in the future, we should have our little friends report whatever suspicious actions they see immediately. That would have saved us an enormous amount of time, money and worry."

"I will so instruct them, DG."

"You're sure the second jar was empty?"

"Yes. They wouldn't have had time to do anything with whatever might have been in it. Odd, that it would have been placed in a niche like the first one, empty. However, we will continue our poking around. They may be more clever than we thought."

"Excellent. Our little stipends pay off now and then, do they not? Now what evidence do you have about Gabriel's involvement in the codex theft? Can you tell me before you arrive, or do we need to wait until later?"

"DG, I can tell you my evidence is indirect and my staff are still trying to verify what we've learned. But I trusted it enough to find him and scare him. If you'll permit me, I would like to wait until I have absolute proof."

"Certainly. If I don't know when I see Gabriel, it will be easier to be nice to him." He disconnected. Avi, put his phone away, rubbed his still tender jaw and gazed out the windshield. *For an academic, he hits pretty hard.*

In Gabriel's Car

Gabriel asked Nicki to drive while he called the hospital. He rode beside her with Trevor in the rear seat. He had not made a note of the hospital phone number so he was fumbling with his copies of all the papers he had to sign that he'd stuffed in his pants pocket.

"Okay. Here it is."

He punched in a number and when the phone was answered asked for the ICU Nurses' Station. He was connected and on the third ring the phone was answered. "ICU. Mrs. Solomon speaking."

"Miz Solomon, this is Dr. Gabriel. My friend Martino Fratini is one of your patients. I was wondering if there had been any change."

"He regained consciousness a little bit ago and asked for a priest who is with him now."

"How is he? Can I speak with him?"

"He's critical, but stable. We don't have phones in the ICU rooms, but I can let him know you called. I suspect after his visit with the priest he'll drop off to sleep again. He seemed very troubled and I think the visit with the priest will offer some relief."

"Do you think if we came by he'd know we were there?"

"Dr. Gabriel, frankly I'd wait and let him rest more. Perhaps you could come this evening. The last family visit is at 8:00 for fifteen minutes."

"Alright. Please tell him we called and we'll see him tonight."

"I'll be happy to do that."

"Listen…one more thing…please tell him he scared the shit out of me and…and…I love him."

Gabriel disconnected before she could respond. He relayed his news to Nicki and Trevor and then everyone was quiet. There was a sense of relief in the car, but also an awareness that Marty was far from recovery. In a very few minutes, they arrived at the DG's office.

In the Intensive Care Unit

The priest entered Marty's room again and said, "My son, I'll begin writing now. As I write a bit, I'll read it back to you to make sure I have it the way you want it. Is that all right?" Marty didn't answer. He seemed to have drifted to sleep or back to unconsciousness. The priest, who really didn't understand such things, looked up at the monitor. There was no flat line; he knew that was good. Beyond that, he was lost. He pulled up the only chair in the room, sat down and clicking open his pen, began to write.

It took the priest about fifteen minutes to complete his work. He spoke to Marty once more, but Marty didn't respond. Unwilling to try to wake him, he put his pen away. He tore off the page on which he had written Marty's confession and folded it to fit his inner jacket pocket and walked back to the nurse's station. "Thank you so much for the note paper," handing back the unused portion. "Dr. Fratini was asleep and I did not wish to wake him. When next he's awake, please let him know I have done as he asked."

"I'll be happy to. He'll know what you're talking about?"

"Oh yes. Thank you. By the way, are you by chance Catholic?" he asked in a warm friendly way. He looked a bit like the old priests often depicted in movies: kind face, snow white hair, light tan, easy smile. He seemed to be a person to whom one could easily confide.

She flushed. "No father. I'm afraid I am nothing."

"Oh my child! Don't say such a thing! In God's sight we are all priceless. You can never be nothing!"

Giggling she said, "Oh, Father, I meant I don't belong to a church. I believe in God though and I think I'm spiritual, but I'm just not religious."

"Yes. Yes. I hear that so often these days. Well, God bless you, young woman." He made the sign of the cross in the air toward her. "And don't forget the message."

"I won't Father. Shalom."

"And also with you. Yes, peace also be with you." He smiled and headed toward the elevator to return to his rectory.

He seemed really nice, she thought, *Maybe I should try his church sometime.*

An alarm began to sound at her desk. "Code Red.

ICU Room 2. Stat!" she shouted. Nurses came running. A crash cart appeared, pushed by a male nurse. Marty had flat lined.

CHAPTER 36

In the Nave of the Co-Cathedral of the Most Holy Name of Jesus, Jerusalem

The visitor couldn't help but notice the beauty of the place. The Cathedral was very light and airy. The stonework was a natural limestone color built in a neo-Gothic style. The ceiling between the arches was painted sky blue and each bay seemed to have a holy figure or scene painted on the blue background. The high altar gleamed from the gold gilding on it. The floor was constructed of white diamond shaped marble with black inserts made from bituminous limestone from the desert of Judea. It was not as old as some churches and sites in Jerusalem, dating from a completion date of 1872, but it was clearly revered. It was located in the Old City and was home to the Latin Patriarch. It was an altogether splendid place in which to worship. Or in the visitor's case, to conduct business.

He turned from looking at the interior and located the confessional he was to enter. He noticed the little light over it was off. He reasoned it meant it was "not available" if the light was on. He also noticed a priest standing some distance away looking toward the confessional. He felt wary. He slowly turned to look once again at the nave, to see if anyone else was just standing around. Then he heard a voice in English, say, "No. No. Grandmother. There is no one available to hear your confession there. Please use one of the other two." He turned to see the priest pointing an old woman toward the third confessional down one of the side aisles. Clearly the priest was there to keep others away from this one. The great cathedral bell tolled out three deep tolls. The visitor moved toward the confessional and entered, nodding to the priest who was guarding it.

Under the seat, he saw a valise. He picked it up and tugged it open. It was full of money, neat packets of hundreds. He didn't even try to count it. He snapped it closed and took out an envelope from under his shirt, tucked into his waistband. He laid it on the floor where the valise had been. He stood and opened the confessional door, nodded to the priest who was still standing exactly where he had been, and walked out the main door. The "guard" wasted no time in entering the confessional and retrieving the envelope. He didn't even close the door. Once he had the envelope, he turned and headed toward one of the side doors of the cathedral. He was on his way to Newhouse. He only hoped there was enough light for the two cameras to get a good picture. One was in the confessional itself, a very small button sized video camera wedged in the screen that separated the priest and the penitent. He would remove it later. The other was mounted on one of the columns that make up an arch. It was aimed at the confessional. The feeds from both were being sent to one of the video rooms in the building adjacent to the church. There will be pictures of this visitor waiting for us.

What this particular priest didn't know was that there were two more priests outside in ordinary street clothes, looking very much like pilgrims. Their mission today was not to see the sites, however; their mission was the follow the person with the valise. They were not alone either. There were others they were in contact with by Bluetooth devices in their ears that looked exactly like cell phone Bluetooth devices. In this way, they could avoid being, as they say on cop shows, "made" by the "target." These religious were dedicated to the Church, answering directly to the Pope but in this task directly to Newhouse. The plan was simple. Follow the bastard, find the codex, and bring it and the Church's money back to Newhouse.

These religious, that is men who had taken vows and who lived in community with each other, had a name, but it was a name known only to a select number. That name was The Order of The Dark Brothers. To the world they were known as the Community of Perpetual Penitents. They could trace their history with some certainty as far back as the Crusades. They had careful records of their work during the Inquisitions. When Holy Mother Church called them in, they came in with no holds barred. The select few in the Church's hierarchy who knew of their existence rarely spoke of them. That did not stop them from using the Brothers who tended to be thorough and ruthless as they pursued their missions. These two were very careful to not be seen. They were well practiced and just appeared to be chatting as they walked along. Indeed they were, except to others who were tailing this man. They suddenly slowed down and seemed to window shop. The target had turned into a women's dress shop.

"He's just entered a dress shop. You suppose he's buying a gift for his girlfriend?" one broadcast to the others. In a few minutes, a team from the opposite direction came toward them. "Okay, we handing him off. We've been standing here long enough." The two original men tailing him, moved on to take up station elsewhere.

Fifteen minutes elapsed. He hadn't come out.

"Is somebody on the back door?"

The answer came back quickly. "Yes. We have it in view. Nothing here."

Another minute went by and he emerged from the shop still carrying his valise and resumed walking in the direction he had been heading. The two priests waiting near the shop fell in behind him at a safe distance. "He's on the move again. Same direction." A few minutes after they passed the door to the shop, a portly woman emerged from the shop and turned in the opposite direction. She didn't look especially well put together, but then not every woman is into how she looks. Up close anyone could have seen "she" was a man dressed in women's clothes.

After an hour of following the first man to no particular destination, the detail leader radioed. "Okay, that's enough. Pick him up. Try not to make a scene. We don't need the Israeli police horning in."

"Roger that. I have the syringe ready. He will appear drunk, but not incapacitated. We're moving in."

It was over in a moment. One of the detail took the valise from him while the others acted like good friends helping someone who'd had a few too many. The one with the valise got an odd look on his face. The valise should be heavier. He stopped and snapped it open. It was empty.

"Take him down the next alley we come too!" In a moment, that was done. The one who gave the order took out his cellphone, snapped a picture of the man's face and e-mailed to his superior along with the note: the money's gone. It only took a couple of minutes until the entire detail heard,

"Shit! It's not him! You've lost the fucking bastard! Bring this asshole back to the office and we'll see what we can learn. Goddamn it! How could you have lost him?"

CHAPTER 37

A Non-descript Office Building

The dark green SUV pulled into the garage beneath the office building that was located on an out of the way street. Five men emerged, two supporting one of the five, all dressed very casually. They half-drug, half-walked the man being supported to the elevator. His casual dress had an accessory the others didn't have--he was blindfolded. They pressed the up button and in a moment the doors, which could have used a paint job, silently slid open. The elevator didn't look like it belonged in this building. The building itself appeared a bit rundown to anyone walking or driving past, but the elevator was nicely appointed. Marble graced the floor and the walls were covered in what appeared to be African Rosewood paneling. The inside of the elevator doors was gleaming stainless steel, highly polished. In a moment, they silently opened onto a nicely appointed lobby.

The supported man was still trying to protest, but his words were slurred and he was still very uncoordinated. He was taken to a room down the hall from the lobby and placed behind a table and told to sit. The room looked exactly like every cop show interrogation room, right down to the one-way mirror and the ring bolted to the top of the table. One of the captors used handcuffs to secure him to the ring. In a moment another person entered and said,

"Roll up his sleeve. No never mind; I'll just inject him in the neck." He then took a couple of swipes with an alcohol-saturated pad and plunged the short needle into the captive's neck. "It'll take a few minutes. Go get coffee or something."

Indeed, in a few minutes, the former babbling incoherent captive was protesting his situation in a very loud voice. His captors returned.

"What's going on? What do you want? I didn't do anything wrong!"

"Please be quiet and we can get this over very quickly and you'll be back home having your TV dinner as if nothing has happened." The captive stopped shouting. "We just want to know three things. One, why are you dressed in those clothes, and two, where did you get the valise. The third thing is this: what happened to the contents of the valise.

"Okay. No problem. I got nothing to hide. See, I'm in the dress shop looking for a dress for my wife. We are planning on a little trip and I wanted to get something special for her, you know? This dude comes over to me and he says, 'Can I talk to you for a minute?' I figure he's shopping too and wants some help. See I have pretty good taste in women's clothes. 'Course, he wouldn't have known that, but I didn't think of that at the time. So I says to him, 'Sure. Need some help picking out clothes?' He says, 'No. I need an odd favor.' I'm thinking, this is weird." He stopped talking.

"That's it?" he was asked impatiently.

"No, there's more. This is really weird. He says to me, he says, 'Look, I know this sounds nutty, but I'll give you a thousand bucks to change clothes with me and take this valise and walk around for an hour.' So I says, 'What? A thousand bucks? You're shittin' me? Right? 'No,' he says, 'here's the money.' He pulls out a stack of hundreds wrapped up like the just came from the bank."

"Pulls it out of what?"

"The satchel." He looked up at his captors looking first from one to the other. The sweat glistened on his forehead and upper lip. Dark rings were visible under his arm pits. "He says, 'Here take it. Just change clothes with me. Walk around for an hour going nowhere and that's it.' Well, I says, 'Hell yeah!' So we go back to the fitting rooms and he tells the woman there we need to use them for a minute to play a joke on our wives. He says, 'We're gonna change clothes and freak 'em out.' Then he smiled real big and she says, 'Sure go ahead.' So we do. That's it. That's the whole story. I swear. Oh, man, I gotta pee real bad. Can we stop and let me pee?"

"Sure." One turned to the other. Uncuff him and take him to the restroom."

As they walked out, the man obviously in charge, pulls out his cell and punches in a number. "He paid some idiot to change clothes with him to fake us off. He'd emptied the valise and told the guy to walk around for an hour with it in hand." There was a pause while he listened. "Yeah. Yeah. We found the money on him when we searched him. A nice neat bundle fresh from the bank." Another pause. "Okay, we'll take him back to where we picked him up and dump him." Another pause. "We'll give him another little cocktail and blindfold him." A pause. "What? Leave him the money. Okay, if you say so." He punched End just as the captive and his guardian returned.

"Okay, here's the deal, my friend. You were made party to a terrorist plot. We only have your word for this story; for all we know you may have been in on it from the beginning.

The captive interrupted. "No! No! Look I'm not a terrorist. You don't have to take my word for it! Go ask the woman at the store. She saw the whole deal!" He was clearly panicked.

"We will. We have also learned where you live. So, we're going to let you keep the money and we will take you back to where we found you. You will speak of none of this to anyone. Hide the money from your wife. Buy a whore; we don't care. If we find out you talked, it will not go well for you, my friend. We are going to blindfold you now and take you away."

"I won't talk! Don't worry. I'm a good citizen. Oh, God! I had no idea the guy was a terrorist."

"We shall see about that. For now, you have a free pass." Turning to the guardian he said, "You heard the plan. Also, stop in the lobby. We will have a little celebratory cocktail for him."

"As good as done."

"Good." The leader pulled out his cell again and as the captive and his guard walked toward the lobby, he ordered the cocktail.

Later In the Captive's Apartment

"How did it go?" the caller asked?

"They seemed to have bought the story. I thought about pissing my pants when they said you were a terrorist, but they had just let me pee."

"A terrorist?"

"Yeah, they said I'd unwittingly become an accomplice. They threatened me if I ever tell anybody about it. Let me keep the money though."

"Excellent. Enjoy it. I hope we can work together again. In the meantime, I still have more to do."

The former captive's phone went dead. He punched End, sniffed the money and started thinking how he'd spend it and the other ten grand he'd already been given. Especially since there was no wife to split it with. Assholes. They'll believe anything. Life did seem good. Except for the god-awful headache their "cocktails" gave him.

Across Town In the Caller's Apartment

The caller congratulated himself on his selection of helpers and on the good planning he had done. Hell, he knew he'd be tailed and he couldn't count on a stranger to help him with that goofy story. Especially one his size and with hair like his. Having an accomplice is the only way to go. Life was good. And it was soon going to be even better. The new plan was to stiff the RCs and not give them the entire codex. That would allow either selling off the rest of the pages to them one at a time, or finding another buyer. The knock on the door told him the rest of their little group had arrived. *Time to celebrate.*

CHAPTER 38

In the Intensive Care Unit

"Charge to 300!"

"Charged!"

"Clear!"

Marty's body lurched upward as the electricity coursed between the paddles and hit his heart. The monitor was still beeping and the lines were still flat.

"Charge to 360!"

"Charged!"

"Clear!"

Again, Marty's body jerked as the electric jolt flashed between the paddles and his heart. Again the beeping continued and the lines were flat.

"Get me an epi! 300. Stat!"

The ICU intern jammed the epinephrine pen directly into Marty's heart and he pushed the plunger. This artificial adrenaline is a last ditch effort to chemically shock a stopped heart and isn't very effective, but may work. Nothing else had worked so the epi pen was a calculated risk.

Nothing. "Turn off that damned beeping!"

"I'm starting compressions. Bag him." The intern jumped up on the table and started CPR compressions, keeping rhythms with the disco song, "Staying Alive." Fitting. But after six or seven minutes, it was clear it was there was no response. He stopped and climbed off. "Okay. We tried. I'm calling it. Time of death 1633." He was soaked with sweat and looked very frustrated and defeated.

The ICU charge nurse had already called the attending physician and now she was calling the morgue. The attending arrived about that time. "What happened," he wanted to know.

"Dr. Fratini expired without warning a few minutes ago. He had awakened earlier today and called for a priest to make his confession. He seemed agitated, but calmed down when I told him we'd get a priest. We saw nothing on the monitor or on his tests to indicate Fratini was anywhere near *extremis* but he insisted. I called St. Anne's as we usually do when we have a priest request and a Father Donlin came. The patient was able to talk with the priest, I guess for ten, maybe fifteen minutes, and then Father Donlin came out to get something to write on. The patient had apparently asked him to write something for a friend. Maybe fifteen minutes later the priest was finished. He spoke to the clerk for a few minutes and left. That was probably half an hour or so ago. Then the monitors started sounding and we tried to resuscitate the patient for ten to fifteen minutes with no response. The intern called it."

The attending, trying to be sure he'd understood said, "He had regained consciousness and spoken, then flat-lined? Odd. I think given the circumstances, especially since he was the victim of a robbery, we'll order an autopsy."

The nurse said, "I've notified the morgue to come for the body. I'll call back and tell them to schedule an autopsy. I've also got to call his emergency contact."

"This is a little weird. His injuries were severe, but I didn't expect this. What did the last EKG show?" The nurse pulled his chart and flipped a few pages to a narrow strip of paper with a graph and tracing on it.

"Here it is. What'd you think, doctor?"

He examined the printout for a minute or so. "It

looks fairly normal. No indication of an irregularity or any damage." The doctor returned to Marty's room and pulled back the sheet that had been placed over him and began to pull back the bandage over the head wound. "Just from a visual, I'd say the swelling hadn't gotten worse. What's the latest CBC show?" Again, the nurse consulted the chart she'd brought with her.

"I'm sure it's normal or we would have let you know when the results came back. Okay. Here it is. Nothing's flagged. His chemistry looked good, even considering. They ran a standard panel with the CBC and there's nothing important out of whack. It's what we'd expect from a patient with these injuries."

"When was the last brain scan done?" Consulting the chart again, the nurse said, "Not long after he came in. Obviously it wasn't good. Lots of trauma. Not enough time has passed to warrant another one."

"Strange. Well, you never can predict these things. I'll alert the morgue to let me know what they find. You say the priest is someone whom we've called before?" She nodded. "Anybody else in there recently?" She said only the priest had been in the room. "Can you give me the priest's phone number? I'd like to speak to him."

"Sure. I still have it written on my scratch pad. Had to call information. Frankly we don't get many requests for priests. Here you go."

"Father Donlin, you say?"

"Yes. Donlin. Listen, just to clarify: we've called St. Anne's before, but I'm not sure I've ever seen Donlin before. I think they send whoever is available."

"The ICU conference room looks empty. I'll call him from there."

The attending opened the conference room door and flopped into a chair. It had been a long shift and wasn't over yet. He slipped off his glasses and rubbed the bridge of his nose. Holding his glasses up to a light, he could see smudges on both lens that he tried to remove using the bottom of his tie that was pulled loose from his neck but still knotted. He slipped the glasses now less smudged but not clean, back on, looked at the phone number and began to punch in St. Anne's number. A few rings and one receptionist later and he heard an apparently older male voice say, "Father Donlin."

"Father, this is Dr. Simon Buchanan at Shaare Zedek Medical Center. Do you have a moment to speak?"

"I do. How may I be of service?"

"Earlier today you came to hear the confession of one of our patients, a Dr. Fratini; is that correct?"

"Yes. I just returned from there. I heard his confession. Is anything wrong?"

"Dr. I'm sorry to tell you he died shortly after you left."

The old priest crossed himself with his free hand and said, "God rest his soul. I must say a mass for him."

"Father, how did he seem when you saw him?"

"He was troubled. He struggled to speak at first, but it came easier as we talked. I heard his confession and he seemed very much at peace when I absolved him. Tired though."

"Did he seem impaired to you?"

"A little. Had to stop and think as if remembering was hard. Sort of talked in little bits, stringing a story together."

The doctor continued, "Did anything unusual happen? Did anyone else come into the room while you were there?

"Something unusual did happen, as a matter of fact. Funny you should ask. He asked that I write down what he told me and insisted it be given to someone he named, a friend, should he die."

"You wrote his confession as he confessed?"

"No. No. I thought it best to hear his confession then absolve him. I told him I would then write it down and read it back to him bit by bit to be sure I got it all the way he wanted it."

"And did you do that?"

"No, it didn't work out that way. I had to step out of the room to get some paper and when I stepped back in, he was apparently sleeping. I really didn't think waking him was wise, so I just stayed and wrote what I remembered. I spoke to him when I finished, but he didn't stir so I asked the nurse to let him know I'd written what he'd asked. I wasn't surprised he was sleeping because as I returned to the room a doctor stepped out and I asked how Dr. Fratini was and he said, 'Resting. Peacefully' and walked down the hall."

The attending's eyebrow went up, "So no one was in the room with you, but in the minute or so it took you to step out and return, a doctor entered and left?"

"Well, yes. I hadn't really thought about it, but yes. He couldn't have been in the room very long, because he entered after I stepped out for the paper."

"Father, you didn't happen to see his name on his ID did you?"

The old priest paused a moment, "You know, now that I think about it, his ID was on a lanyard around his neck and it was turned so the back showed."

"You're sure, Father."

"Oh yes, I can picture it very clearly now."

"No name written over his pocket?"

"If there was, I didn't notice it."

"Thank you very much Father."

"I hope I've been able to help."

"Oh, yes, Father, you've been a big help. Thank you."

"One thing, doctor, if you need a place for his funeral, St. Anne's will be glad to provide the requiem mass."

"He has an emergency contact, no next of kin, so I guess it will be up to that person. I'll pass along your offer. Thanks again. Bye now." The priest responded and they both disconnected. The attending returned to the nurse's station. "Would you please call the chief of security and ask him to meet me up here. Don't let the morgue take the body yet, either."

"What's wrong, doctor?"

"I think our patient was murdered."

CHAPTER 39

At the Offices of the Community of Perpetual Penitence

The only surveillance team member not present at the conference table was the one delivering the target back to Old City. He was expected back shortly. The leader, a priest named Donovan, said, "Something has been bothering me, that's the reason I wanted us to debrief. Why did we follow this guy? Tell me."

Another priest, Joseph, spoke up, "He was a man coming out of a dress shop carrying the valise."

"Right."

Said a third, "Plus the clothes were right."

Joseph added, "Yeah and his build and hair looked the same."

Donovan looked at the three of them. "The target's story--what's his name by the way?"

Another priest said, "I have a copy of his driver's license. Name's Heywood, Robert Heywood."

Donovan resumed, "Okay, Heywood's story is he's in a dress shop shopping for his wife. Now what we have is two men of approximately the same build, with hair about the same, who just happen to be in a dress shop--a dress shop, mind you--at the same time. What are the odds?"

"You're saying it was a set up from the beginning."

"I'm saying," Donovan said, "it's damned convenient for our thief to find the nearly perfect match--in a dress shop--in a city of nearly a million people. Of all the places he could have gone, why a dress shop?"

The third priest said, "We need to see if he's even married, and if he is, how often he shops for his wife's clothes."

"Get on that," Donovan ordered and immediately, the priest left for a computer terminal.

Joseph said, "Shit! Our thief went to a dress shop so he could leave in women's clothes!"

"Bingo!" said Donovan. "The prick figured we'd tail him, so he planned a two pronged scheme to throw us off. I need to call the bishop."

The third priest came back into the room. "If his name actually is Robert Heywood and he actually lives at the address he gave us, he's not married."

Father Donovan stood, leaned forward with his knuckles on the table top. "Get some more help and get to his apartment. If the same guy comes to the door, rough him up in his apartment, look for the money, and then drag his ass back here. And don't get caught. We don't need the police involved."

With nods of agreement, the three stood, Donovan made the sign of the cross over them and said, "God is your right hand!" Joseph had his phone to his ear calling for reinforcements as they walked out.

Donovan punched in Newhouse' cell number from memory. When he answered, Donovan said, "We've got a lead; we may yet get the codex." He quickly filled him in on their conclusions. "We'll get him back here and he will--let me stress this--he will give up the thief. We are also still trying to match the photos we got while he was in the Cathedral with several databases we have access to. If that doesn't work, I have a contact with the Israeli Police who may be able to help us. We're closing in. Can you string him along a little longer?"

"I am to talk with him tomorrow at noon. By then we hope to have the text from the photocopied page he gave us. If it is at all promising, I can offer more money and ask for time to raise it."

Donovan replied, "Perfect, Your Grace. I'll be in touch as soon as we have more information."

"Thank you, Father. I knew I could depend on you. I knew losing him earlier was only a temporary set back. Donovan, God is on our side!"

"Yes, Your Grace. He is." They disconnected and Donovan went back to his office to await Robert Heywood's return. *I show the little prick you can't get away with shit like this with us. He'll regret he ever tried.*

CHAPTER 40

The Director-General's Office

The DG, Gabby, Nicki, Trevor and Avi the investigator, had been in the DG's office for nearly forty minutes. Doormann had apologized multiple times to Gabby and reamed out Avi a couple of times. Avi had apologized to Gabby and to the DG more than once. The DG had explained to Gabby how the IAA sometimes uses outside investigators when the IAA staff was occupied and that resulted, on occasion, in this kind of sloppy work. Gabby was assured Avi would never do any work for IAA again. Avi looked appropriately chastised and downcast as he was dismissed while the others remained.

"Now, my friend, we must clear the air between us," said the DG. "You kept extremely important information from me, Gabby. I'm very saddened by your lack of trust." Gabby interrupted,

"That's not exactly the reason." But, the DG went

on,

"No matter the reason, the discoveries you made have great potential for our field and for our country, certainly for Christianity and maybe Judaism. Because of that, we could have safeguarded the codex, Gabby. We would still have it. You and we could now be studying it. Now it may be lost forever. What if the thief destroys it? What if he sells it to a third party who wants to suppress whatever Mary is telling us? What if a third party controls it and distorts what it says? Forgive me for saying this, but after the Dan Brown business, don't you think the Catholics would pay anything to have it for fear it will tell of a marriage of Mary and Jesus? All these things are catastrophes, Gabby."

"DG, if I had it all to do over, I would have made different decisions. But, you know what they say about hindsight. We were going to photograph each page under varying conditions to protect the codex, then we were going to turn it over. One more day and we would have it done and we could both be happy. There was no reason to think anyone knew we had it, much less that our apartment in the hotel was where we were working on it. How could we have predicted any of this?"

"Yes. I understand. You were doing what you thought was best for your interests, while trying not to interfere with ours. It is all most unfortunate. But, Gabby, my friend, we both must learn from this exper..." He was interrupted by Gabriel's cell phone.

"DG, I'm sorry. Normally I would ignore the call, but with Marty..." as he was speaking he pulled out the phone. "Uh oh! It's the hospital." He answered, "Dr. Gabriel." The look on his face made it clear to everyone the news was bad. He interrupted the caller to ask "When" and "How" but listened more than talked. Then, "What! Who did it? Have you anyone in custody?" He listened again. "I'll be there as quickly as I can." He pressed End and turned to the group, "Marty's dead and the hospital thinks he was murdered. The police are on the way to the hospital and I need to be there too." He was standing as he was talking, obviously ending the conversation.

"Yes, Gabby, you must go. My God! My sincerest sympathies. Please call me when you know more. And if IAA can help in any way, let me know."

Trevor and Nicki had stood when Gabby did and now the three of them headed for the door. "Thank you DG. I'll keep you informed. From now on."

As soon as they were out the door and out of earshot of Doormann, Nicki and Trevor began to pepper him with questions. All he could tell them was, "They are a little suspicious of a priest who heard Marty's confession, but what the doctor thinks really happened is someone impersonating a doctor somehow killed him. That's really all I know."

They were at the car and Gabby said, "I know one other thing. That was a charade we were just a part of. All that apologizing and firing Avi; that was solely for show. IAA knows more, the DG knows more than he's telling us. Oh, shit!" A new idea hit him, "Could they be involved in the murder?"

The Director-General's Office

Doormann had just completed punching a number into his phone. On the second ring, he heard a pick up.

"Avi! Someone may have murdered Marty, Gabriel's number two man. Reassure me."

"It was not us, DG."

"Good. See what you can learn about all this. I have little faith Gabriel will keep me advised in a timely fashion." The DG gave him the name of the hospital and other particulars and finished up by saying, "It would nice if we could get ahead of this. If we find the murderer, we find the codex."

"I understand sir. We'll do our best."

"Ah, Avi. I know you will. I know you will. Keep me informed." He replaced the receiver and settled back in his chair thinking that Gabriel had fallen for the whole, how do they say, kit and caboodle, earlier. *That,* he thought, *might keep him somewhat in line. For now, anyway.*

Somewhere in Jerusalem

"So, how did it go?"

"Easy, peasy. I walked in as if I were a visitor with flowers in my hand and asked at the information desk for Mr. Fratini's room number. She told me and said he could only have visitors for five minutes each hour. I thanked her and headed to a restroom. I went in and stepped into a stall, waited a minute until the guy washing his hands was finished and left. Then I slipped on a white coat and stethoscope I had smuggled in. I had an ID on a lanyard I've used on other jobs, so I put it on and used double sided tape and stuck it to my coat to make sure it would keep only the back of it showing."

"Clever. What about the flowers?"

"I left them on the back of the toilet in the stall."

"Then what?"

"I took the elevator to the third floor where the ICU is. I walked into the ICU like I belonged, quickly spotted Marty's room and walked in. There was nobody there. That was a help. Then I stuck the syringe into his Ringer's bag, squeezed, and put the syringe back in my pocket with the cap on it. I walked out. I walked to the stairway and walked down one flight and kept going until I was outside. The bag was nearly empty so I thought he'd get the dose pretty quickly. I stuck it in just above the level of the liquid. I thought that way there wouldn't be a needle mark in case they got suspicious."

"Just like that?"

"Just exactly like that."

"No hitch?"

"The closest thing to a hitch was that was I was walking out of his room, a Catholic priest was walking in and spoke to me."

"What'd he say?"

"How's the patient."

"And?"

"And...I said 'resting'. He was resting all right. He probably was having the best 'rest' of his life." They both laughed.

"Tell me about the priest."

"There's nothing to tell. We spoke and I kept going."

"So he saw your face and heard your voice?"

"For just a second, but yeah, I guess you could say

that."

"I could say that because it's true. He may be able to identify you."

"What? Naw. It was over in a second, maybe two."

"Like that's not enough time? Is that what you're telling me?

"Okay, Maybe he could describe me, but what's the chance anybody can put that description on me?"

"I don't want to risk it. We've got to find that priest and eliminate him. We can't take any chances."

"Don't you think a second murder is pushing our luck?"

"You know, I'm aware we wouldn't have gotten this far if it hadn't been for you. I appreciate your brains, your planning, but you've made two mistakes. If you'd finished Marty off when you took the codex, we wouldn't have to deal with the priest. If you'd timed it better, the priest wouldn't be an issue anyway."

"How the hell could I know the priest was going to be going in that room?" Some anger was creeping in. "It was empty when I glanced in, so I took my shot."

"Okay, I'll give you that. You couldn't have known. But you were seen. We've got to deal with that."

“By ‘we’ you of course mean me, right?”

“Yes. Look, we’re both in this up to our eyeballs. I made the calls to the Catholics and I took the chance at the church. Bottom line: it doesn’t matter who offs him, if we’re ever caught, we’ll both hang. You’ve got the knack. Don’t tell me you didn’t like beating up Marty. Plus, I didn’t notice any hesitation when I said I thought we’d need to finish him off.”

“All right! It’s a power trip. You find him; I’ll finish him, but let’s get this part over with in a hurry.”

CHAPTER 41

At the Intensive Care Unit

Gabriel, Nicki and Trevor rushed down the hall from the elevator and banged through the double doors of the ICU. At the nurses' station, Gabriel said, "Someone called me about my friend Marty Fratini! I'm his contact person, Dr. Gabriel. What's going on?" Before the nurse could answer, one of the hospital security officers approached him.

"You are the next of kin?"

"He has no family. I'm his employer and emergency contact. My name's Gabby Gabriel."

"Please come with me."

"To where? I want to know what's happened!" Gabby practically shouted.

"To a conference room just down the hall. Who are these other people?"

"My wife and son." Both Nicki and Trevor looked surprised, but only for a moment. "They're coming with us."

"Very well. This way please."

The four of them walked down the hall and stepped through the door the officer held for them. They could see before they entered there were two men in suits and a doctor and a nurse sitting at the table. Introductions were made, including the names of the two men in suits: Lieutenant Schmidt and Sergeant Aamir, both of the Israeli Police. After the introductions, the Lieutenant said, "We are so sorry for your loss. Thank you for coming. We have questions we need to have answered for our investigation; you can help us."

"I'll...we'll...do whatever we can. Can you tell me why you believe he was murdered?"

"At this point in the investigation, I can only say there were some odd things that have piqued our interest. I can tell you we have reason to believe an imposter dressed as a physician may have done something to him. We will not know until the Medical Examiner has completed an autopsy and we have done tox screens. At the moment our crime scene people are in the room looking for evidence."

"I can't believe anybody would want to kill him.

He was here because he was beaten in a robbery at my hotel apartment, but he couldn't have been the target."

"We have a report on this robbery, yes?"

"Yes we called the police and officers and two detectives came as well as crime scene people."

There was a knock on the door as it was pushed open. "Lieutenant, may I see you a minute?"

The Lieutenant rose, asked the table to excuse him, and stepped outside into the hall. "Moshe, the crime scene guys have found something. Come see." The two of them walked to Marty's room where his body still lay, just as he had died.

"Oh, hey LT." One of the techs said. "Listen, we guessed he might have been injected with something because that would be easiest to do quickly so we check the tubes and shit and didn't find anything. But that wouldn't be a surprise, because something could have been inserted into this little port in his vein or even just stuck in his body. But, we're thinking what if the killer isn't a medical person?"

"Does this story have an ending, because I've got grieving people waiting to be questioned?"

"Sorry LT. Bottom line. We found a tiny hole in the back of his Ringer's bag. See. The bag was nearly empty, so it wouldn't have taken long for whatever what injected to make it to the bloodstream."

"So, the killer stuck a needle into the bag, injected a solution, and then it dripped into the dead guy's vein. Hmm. Get the bag to the lab and find out what was in it. Good work, men." The Lieutenant walked from the room and back to the conference room. "Sorry, for that. We found something the CSI people thought I needed to see."

"What? What is it?" Trevor asked.

"Sorry. I can't say right now. Look, I need to ask you a few questions to help us in our investigation." He was interrupted again by the same man.

"Sorry again LT. The Medical Examiner is here. You said you wanted to be notified."

"Thanks. Come back for me as soon as he's finished his preliminary look."

"Got it."

What followed for the next fifteen or so minutes was a lot of questions on background matters. While Gabriel understood the importance, he was becoming increasingly impatient with the process. A few times Nicki had put her hand on his arm and he would calm down. Finally, the Lieutenant said, "Thank you so much for your time and patience. I know this is a difficult time for you.

Let me tell you what will happen next. The ME will take your friend's body to the morgue and perform an autopsy. Various tests will be run on blood and other fluids. All of this will help us pinpoint the cause of death that can help point us in the direction of the killer. You'll be notified when you may have the body. I wish I could say when. It will depend on our findings. You understand, I hope. If you think of anything else, please call me. Here's my card; I've written my cell phone number on the back."

The door opened for the third time. "Sorry again LT. The ME's finished."

"I'll be right there. We're through here."

Everyone rose and headed for the door. "Can I see him before you take him to the morgue?" Gabriel asked.

"Certainly. Come with me."

After Gabby, Nicki and Trevor saw Marty's body, they left the hospital. Nicki was teary watching the horror and loss on Gabby's face. Trevor looked lost himself. He never signed up for anything like this. They agreed that Trevor would go back to the dig sites and clue in everyone, while Gabriel and Nicki went to the hotel to decide the next steps.

Back in the ICU, the police and ME took over the conference room again. The ME agreed that in all likelihood something was injected into the hanging bag. What? He could only guess. The Lieutenant summarized what they knew which was a probable imposter entered the room and did the injection. He wanted to talk to the priest face to face, so he was heading out to St. Anne's. He decided to call on the way to be sure Donlin was in. Everyone else headed back to their offices.

St. Anne's Parish Church

Father Donlin was waiting for him at his office at St. Anne's. While the Lieutenant had seen murderers of all kinds, after a few minutes of interviewing him, the policeman's instincts were pointing away from Donlin having anything to do with any of this. "Father, what was it you wrote for Mr. Fratini?"

"Oh, Lieutenant, I'm sorry. It's protected under the seal of the confessional. I can't divulge it."

"Father, it might help us in our murder investigation; we really need to know what it said."

"I wish I could help, but my hands are tied. All I can say is that it was an apology to a friend."

"An apology? For what?"

"I'm sorry. I'm skirting the edges by telling you anything."

"Can you at least tell me who the friend is?"

"I suppose I can. It is a Dr. Gabriel."

The Lieutenant tried to keep his non-committal face on, but there was a slight twitch. Suddenly the grieving friend was looking like a suspect. He might have had reason to kill depending on what Marty was confessing.

"Are you to contact Gabriel, Father, and give him this information."

"Yes. I've tried his phone, but it went to voice mail. I'm hoping he'll call me back soon." As if by magic, the priest's phone rang, and after excusing himself, he answered it. The officer couldn't help overhearing. Gabriel was returning his call. Donlin and Gabriel made plans to meet at St. Anne's as quickly as he could arrive. When the conversation ended, the policeman said,

"I assume Dr. Gabriel can tell me what's in the message if he wishes to do so? No Church law against that is there?"

"Oh, no. He's free to do whatever he wishes with it. But I can't..."

"I understand Father. Thank you for your time. I'll show myself out."

The Lieutenant walked across the parking lot to

his car and decided he needed to move it so he could see the front of the church. That way, when Gabriel came, he could wait for him and grab him and the note.

Almost as soon as the priest left Donlin's office, the priest's phone rang again. "Father Donlin," he said.

"Father, this is Dr. Gabriel. We spoke a moment ago. Listen, we have a lot going on right now. Can you just read the message to me and let me pick it up later? It would be a great help to us."

"Yes. Yes, I can do that. Just a moment while I get my glasses." He fumbled for his reading glasses, put them on and adjusted them on his nose. Ready?"

"Yes."

As the priest read the message, Gabriel's face drained of all color. He sat down, feeling very weak and confused. What he was hearing was surreal, unbelievable, and yet it answered so many questions. He thanked the priest and was about to hang up when Donlin said, "Dr. Gabriel. I don't know what your religion is, but your friend has done a courageous thing in telling you all this. I hope you can find..." The phone went dead. Gabby had disconnected the call.

CHAPTER 42

At the Palatin Hotel

Unable to bear the thought of returning to his apartment and feeling as if there was still the possibility of danger there, Gabriel and Nicki had checked into the Palatin Hotel in adjoining rooms. They were in his room as he ended the call with the priest and sat down, his face ashen. Nicki demanded, "Gabby, what is it? What did he say?"

"He read me Marty's confession. But I can't believe it. Marty is the one who leaked the information, but not to the IAA. He was working with someone who was going to broker a deal for the codex with the Catholic Church. He said he did it for the money. He'd been gambling at an Indian casino in Kentucky not too far from Nashville and he'd lost a huge sum, including money from his 401(k). He said he needed the money to get out of debt and be able to retire. I had no idea this was going on. I swear, not an inkling."

"But who beat him and stole the codex. Surely," Nicki asked, "that wasn't part of the plan was it?"

"He didn't say. I'm sure his beating wasn't originally a part of the plan, but somebody decided he wanted Marty's cut of the money, would be my guess. No doubt in my mind, the person who beat him, killed him. I'm calling Schmidt. Plus, there seems to be two different people out to get the codex. How in hell did this exciting discover come so unraveled?"

Reading from the policeman's business card, he punched in Schmidt's number and in a couple of rings, the Lieutenant answered. Gabriel identified himself. "I just talked to the priest who heard Marty's confession and he read it to me. Marty was in on a plan to use photos of pages of the codex to get money from the Catholic Church. Trust me when I tell you, the Church will pay almost anything for this codex, even photos of pages. He needed a lot of money for reasons we don't need to go into right now. He told them how they could get copies of the pictures we took. Evidently somebody decided to take the codex instead and eliminate Marty making the money split go to fewer people."

"Holy shit! Your own guy dimed you out? Man, that's low."

"Listen, asshole, he was a good man who made a bad decision and it cost him his life. I don't fucking care what you think about him. Just find the damned killer and the codex."

"Sorry. I know he was your friend. Where are you? In case I need you."

"I'm safe right now. We've left the Agripas and moved into another hotel for now. But, I'll tell you the truth: right now, I'm not sure I should even trust you." Gabriel ended the call with a promise to stay available.

The Intensive Care Unit

"ICU. Ms. Rabanowic."

"Ah. Yes. I'm Sgt. Metzler with the Israeli Police. We are investigating the death of one of your patients, Mr. Fratini. I was there earlier. I seem to have misplaced the name of the priest who was there with Mr. Fratini. Can you help me?"

"I gave it to your Lieutenant when he was here."

"I know, but he asked me to follow up and I misplace the name. I don't wish to tell him of my mistake. So sorry to inconvenience, but it would be a great help to me."

"Sure. I understand. Just a second...Here it is:

Father Donlin at St. Anne's."

"You are so kind. Thank you. Shalom."

"Shalom."

Somewhere In Jerusalem

"Here you go. Father Donlin at St. Anne's. See how easy that was."

"I'm impressed. How do you think this should go down?"

"Off the top of my head, I'd say lure him to some location with a sad story and do it there. Pick a place that can't be tied to either of us."

"He was an older guy. Maybe I could just go see him and inject him with our little friendly Go To Heaven goody."

"That could work. If no one else saw you."

"I need to mull this over. This is all still new to me. Marty is not the first person I've smashed in the face and beat up, but he's the first person I've killed."

"Really? Who'd you beat up?"

"Someone who came on to me and wouldn't take no for an answer."

The Director-General's Home

Doormann saw who was calling on Caller ID and answered with, "Yes, Avi. What have you learned?"

"Sir, I checked with a contact I have with the police. Their working theory is that a person disguised as a physician entered the room and injected the guy with something. He was in and out in less than a minute. They have no leads. However, Marty dictated some kind of confession to a priest. They're trying to find out what it was. No go from the priest though. Some Catholic nonsense. But guess who the confession was for. Gabriel."

"Has Gabriel read the confession yet?"

"My contact didn't know."

"What the hell does Marty have to confess to Gabriel about? Was he in on this thing somehow, I wonder?"

"No clue. I've got someone trying to locate the priest and someone else trying to find Gabriel. They both seem to have disappeared."

"What about the woman and the student he had with him?"

"No luck there either. May all be together."

"Very well. Stay after it and keep me posted."

Speaking to himself out loud, Doormann said, "Well, well, well. Marty confesses something and is killed. Gabriel vanishes with the woman. Something tells me something's about to happen, something big." He smiled. "I love this job! One exciting discover after another. Wonder what's next."

CHAPTER 43

Palatin Hotel Jerusalem

Gabriel punched in Trevor's phone number and when Trevor answered, he said, "Trevor, this is Gabby. Look Nicki and I have checked into the Palatin Hotel. You know where it is?"

"No sir."

"It's in the shopping district near Mache Yehudah market and Ben Yehudi Street. You need to move in here tonight. We've got a room for you. Get your stuff from the hostel if you can do it quickly. If not, we'll just buy what you need. Come to room 1114 and we'll give you the key to your room."

"Sure, but why? What's going on?"

"We think we're in danger, but just from whom, we don't know. Get here as quickly as you can and we'll figure out what to do next. Don't check out of the hostel and don't tell anyone where you're going."

"Shit! This is getting freaky, if you don't mind my saying so. I'm just a student and a photographer."

"I get it, man. I get it. C'mon. We'll get this all straightened out."

"Okay. Forty-five minutes tops."

"Great. Good luck." With that Gabby punched End and stopped pacing. He sat in one of the two chairs in the fairly ordinary hotel room. There were two double beds, a chest, a small flat screen TV and a table and two chairs. All were clean but non-descript. The drapes had been pulled tight over the wall of windows and the door had been deadlocked and chained. Nicki sat in the other chair waiting for Gabby to speak. "He's on his way. He's scared. I get that; I'm pretty shaken up myself."

At the Community of the Perpetual Penitents Headquarters

"Mr. Heywood. How nice to see you again." Heywood was back at the CPP headquarters and once again, handcuffed to the ring attached to the interrogation room table. Heywood was just lifting his head from the table top.

"What the fuck! What's going on? Why am I back here?"

Donovan said, "Mr. Heywood, it seems your little story has a few holes in it and we are going to give you another chance. I don't want to waste your time, so let me tell you the biggest hole: you're not married so you couldn't have been buying clothes for your wife."

"I can explain. I can. Okay. Look. I was lookin' to buy something for myself. I dress up sometimes. You know what I mean? I was just too embarrassed to tell you."

"A cross-dresser, is that it?"

"Right. I'm not proud of it, but I can't help myself. That's why I'm not married. Can't find a woman who'll let me do it."

"That's very sad, Mr. Heywood. One wouldn't imagine a little perversion like that would put off all women. Surely there is a woman out there for you."

"I keep hoping, but so far, no luck."

Donovan slapped him hard. "Cut the shit, you little prick! We searched your house. There are no women's clothes there. You know what was there, though? Eleven thousand dollars, American. In $1000 bundles of $100 bills. Now I could have sworn that when you left here you only had one of those bundles. How did you happen to get so much more?"

"Hey, man, you don't need to be hittin' me. I ain't done nothing wrong. I just helped a guy out like I told you."

"If you didn't like the slap, you're really going to hate what else I plan to do. You are going to tell me the truth. We know it was no accidental meeting in that clothing store. It's all just too pat and unlikely. So we know that you know the guy with the valise. You're not leaving here until we know who he is as well. Understand?"

"You can't do this. I'm a citizen. Hell you guys are not even the cops. This ain't no police station."

"Yes. You're right. We're not the cops. That's bad news for you because we're not bound by the law." Donovan slapped him again. "See if we were the cops, I couldn't do that. And I couldn't do the other things we're prepared to do to get the information we want."

"You're bluffin'. You wouldn't hurt me."

"You're right. I'm sorry. I'm just carried away. We should release you." Donovan got up from his chair and walked around beside Heywood. He reached down and unlocked the handcuffs. "Please. Stand up. You're free to go." Heywood stood and faced Donovan and was about to say something when Donovan kneed him as hard as he could in the groin. Heywood collapsed in agony and began to writhe on the floor. "Hurts like a mother, doesn't it. Can you imagine my doing that every fifteen minutes until you tell me what I want to know? Think about that. Oh, my goodness. You've peed all over yourself. At least, I hope that's piss. Lie there a few minutes and think about my request. I'll be back." At that, he left the room and walked down the hall. The guard on the door nodded as he exited.

At Avi's Office

"Boss, we have a break. You know that vinyl glove we found in the alley when we went back to Gabriel's warehouse? The one we 'forgot' to tell the police about? We've been trying to get a print from the inside of it and we raised one. We also got a hit. I didn't get any thing from my contact with the Israeli Police, so I called in a favor from a contact at the FBI and my friend ran the prints through IAFIS."

"Who is it?"

"His name is Andy Kelly. He's a contract worker on dig sites. This season he's working Gabriel's site. The FBI had his prints because of a problem in the States. He tried to extort someone there who cooperated with the cops."

"Excellent!"

"Yeah, but there's a problem. We sent his picture to the hotel where the codex was stolen. Nobody recognizes him. He wasn't the guy who rented the apartment."

"Where is he now?"

"At this hour, probably at home or else out somewhere for the evening."

"Go to his home. If he's not there, stake out the place till he arrives. Grab him and bring him here."

"We're not going to tell the cops?"

"In due time."

"Got it. I'm on it."

"Call me when you have him."

"Will do."

Avi thought for a minute and picked up his phone and began to punch in the DG's home number. When Doormann answered, Avi said,

"We have a break. We know who broke into the warehouse. His name is Andy Kelly, one of Gabriel's contract workers. He got caught in the States a few years ago in an attempted extortion."

"Good work, Avi! What now?" asked Doormann.

"We're going after him. If he's working for Gabriel in some 'extra-curricula' way, we'll find out. I'll start work immediately on finding out where he lives."

"What more do you have about Gabby's involvement?"

"DG, our sources on the street could only say it was some kind of inside job. We thought it too convenient that Gabriel and the others left Marty alone and that's when he's beaten and the codex taken. That's the main reason we thought it was him. Maybe Kelly is the inside person. We don't know."

"I've never believed Gabriel could have been a party to Marty's beating and death. They've been too close too long. Let me call him and find out what I can about Kelly."

"You're sure that's what you want to do?"

"Yes. I'll call now."

"I call you after we've questioned Kelly."

"Very good. Excellent work." said Doormann and pressed End.

At the Director-General's Home

Doormann punched in Gabriel's number and

waited for a few rings. Gabriel answered, "Gabriel."

"Gabby, I'm so sorry to bother you at this time of grief. How are you?"

"In shock." *For more reasons than one,* he thought, but didn't say.

"Yes, I can only imagine. Gabby, one of my other investigators has turned up some information that requires that I check something with you. You have an Andy Kelly working at the dig; is that correct?"

"Yes. Why?"

"What can you tell me of Mr. Kelly?"

"He's a US citizen living here he says for religious reasons. He said he wants to be close to where Jesus lived and died. He's a contract worker. In fact, he's the one that discovered the second jar."

"While I don't know the details, I have been informed that there is strong evidence he broke into your warehouse."

"Kelly? I can't believe it."

"I'm told fingerprints were found in a location that only the intruder could have left them."

"Mr. Doormann, he did a great job of convincing me he was a devout Christian. I'm shocked. What now?

Do the police have him?"

"That's all I know at this moment, Gabby. I'm sure the police are involved in some way, though it was one of my other investigators who called me."

"Thank you for calling, DG. Please, if you learn more, let me know."

"I will, Gabby. I'm sorry my friend. So much to bear in such a short time."

"Yeah. Too much. Shalom."

"Shalom, my friend."

At the Palatin

"Gabby, what's wrong? What about Andy?" Nicki asked.

"Andy apparently is the one who did the break-in at the warehouse."

"He seems so nice and such a devout Christian guy. It's hard to believe he could do anything like that."

"I need to call Schmidt." Looking again at the card, he punched in the number. When Schmidt answered, Gabriel said, "I just learned something else you need to know. I just heard from the Director-General of the IAA. He tells me his investigators have discovered who broke into our warehouse. His name is Andy Kelly. He's a contract dig worker who works for me."

"Did the DG say how his investigator learned of this?"

"Not the specifics."

"Where can I find this Kelly person?"

"Beats me. I think he stays at the same hostel as many of the dig workers, but I haven't seem him lately because I haven't been to the dig site."

"Thank you, Doctor. We will pick Kelly up for questioning. Shalom."

"Goodbye," Gabriel said and disconnected.

"I can not fucking believe this. I know Marty. I thought I knew Kelly. How could I have been so fucking stupid?"

"Gabby, you aren't stupid. You didn't have any reason to suspect anything was going on." She took his hand. "Look, you have two big shocks today. You're not yourself right now. God knows, I know what it's like to be hit with something like this. The cops will get to the bottom of this. Please…don't beat yourself up." She turned his face to hers and she kissed him. "You aren't alone; I'm in this with you." She was about to say more when there was a knock on the door.

"Who the hell could that be? Nobody knows we're here."

He rose and started for the door. "Be careful, honey," Nicki pleaded.

CHAPTER 44
At the Palatin Hotel

Gabriel looks through the peephole. It was Trevor, looking very nervous. "It's Trevor," he said as he unlocked and opened the door. Trevor had checked in, and as instructed had come to 1114. Once he was in the room and the three of them talked about what was going on in their lives, Nicki suggested they needed food. The ordered room service and continued to talk until it arrived.

The food was fine, but none of them really tasted it. Too much was happening and their anxiety level was off the charts. As they were trying to decide what to do next. Gabriel's phone chirped. When he pulled it out, he saw if was Marge. "Oh, shit! I didn't call Marge to tell her about Marty." He punched a key to take the call and began talking, "Marge, I'm so sorry I haven't kept you up to date. Things have been crazy here. I have..." Marge interrupted him.

"Gabby, listen to me! We've read some of the material that Trevor e-mailed before you decided to switch to thumb drives--which I got by the way. I hope you won't kill me; here's what I did. I called your journalist friend. I filled him in and we made plans to meet, but I sent him the file Trevor had sent me. Gabby, you will not believe the resources Harry has access to. The magazine doesn't personally have the technology to read anything like this, but he has friends in high places. Friends who are so happy about what he did with the Scrolls, they will do anything he asks. The infrared images Trevor took turned out to be the best and they're legible. Bottom line, Gabby, we've read some of the codex."

"What? Already?"

"Already. Trevor did such a good job with the various lights, filters and stuff that when they went after it with their software, we could begin to cut through whatever had stained the pages so badly. We've got a good percentage of the beginning read. Gabby, it's exactly what we thought it was! It's from Mary! Let me e-mail a translation to you."

"No! It's not safe to e-mail anything. We'll figure out something else, but for now, just read what you've got."

"Okay. We've made educated guesses at some of the words, but we think we've got the sense of it. Let me read it and where we guessed, I'll say 'brackets'. Some guesses we feel better about; some we're uncertain. We put a question mark after those. Some parts are illegible and I just say that. Okay?"

"Yes. Read."

"*Now when Mariam, Yeshua's mother died in the* [thirty-first year after] *his Resurrection,* [illegible] *closest to Yeshua along with Mariam's children* [laid her in a] *tomb in Jerusalem.* [illegible] *laid her in the tomb, Yaakov* [spoke] *to us. He told those of us who* [were closest?] *to Yeshua before the Resurrection* [illegible] *the room that* [was our place] *of prayer and worship.* [On the first] *day of the week, we gather before sunrise* [in this room] *and break the bread and drink from the cup as he commanded us. We tell and retell the stories we remember to keep* [his memory?] *alive in our* [hearts].

When we had come [illegible] *spoke to us saying, "Last year our* [illegible] *Peter was executed in Rome. Now Yeshua's and* [my] *mother have died. If Peter* [and also?] *Yeshua's mother die before he returns,* [illegible] *face that we may well die* [before he returns]. *Soon it may be that none of us will be* [left to tell?] *the story of what Yeshua said and did and who he was. We* [have believed] *that he would soon return to restore the land* [illegible] *God's Kingdom, but he has not. He may come today; he* [may come] *in forty years. As he told us, no one* [knows but the] *Father when that time is."*

'*We Jews* [illegible] *and plots to revolt* [are

everywhere]. *Soon* [illegible] *an armed clash with Rome; it cannot be* [avoided?]. *While God is on our side, God's* [side has not] *always won each battle.* [illegible], *but from the gladius or spear* [of a Roman?] *solider. Therefore, it seems good to me that we must begin to write down what we* [remember] *of his* [time with] *us. In this way, our witness* [will continue]. *Because we knew him as no one else did, because we saw* [with our] *eyes and* [heard with our] *ears, each of us must undertake this task. We must leave something* [for we were the first] *witnesses." Since Yaakov has told us to write our memories, I have decided to share what I have kept private all these years.*

Marge stopped reading. "That's it."

Gabriel had put the phone on speakerphone so the others could hear. The room was deadly quiet. Finally, he broke the silence, "My God in heaven. Oh my God!"

Marge said, "I hope I did the right thing Gabby."

"Yes. Oh, yes! You did the right thing, Marge. I'm just stunned. I'm reeling. As wonderful as this news is, it's kind of another body blow."

"Why? What's happened? Is Marty okay?"

"No, Marge. Marty's dead. The cops think he was murdered. Several of us have moved from our hotel to a different one because we're afraid."

"Murdered? Oh Gabby! No! No! He can't be

dead! He just can't be!"

"I can't believe it either, but he is. I saw the body. You guys keep at it with the material on the flash drive. Don't use e-mail. I'm going to get another phone and I'll call with that number. For all I know, somebody's monitoring this one."

"For Marty, Gabby. I'm going to work my ass and everybody else's ass off for Marty."

"That's great, Marge. Stay after it. I'll call later. And, hey: fantastic work. Give our mutual friend my regards and undying thanks."

"I will, but he's at least as excited as we are."

"So long, Marge." Gabby clicked off the call. Turning to the others, "It just occurred to me, this phone has GPS in it. Somebody with my number can find me. So, it goes off this second."

"What about ours?"

"We'll all need new phones. First thing tomorrow. But back to what Marge read to us; it's just what we speculated. As Jesus doesn't return and the eyewitnesses begin to die, the community decides to begin writing down what they remember. This makes perfect sense. It's why the Gospels came into existence. Mary apparently had been writing things down all along, so it was easy for her to share what she had already written. We have Mary's Memories, just as the jar said."

They wrapped up the conversation without a clear plan about how to get back to the warehouse to see what was in the leather sack. Fatigue, shock, raw nerves had finally won. They were emotionally and physically exhausted. Trevor left for his room and Nicki and Gabby looked at each other. The sleeping arrangement had just been decided. And, as it turned out, sleeping was all they were going to do.

CHAPTER 45

At the Community of Perpetual Penitents Headquarters

"Sir, after he got over the kick you gave him, he spent a good bit of time pounding on the door. He used a chair to try to break the mirror. I went in and while he was covering up his nuts with both hands, I busted his nose. He yelled some more, but finally went to sleep about an hour ago."

"Good. Maybe he'll be ready to talk." Donovan entered the room with two cups of steaming coffee. "Have a restful night, Mr. Heywood? Ready for coffee?"

"What do you want from me?"

"The name of the man with the valise."

"I don't know."

"Here have some coffee." Donovan threw the coffee at his neck and chest, careful to miss his face.

"Son of a bitch! Why'd you do that? That's burns, you asshole."

"Mr. Heywood, please. Such language over a little spilled coffee. Now, shall we cut the shit and finish our business here. Surely, you understand I can do this as long as I like. Far longer than you will like." Donovan pulled a stun gun from his pocket and tossed it from hand to hand. "Ever had one of these stuck to your nuts for a couple of jolts? I'm told the pain is unbearable."

Heywood slumped to his chair. "Okay. I'm done. If I tell you what you want to know, can I keep the money?"

"Absolutely, in fact I'll be glad to make a generous donation myself. Say another ten grand? How's that sound?"

"When do I get the ten grand?" Heywood asked.

"As soon as we have your friend in our custody."

"How do I know you won't screw me?"

"Mr. Heywood, we're Catholic priests. We would never break our word. We might break your neck, but our word is good."

"The guy's name is Ezra Dyan. I don't know how he gets his information, but he finds out stuff that's going on and how to get ahold of artifacts he sells. Sometimes he asks me to help in some way. This time he said when to be at the store and what to do. I don't know why. He never gives me any details. I show up and do my bit and get my money."

"So where does Ezra Dyan live?" Heywood provided the address.

"Hey, you can't tell him I ratted him out, okay? He might hurt me. He don't work alone, I know that much. He's bragged about having to rough people up now and then. Can you just leave me out of it."

"Certainly, Mr. Heywood. You've been so very cooperative. Finally. When we talk to him, he'll never know your part, your betrayal."

Donovan stood and approached Heywood, who shrank back. "Mr. Heywood! You have nothing to fear from me any longer. I know you'll never speak of our time together."

"No. No. Not to anybody. This never happened. I swear to God."

"Yes. Well. The oath of a thief and rat may not be worth much, but you know that we know where you live. I merely want to help you up. My friends will help you get cleaned up and fed. You'll stay with us a bit longer while we go find Dyan."

Donovan gave instructions to see to Heywood and then he called several men into his office to discuss bringing in Dyan.

CHAPTER 46
At Police Headquarters

They couldn't find Kelly in any of their directories. He was staying at the hostel, so he really didn't have a permanent address. But, the Lieutenant had an idea. If Kelly felt safe, he would probably act as if nothing had happened. That would mean he'd be at the dig site when it opened. Schmidt made arrangements for someone to go to the dig site and pick him up first thing in the morning. Realizing he was bone-weary and that some sleep would make him sharper, the Lieutenant went home.

The next morning Kelly was waiting for him at headquarters, sitting behind a table in Interrogation Room 3. As Schmidt and the arresting officer stood outside the door of IR 3, the officer said, "He didn't resist. He wanted to know why we were taking him in. He asked if he were being arrested. When I told him you just wanted to talk, he didn't say anything else. In fact, he hasn't spoken since then."

"Thank you, Rafi. Please make sure the video is going." Rafi stepped next door and the Lieutenant opened IR 3's door.

"Mr. Kelly, sorry to have had to ask you to join me today. My name is Lieutenant Moshe Schmidt and I need to ask you some questions. You are not under arrest, however you still have the right to request counsel. Do you wish to do so?"

"No sir. I'm just confused as to why I'm here." His face showed a relaxed expression tinged with curiosity and openness. A cross hung from a chain around his neck and he was fingering it gently.

"That will all become clear as we talk. I understand you are a US citizen living here; is that correct?"

"Yes. I moved here about two years ago."

"And what prompted that move?"

"I'm a Christian and I felt very deeply I needed to be in the Holy Land. I needed to see where Jesus lived and died and was resurrected. Once I got here, I felt so close, so changed, that I knew I didn't want to leave. I've even given thought to becoming a citizen." Kelly slumped in the chair a bit, looking even more relaxed than before.

"How long have you worked for Dr. Gabriel?"

"This is my first season with him, so about a month, give or take."

"And before him?"

Kelly named several other dig directors and sites on which he'd worked since his arrival, a couple in Jerusalem and the other in Petra, some distance away.

The Lieutenant asked, "When you are not working digs, what work do you do?"

"I work in Avram Shlomo's shop."

"What kind of shop is this?"

"He sells antiquities and reproductions of antiquities. He says it all legal. He has a license and everything."

"Mr. Kelly, do you know where Dr. Gabriel's warehouse is located?"

"Not exactly; some industrial park I think. Most of us don't have any reason to go there. He has a few people who work on finds there, but most of us aren't involved."

"So, you have no reason to ever have been there, is that correct?"

"Why are you asking me about his warehouse?"

Kelly's composure was slipping a bit and he squirmed a little in his chair. He pretended to brush the hair from his forehead, allowing him to wipe at the tiny beads of sweat forming there.

"As annoying as it is, I'm afraid I am the one asking questions. So, never been there or even near there, is that correct?"

"That's correct. Or maybe I should say if I've ever been there I don't remember."

"Mr. Kelly, you will forgive me if I say you are a fucking liar."

"What? What are you talking about?" Kelly's guard went up instantly.

There was a knock at the door and Rafi let himself in. He whispered to Schmidt. Schmidt asked, "You brought it?" and Rafi nodded yes. "Mr. Kelly, you are a fucking liar because I know you broke into the warehouse just a few nights ago. We have your backpack from your room. Rafi tells me that in it were found tools including a hammer and chisel. They had concrete dust on them. I suspect when we do some tests we will discover it is dust from the concrete blocks you broke. We also found some small glass shards embedded in the claw of the hammer that I suspect is from the broken window inside the warehouse. So, you see why I say you are a fucking liar?"

"Am I under arrest?" Kelly was stiff. His face drained of color.

"If you like I can arrest you. Or perhaps if you help me, we can avoid such a blemish on your record. It would certainly interfere with your staying in Israel, much less becoming a citizen."

Kelly didn't even try to disguise wiping the perspiration from his upper lip. It would have been pointless anyway. Dark circles were appearing from beneath his armpits. "What kind of help?"

"We have a missing artifact which we think you were trying to steal when you broke into the warehouse. It is a very valuable artifact. It is connected to a murder. So, the kind of help you can provide will be information about these things.

"What kind of deal can I get here?"

"Tell me what I want to know, and who can say--you may walk free."

"Can I get that in writing?"

The Lieutenant stood, "I think I am through talking with you Mr. Kelly. Have you ever spent any time in an Israeli jail or prison? I'm told it's not as 'cushy' as those in the US. At any rate, I'm through wasting my time with you."

"Wait! Okay, here's the story. Someone hires me to give them information about finds at dig sites. When I have something, I let them know. Sometimes, they contact me first. We found something important at the dig a few days ago. There was a lot of ruckus. My contact was on the walk above the site and saw what happened, and before I could contact him, he called me. So I told him they'd found a jar with some writing on it. The next day, I found a second jar, so I called him about that."

"So which of you killed Marty Fratini?"

"What? Are you nuts? I didn't kill anybody!" He rose from his chair in his excitement and Schmidt pushed him back down.

"Somebody killed him. Either you or your boss or partner. Either way, you'll both get the death penalty. Unless, of course, you were to roll over on him."

"I swear to God, all I did was sell the information about the jars and break in to the warehouse. He paid me $200 for the information and $200 for the break in. I was going to get more, but there was nothing in the jar to steal and when the alarm went off, I didn't have time to look for the second jar. You have got to believe me. I may be a fucking liar and a crooked bastard, but I didn't kill anybody!"

"Who is your partner in all this, the man who gave

you the money?"

"Shlomo. We do this every season. I don't know what was in the jars and I didn't kill anybody. You've got to believe me."

"Mr. Kelly, you're under arrest for breaking and entering and a few other things I'll add. We're keeping you here for your own safety while we check your story further."

"What about a lawyer?"

"Maybe later." He rose and opened the IR 3 door and told the officer stationed there to escort Kelly to the holding area. He was not to make a phone call or have any visitors.

Later At Avram Shlomo's Antiquities Shop

"Everybody in place?" A series of clicks came over the mike. "I'm going in with my mike open. When you hear me say 'riot' come in force." Schmidt and Rafi walked into Shlomo's shop and asked a clerk if they could speak to Mr. Shlomo. The clerk pointed toward the back of the shop where they saw a short man but a man of huge girth: Mr. Five by Five. His white hair was wispy and unkempt, a little yellowed and his glasses were perched on the end of his rather large red nose. His white shirt was yellowed too and needed pressing badly. "Mr. Avram Shlomo?"

"Yes. How may I help you? Are you looking for a nice piece to take home to the wife perhaps?"

"Mr. Shlomo, I'm Lt. Moshe Schmidt and this is Officer Rafi. We need to talk to you. We can do it here, perhaps in your office, or we can go to police headquarters."

Shlomo, yelled to his clerk, "Go get yourself a coffee. Put up the closed sign when you leave." The clerk, looking unsettled, did as he was told. "We can speak here, gentlemen."

"Do you know a young man named Andy Kelly?"

"Yes. Yes. Andy works here in the shop when he's not at dig sites."

"Sir, Mr. Kelly has implicated you in a serious crime, murder. We're here to let you tell us your side of the story."

"He what? The little bastard. I didn't murder anybody. Look at me. Who do you think I could kill?"

"He also told us you hired him to break into a warehouse that is connected with the crime."

"Look, I didn't murder anybody. You said you wanted my side of the story. Here it is. The kid tells me the dig he's working found something important, a jar. I ask why he thinks it's important and he tells me this story of the dig director going all ape shit over the find. He wants to know how much the information is worth and how much the jar is worth to me. I thank him for the information and tell him I can't comment on the value of the jar without seeing it. That's it. Next thing I know he tells me he broke into the warehouse but couldn't get the jar. I swear to God, that's the whole story."

"Mr. Shlomo, you're under arrest for soliciting antiquities and for murder. And you know why, Shlomo, because you're wasting my time and pissing me off. Given the means I used to question Kelly, I believe his version. That makes you a lying piece of shit. Handcuff him Rafi."

"Wait. Okay. I wasn't entirely forthcoming. I'm walking near the dig site, see, and I witness a big commotion. I called Kelly and for $200 he told me what happened. Later, Kelly tells me he's found out that the jar contained a codex. I asked him how he found out, and he says something about being able to clone a phone--whatever the hell that means. He tells me the codex may have been written by Mary Magdalene. I decide the codex is too big a risk, but the information about it may be valuable. So I call the Director-General of IAA and cut a deal to sell the information to him. I made him think I could get the codex too, but I had no idea where it was. That's it. The whole story. Swear to God."

"Fascinating. Maybe even bits of truth here and

there. Even so, you're still under arrest."

"Wait. Wait. I told you everything. Check with the DG. He'll tell you a Judas has been talking to him and sent him an e-mail by courier as part of the negotiation. Kelly gave me an e-mail he said he got off the cloned phone."

"Thank you, I will. But you're still under arrest for murder."

"I didn't kill anybody. I was trying to extort some money; that's all."

Shlomo's face was covered in sweat; he was red as a beet and breathing hard. "Please. I'm not well. Let me sit down a minute." Schmidt nodded to Rafi and he help Shlomo sit on a stool behind the counter trying to slow his breathing. In a minute or two he spoke. "I've told you everything. I may be a crook, but I'm not a murderer."

"I'll tell you what," said the Lieutenant, "Show me your copy of the e-mail you sent to the DG and we'll reconsider murder."

"Yes! Yes! Come, it's in the back in my office." As they started toward the office, Schmidt pulled out his mike and keyed it. "Somebody ask the DG of IAA to come to our office as soon as possible. Tell him we have information vital to him. By the way: stand down."

At Police Headquarters

"Mr. Doormann," said the Lieutenant, "thank you for coming." They sat at a table in an interrogation room. "I'm sorry to have to speak to you in such a room, but we don't have enough space for each of us to have our own office." Sliding a copy of the e-mail Shlomo had given them across the table, Schmidt asked, "Sir. Have you ever seen this before?"

The DG slipped on his glasses and picked up the e-mail that was in a plastic sheath. He spent a few moments looking at it. It was an un-redacted version, but there was no mistaking it. "Yes. Lieutenant. Or rather, I should say, I saw a copy of this--much redacted--but it is obviously the same."

"How did you come to possess that e-mail, Mr. Doormann?"

"It came by courier without the name of the sender."

"You're saying it just appeared?"

"I knew it was coming. Someone called and said he was sending it and that I might find the information useful."

"And who was this 'someone' may I ask?"

The DG slipped off his glasses and returned them to his pocket and chuckled. "He would only say his name was Judas."

"Judas. Good. Mr. Doormann, we have reason to believe that this e-mail is somehow connected to the murder of a Mr. Marty Fratini. Would you know anything about that?"

"I'm astonished!" Doormann quickly replied, sounding every bit as astonished as the word would denote. "Let me tell you everything I know. If my information will assist in finding Marty's killer, I'm happy to help." Doormann then told the entire story, from beginning to end, including using his investigator to try to discover information or the whereabouts of the codex. "I suppose in retrospect, I should have called the police, but I thought we could operate out of sight and perhaps be of some small service."

"I'm not an old man, Mr. Doormann, but I've been on this job for almost twenty years. During that time, though I'm not proud of it, I have developed a very well developed tendency toward skepticism. You will forgive me if I tell you my bullshit detector has just rung in my ear. Because of that...no, please don't interrupt...I am guessing most of your story is true, but there is a bit that isn't. You kept the police out of this so you could recover the codex yourself for IAA. I've read the e-mail. The codex is literally priceless. But, it has great value for many other purposes. To control the codex would be a terrific windfall for the

IAA and for our country. Yes? This is closer to the truth? Correct?"

"Your detector is fine-tuned, Lieutenant. Yes, we were trying to recover it on our own for many of the reasons you suggest. Judas wanted a lot of money, a million US in fact. The e-mail, my copy of which was very redacted, was his offer of good faith that he could provide more. My copy only had one name: Trevor. I eventually traced that to a graduate assistant who works for Gabriel, the dig director, the person to whom the e-mail apparently was sent. However, you have learned much more than we were able to learn. Except for this: we had reason to believe someone inside the Gabriel camp was involved. But we haven't pinned down who."

"Thank you, Mr. Hoffman. No sign of my internal alarm this time. In fact, your being forthcoming prompts me to be as well. We have the inside person in custody. We also have Judas, which is how we obtained the e-mail. I will want you to identify Judas' voice to provide corroboration of his identity. You will be willing, yes?"

"Of course. May I ask one question: this insider and Judas murdered Mr. Fratini?"

"The evidence we have doesn't support such a theory. But, we are still developing leads. Sir, while I understand why you didn't come to us, you're aware not doing so has hampered our investigation. However, we will speak no more of this. I will need your redacted e-mail and any other material your investigators have developed. And sir, please call them off. We take a dim view of people who interfere with our investigations."

"Of course. Of course. At once. I'll have the e-mail and anything else we have, including reports, sent to you later today."

"Thank you, sir. One of my men will take you to another room. We want you to listen to Judas over our phones to make sure you recognize this voice. Shalom."

"Shalom, Lieutenant. Shalom"

Later At the Director-General's Office

"Avi, thank you for coming. The police have arrested Judas and the Gabriel camp insider. They've asked me to back off as they continue their investigation.

"Did they tell you who they arrested? We haven't found Kelly yet. I wonder if it's him?""

"They didn't give me a name. I listened to his voice over a phone and there is no doubt it's Judas, but they didn't identify him to me."

"One of my men picked up a rumor today that Avram Shlomo was arrested at his shop earlier today. I wonder if there is a connection?"

"Avi, it doesn't matter any more. Judas doesn't have the codex. We're no closer to it than we were. He was using information he'd gotten from an insider, according to Lt. Schmidt, to tease money out of us. He hoped he'd get more information, maybe pictures of pages, but that hadn't happened. It's also unlikely they were involved in Marty's murder."

"If they didn't murder Fratini and take the codex, who did? That's the big question. I can shift our resources toward that direction and see what we can find."

"Avi, you must be very careful to not be detected. I promised the police we'd pull out of the investigation so you can't be discovered as you poke around, as it were."

"I understand, DG. Don't worry. We will be like shadows on a cloudy day."

CHAPTER 47

At Ezra Dyan's Apartment

"I'm coming! I'm coming! Who is it?" Dyan looked through the peephole and saw someone in a uniform.

"FedEx. Need a signature."

"Just a minute." Dyan took off the chain and threw the deadbolt. As he opened the door he said, "I don't remember order..." He was interrupted as the men in police uniforms rushed him, slamming him against the wall, pinning his arms behind him.

"Ezra Dyan, you're under arrest for dealing in stolen antiquities."

"What the hell are you talking about? I haven't done anything!"

In a very calm voice, Donovan said, "You have a friend named Robert Heywood. He ratted you out. We're going to take you for a little ride right after we toss your apartment. But you are so anxious, we need to give you a little sedative to help you relax. Donovan nodded to one of the men who plunged a needle into Dyan's neck.

"You're not the police!" Dyan shouted and then went slack.

They half dragged and half carried him to the broken down sofa in the sitting area and laid him on it. Then they set about searching for the money and the codex. It didn't take long to find the money, but there was no sign of the codex. The money was still wrapped in packets of $1000 and stacked in the oven. "Not a very original place, but if there was a fire, the money was at least in an insulated place. Okay. Let's get him back to headquarters."

Getting him out of the building and into the car was uneventful. The drive to CPP headquarters was equally uneventful. Dyan was slumped against the back seat of an ordinary looking car with two casually dressed men, one on either side. The faux policemen followed at some distance in a dark blue SUV with heavily tinted windows. Once back at their headquarters, Dyan was hustled up the elevator and into an interrogation room and handcuffed to the table ring. He was left there to sleep off the sedative and to give him time, once awake, to consider his life had just turned to shit.

Finally, Donovan entered the room where the fully awake Dyan sat. Dyan started to say something, but Donovan struck him across the face with an open-handed slap. "Shut up. You don't get to ask any questions. You have something I want and I want it very badly. If your friend Heywood could talk, he'd tell you to what lengths I go to when I want something badly. Where's the codex?"

"I don't..."

Donovan slapped him again. "Damn it, Ezra, don't tell me you don't know what I'm talking about or don't know where it is. I don't have time for that kind of shit."

"Please, don't hit me again. I'm not the one who stole it. I'm just the negotiator. Somebody else took it. I swear."

"What do you call yourself when you negotiate?"

"Matthias. I call myself Matthias."

"Good. The truth. I like that. With whom do you negotiate?"

"A bishop. Bishop Newhouse." The fear in Ezra's voice closely matched the fear etched into his tanned face. His eyes were wide and his breathing shallow and rapid.

"Excellent! Two correct answers. I love it when people cooperate with me. Now, if you don't have the codex, who does?"

"I don't know. Wait! Don't hit me! Hear me out! Please!" he begged.

"I'm listening, but I'm also an impatient man. Remember that."

"Okay, somebody contacted me and said he was with the dig, see. He offered to get me information about any major discoveries they made, but we'd have to split any money I got. We never met face to face; he said it was too dangerous. Several weeks into the dig, I get a call from him."

Donovan interrupted, "Cell or land line?"

"Cell. He had my cell number, but whenever he called me his number was blocked."

"Keep talking."

"Okay. He says they found a jar and inside the jar was a codex, a book. He says it's priceless, okay. He says the Catholics will pay a butt load for it. He thinks he can get me pictures of pages from the book and that I can use those to convince the Catholics we have the book. The plan was to offer a copy of a page for a million bucks, then stiff them on the codex."

"Stiff them? What're you talking about?"

"See, we didn't have the book. The guy calls me and says somebody has stolen it but he thinks he can still get some pictures of pages. Enough to get the rest of the money we'd asked for."

"Which was how much?"

"Ten million more. But we knew we'd have to settle for less. Probably."

"So the guy can't get the book, only pictures of pages from it. And you claim some third party stole the book, not you. Right?"

"Exactly. We were bummed because we were afraid if we couldn't produce enough pages or pieces of pages to hook Newhouse, we wouldn't get our money."

"Why don't I believe your story? I think it's because you told me so much with so little persuasion on my part. I think you just want to avoid some pain. Am I right Ezra?"

"No! I mean yes. I mean...I swear. Everything I told you was true."

"No. I don't believe it. Here's what I'm going to do. I'm going to let you sit here and think for a bit. Then I'm coming back and we're going to try again. If I don't get what I want, I'm afraid I'll have to try some other tactic."

As Dyan was protesting his truthfulness, Donovan got up, walked over to the light switch and clicked it off. "Do you like the dark, Ezra?" He opened the door and stepped out, locking it behind him. One of the other priests was in the hall. "Get his cell phone records. Go back to the beginning of the dig season. Look for calls from blocked numbers and calls to the Chancery." The priest nodded and walked toward his workspace while Donovan walked to his office.

Donovan thought a few hours in the dark might be helpful. Plus, it gave his team time to do some checking. When later he got what he asked for from them, he returned to the darkened room. "Ah, Ezra," he said as he entered the room and clicked on the lights, "I have some good news and bad news." Ezra had raised his head from the table when the priest entered. He blinked against the light and his eyes teared up. He looked expectantly at the priest and said,

"Can I go to the restroom before you tell me your news? I need to pee real bad."

Donovan replied, "You may piss whenever you like."

Dyan rose thinking the priest was about to take

the cuffs off, but Donovan said, "Sit down. I said you may piss, I didn't say in the restroom. Now here's my good news." Dyan sat down and grimaced, trying to hold his water. "We checked for phone records, and by golly, you were calling the Chancery office just as you said."

"I told you I was telling the truth."

"Ah, but the bad news. The bad news is there is no record of someone calling you from a blocked number, so the story of getting such a call is another lie. There was an interesting coincidence in the list of calls, though. In the very recent past, you received two calls from the Agripas Hotel lobby phone. Who do you know from that hotel? Hmmm, let me see, that's the hotel where Dr. Gabriel lives along with Dr. Marty Fratini--the late Dr. Marty Fratini. You see, Dr. Fratini was savagely beaten in the commission of a robbery during which the codex was stolen. Don't you find it odd that you got a call from that lobby?"

"I don't know what it means. I don't know who could have called me. Please, let me go to the restroom. I don't have to just pee now." He was pleading.

"Ezra, it would be so disgusting if you shit yourself while we talked. But, sorry, no restroom break for you because you're not cooperating."

"Okay. I'll tell you who called me. Then will you

let me go to the john?"

CHAPTER 48
At the Chancery Office

Bishop Newhouse' phone rang on the receptionist line and he answered immediately. "Bishop, on line three there is a caller, a woman who said she is a friend of Matthias, and asked to speak to you."

"I'll take it." He pressed the button for line three and said, "Bishop Newhouse speaking."

"Bishop, we've met. At a coffee shop. I just never introduced myself. I'm Anna and I'm calling for Matthias. It seems he's had an unfortunate experience." The truth was they hadn't met. Heywood had sent a female friend of his who really didn't know what was in the envelopes that were exchanged. But the caller thought is was a helpful lie to move things alone. And if the bishop tried to identify her by using that description he would just be providing cover for her.

"Anna, I'm sorry to hear about his experience. I

trust he will be fine?"

"Gee, I don't know Bishop. As well as I can figure it out, your goons picked him up and tossed his apartment. I imagine you know better than I how he's doing."

Newhouse tried not to let his anxiety show in his voice. "Anna, I'm not sure I know..." She interrupted him.

"Bishop, please save us time but not trying to bullshit me. Look, I don't really care what happens to Matthias, or I should say, Ezra. He doesn't know where the codex is because I have it. So, here's what I want to know. Did you enjoy your taste of the codex?"

"Anna, so harsh. I'm surprised. But, to address your question: I was disappointed that you gave me only an inkjet copy of a page. Scanned on your home printer no doubt. I really thought we were paying for an actual page."

"Well, you see Your Grace, I wasn't sure I could trust you. But since you played fair with the down payment, I'm feeling better. Of course your goons took the money. So I've got zero and you've got proof of the codex. Not very fair, if you ask me. Still, even though it was only a copy, what'd you think?"

"Of course, I was unable to read it. But I have turned it over to those in our community who can, people I suppose you would call 'our lab guys'. When I hear from them, I'll be in a better position..." His office door flew open and a priest rushed in excitedly, trailing the receptionist.

"We've read it! You won't believe what it says!"

"Anna, please excuse me. It seems my 'lab guys' have come with a report."

Laughing, she said, "So I heard. Let me call you back in thirty minutes. It will take me that long to find another pay phone. Those things are a bitch to find in this day and age." At which, she hung up.

"All right, Father. Calm down, please. Here, let's go over to my sitting area and you can tell me what you've discovered." The priest was almost panting with excitement and exertion from his run from the lab.

"I'm sorry, Your Grace, I shouldn't have barged in. I'm just so excited, I let myself get carried away." The priest clutched a folder tightly to his black shirted chest, eyes wide, pupils dilated.

"*Ego te absolve*, my son." The priest-technician crossed himself and resumed clutching his folder. "Now, what have you discovered?" asked Newhouse.

"Your Grace, it appears to be a page of a codex describing an event in Jesus' life from a first person perspective."

"Please read it to me."

"Yes, sir." He released his death grip on the folder and opened it. "It starts mid-sentence and ends the same way, but the text is clear and unmistakable. It's written in Koine Greek, but well written. There are some words we're unsure of, but we think we know..." The Bishop interrupted.

"Please, later a report. Now: read."

"Yes. Of course." He began reading one of the most important documents in human history.

"...youth I have followed the Lord Yahweh of Israel. I obey the commandments, I help the poor. I am a woman of means and I share the blessings Yahweh has given me with those who have less. My illnesses and my demons are drawing me away from my Lord, though, and I am forlorn."

"What is your name?"

"I am called Mariamne Magdala."

"And you have come out to find me that you might be healed?"

"That I might be healed so I can resume doing Yahweh's will and feel alive again."

As he touched my arm he smiled and said, "Mariamne, your faith has made you whole. Your demons have departed and you will be sick no more. Go and serve Yahweh in Magdala as you have been."

Immediately the heavy burden crushing my soul lifted. I could tell my physical problems had disappeared--I don't know how I knew, but I was certain. It was as if the demons within rushed from my eyes, my nose, my ears, my mouth and I was free of their tyranny. The sun seemed to..."

"That's all there is," said the priest with tears brimming in his eyes.

"Who else knows of this?" asked the Newhouse.

"Only the three of us who have been working on it."

"You will go to them and command them under the threat of excommunication to speak of this to no one. None of you shall even hint this discovery has been made. Bring the copy you were working from and any other material you've developed as you worked to me immediately. Am I clear?"

"Yes, Your Grace. Absolute silence."

"Do not talk about it among yourselves. It must be as if it had never happened."

"Absolutely. I understand. I will tell them at once."

"You may go my son. Please convey to your co-laborers the Holy Father's deepest appreciation. I'm sure when we inform him, he will reward you all. Now. Go. I have more of God's work to do." The priest left. Empty handed.

Newhouse pulled out his cell phone and keyed in Donovan's number. After a few rings Donovan answered and the bishop said, "The man you're talking to, Ezra, he does not have the codex. I have received a call from a woman calling herself Anna who says she has it. You must find out from him who this Anna is and how we may find her. Quickly, Father. Quickly."

"I will resume my discussion with him immediately." Both disconnected.

At the Community of Perpetual Penitents Headquarters

Donovan had taken the call from Newhouse just as Ezra was going to identify the person who called him from the hotel lobby. "Ezra, I've decided to let you go to the john. When you return, I want to speak to you about a woman you know. Be prepared to tell me everything I want to know about her."

The fear in Ezra's eyes was immediate, but just as quickly, the fear turned to embarrassment as his bowels and bladder let go. "Oh God! Oh God! I'm sorry! I'm sorry! I couldn't hold it. Oh God!"

"Well Ezra, it appears as if we've saved a little time. I would have preferred you to use the restroom, but

I guess I am partly to blame. Apparently, my friend, something about my mentioning a woman frightened you. Tell me about her and why the very mention of her caused you to shit yourself. And please, hurry. The odor is foul."

"Look, the guy who called me from the lobby, that was a guy named Fratini. He's...was...the co-director of an Old City dig site. He wanted money but he had to be hands off. He said he had a woman who could help us, but I never met her. I just know she's a mean bitch."

"Ezra, was that so hard? Now we need to get you cleaned up. Donovan rose and stepped out of the room. To the guard outside the door he said, "Get some help. Take him to the showers and strip him. Make him take a cold shower and then take him to the basement level. I need to question him further. Make it quick. I'll be down there within fifteen minutes."

At that, Donovan started to his office, punching in Newhouse' number as he walked. When they connected he said, "It appears the guy who died in the hospital, Fratini, was in on this. I will have to question Dyan more strenuously to find out about the woman. He claims he never met her."

"We must find her. She's going to be calling me back in a few minutes to negotiate further. We must have the codex. We've translated the page they gave us and it's clear this codex will change religious history. Clearly we must control it to be sure any change in history or faith will be guided by Mother Church."

At the Chancery

"Bishop, an Anna on line two."

"Thank you." Newhouse punched line two. "I see you were able to find a suitable phone."

"So, did you like the material?"

"It is very interesting. If it is genuine. A photocopy can't be tested for age. An actual page can be."

"Bishop, I'm really getting tired of fucking around with you. I have the codex and we both know you want it. You know it's genuine because you know where it came from. So, here's the deal. The codex for fifteen million US. Tomorrow. No more wasting time. I've got things I need to do. And I don't need to be giving you more time to have your goons hunt me down."

"Anna, Ezra had said ten."

"I don't give a shit what Ezra said. I have it and he doesn't. You want it? Fifteen. I want another million in cash tomorrow and I'll give you an account number. When the other fourteen is in the account, you get the codex."

"I hate very much to be so cynical, but to give you

the money without the codex in hand doesn't seem to be a fair business arrangement. Already, you have not played fair with me. You gave me a copy when you promised an actual page. You said ten, now you say fifteen. I'm afraid we have to have a different plan."

"Fair enough. You're gun shy. I'm partly responsible. Okay. Here's what we'll do. We'll meet at an Internet cafe. I'll show you the codex and I'll watch you transfer the money electronically. When the money is in the account, I'll walk out leaving the codex behind."

"That sounds fair." Newhouse replied, his mind already thinking about how to get the codex without having to pay a penny.

"Bishop, just how stupid do you think I am? Your pious thugs would be all over me before I even sat down. You'd have the codex; I'd have *nada*. No, the little Internet idea won't work. Here's what I'm going to do. I'm going to give you a couple of hours to come up with a plan that assures my safety and my money. I'm going to call you again and we're going to wrap up this little transaction." She disconnected.

Newhouse called Donovan and explained what had happened. "Look. I'd rather pay nothing for it, but I'll actually pay anything for it. Let's assure her safety and get this over with."

"I'm going to finish my little talk with Ezra. We might still be able to get it for free."

CHAPTER 49

At the Community of Perpetual Penitents Headquarters

Donovan left his office and took the elevator to the basement level below the garage. The area was secure. The button in the elevator for the basement was a fingerprint reader. Unless your fingerprints were on file, the elevator would not descend. Of course, Donovan's was in the system. The basement appeared much like a typical office building floor. There was a central hallway with doors opening off it on both sides. Most of the rooms behind the doors were filled with equipment of various kinds needed to keep this particular group of Dark Brothers well connected to everything they needed.

At the far end of the hall, there were two doors

that opened into rooms holding something quite different from the others. Donovan pressed his thumb onto another fingerprint reader and heard the lock click. He opened the door and entered what can only be called a modern torture chamber. Dyan's nude body was strapped to a stainless steel table in the center of the room. He was strapped in such a way as to have his arms stretched out as if he were on a cross and his legs spread creating about a forty-five degree angle. The temperature in the room was uncomfortably cool, even if you were dressed. Dyan was shivering.

"Ezra, I hope they have been gentle with you."

"Why are you doing this to me?" Tears ran down his cheeks into his ears. "Please don't hurt me. I've told you everything. Please."

"Anna has been in touch with the Bishop and is working out a deal that doesn't include you. I think he said her actual words were, 'I don't give a shit what happens to him.'"

"Anna? Anna who?" Dyan's voice was still full of pleading. "I don't know anybody named Anna."

"Really? She knows you." Donovan walked closer to Ezra. On a stainless steel table were arrayed various instruments, all designed to heal or cause enormous pain. He picked up a scalpel. "Do you enjoy sex, Ezra?"

Without waiting for an answer, Donovan picked up Dyan's exposed scrotum and made an inch long cut near where it joins the penis. Dyan screamed and Donovan said, "I bet that hurt."

Dyan's moaning and whimpering subsided and he said, "Okay. Okay. The woman I work with is named Ellie Steinburg. She's probably Anna. She beat up Marty and then she killed him."

"Really, Ezra. How did she manage that?" Donovan rubbed the side of the scalpel along the side of Dyan's shriveled penis.

"Please! Don't hurt me! I'm telling you everything!" Tears were still leaking from Dyan's eyes and his panic was at its peak. "She's a stocky, strong woman. She's butch, a dyke, you know what I mean? She has short hair and she wears it kind of like a man. She dressed up like a male doctor and injected something into Fratini's IV bag. She took the codex after she beat up Fratini and she still has it. I kept the money; she kept the codex."

Donovan removed the scalpel from Dyan's penis and placed it only inches away from his left eye. "Where can we find her?"

"I don't know. She never told me where she lives. We met at my place after she did the guy. Other times we'd go to a coffee shop or someplace like that. Please, it's the truth. Please don't hurt me any more." He began sobbing and trying to talk at the same time. "Nobody...was supposed...to...get hurt. We just...were trying...to make a....little money. You can have...the codex...Keep the money. I don't care. Just...please...don't hurt...me." Mucus ran from his nose down onto his lips and cheeks, mixing with the tears.

"Ezra, you are such a pussy. First you shit yourself and now you whimper like a baby. Here's the thing. You shouldn't have fucked with the Church. You understand that, right?"

"It just all got out of control. Please, let me go. Don't hurt me any more."

"Well the thing is, Ezra, I can't let you go. First, we don't have Ellie. Second, we don't have the codex. Third, I don't think I can trust a thief and a liar to keep secret our time together."

"You can! You can! I'll leave Israel! Nobody will ever hear about any of this from me."

"I'll tell you what. You just lie here and rest while we hunt for Ellie. Then we'll see." Donovan took the scalpel and cut the flesh at the scrotum again, almost peeling it back and exposing Dyan's testicles. Dyan screamed. And screamed. Donovan tossed the knife back on the tray and picked up a syringe. "If everything goes well, I'll come back and sew you up good as new. If not, I will cut off your nuts and feed them to you one at a time." Dyan lay whimpering and sobbing as Donovan left the room. He said to the guard who apparently was also a medical person, "Don't let him bleed to death and hook him up to an IV to get him hydrated. Warm up the room a little, but don't cover him. I don't want him comfortable."

"Mr. Heywood is across the hall. When you finish here, go next door and beat Mr. Heywood as if he were in a mugging. Make sure he has defensive wounds on his hands as if he fought for his life. Inject him with this sedative, and then as soon as it's possible, take him to one of the less desirable areas of our city and stab him, once in the stomach and then in the neck; make sure you cut the carotid. That should do it. We don't need this particular sinner to connect us to Holy Mother Church."

CHAPTER 50
At the Palatin Hotel

Gabriel, Nicki and Trevor were finishing their coffee from the restaurant off the lobby. Sleep, food and now a second cup of coffee had refreshed all three of them. "So, Trevor, you estimate we were able to photograph maybe a third of the codex, right?"

"We got all the worst damaged pages and a number of the least damaged pages done and on the thumb drive we sent to Marge, so yeah, I'd say about a third, give or take."

"Good. I'm afraid we've lost the codex for good. Whoever took it is likely the person who also killed Marty. I think we need to go public with what we have. I'm not so much worried about credit for the find as I am the stuff being in the wrong hands and used in the wrong way. We have to think of it primarily as an important archeological find and try to be neutral to any religious implications, so that's the way we'll spin it in our press release. The other thing I want to do today is get back to the warehouse and get the pouch from the second jar."

Turning to Nicki, he said, "Nicki, you mentioned the contents of the pouch felt 'lumpy.' What did you mean exactly?"

Nicki smiled a little embarrassed smile. "Well, lumpy was probably the wrong word. I didn't really try to feel its contours or anything, but it felt solid and kind of like a cylinder. I really didn't get a good feel though."

"Any idea what it was," Gabby asked?

"No. I've tried to remember having it in my hands and seeing if I could imagine anything that felt like that, but it was all over too quickly and I was scared to death."

"Okay. Trevor, can you get to the dig sites and get people working? Pull everybody off the first site and get them to the Old City site. Let's bear down there. Who knows what else we'll find. While you do that, Nicki and I will go to the warehouse and get the pouch."

At the Dig Site

"What'd you mean we can't go on the site," Josh asked, not very pleasantly of the IAA representative who stopped the workers as they got off the bus.

"What I mean is that IAA appreciates your work so far, but we have freed up internal resources and we will no longer need the Vanderbilt group. We have tried to call Dr. Gabriel, but his phone keeps going to voice mail."

"Fuck! This can't be happening! And why did the cops take Andy? A couple of them showed up and grabbed Andy right off the bus. What the hell is going on? Ellie, you live here, who can we complain to?"

"I don't know, Josh. If we can't find Gabriel, we're screwed. We're probably screwed anyway. IAA is pretty powerful."

"Where the hell is Nicki? Did you know she has more money than God? Hell, we'll get her to bribe some prick and get this show on the road."

Trevor came rolling up in the pick up truck and walked over to the bus and the knot of workers as Nicki's status was being discussed. "What's going on?" Josh told him. Trevor tried to talk to the IAA representative, but got nowhere. He excused himself from the group, stepped a few feet away and punched in Gabriel's new phone number. When Gabriel answered, Trevor quickly filled him in. While they were talking, Ellie wandered away from the dig and up to the walkway and then walked away.

"Let me talk to the IAA guy," Gabriel ordered.

Trevor walked back to the group and handed the

phone to the IAA representative and said, "It's Dr. Gabriel."

"Ah, Dr. Gabriel. We've been trying to reach you."

"Who the fuck ordered my people off the site?" Gabriel demanded.

"Why the DG, of course."

At the Chancery

"Bishop, it's Anna again on line four."

"Thank you." He punched line four and said, "Good morning, Anna. We have a plan."

"Bishop, I hope it's a good one because things are getting a little dicey where I am. Let's hear it."

"Anna, we want the codex. We value it more than money. I have decided to wire the money into whatever account number you give me and trust you to provide the codex. I also want to, as they say in the business world, give you a disincentive to short me this time, so we're upping the ante to twenty million US. I understand it's a seller's market, but we want the codex."

"Bishop, that's a very generous offer. I admit I considered stiffing you by giving you only some of the pages. But, I don't like some things that are happening, so I want to get rid of this thing. How's this sound to you: I'll give you the account number. As soon as the money is there, I'll tell you where you can find the codex. How long will it take for you to get the money wired?"

"I have already received clearance, so the money can be moved as soon as you give me the account number."

"Bishop, I know you have no reason to trust me. But you can trust me on this. I will need about an hour to move the codex to a location you can find. I'll call when it's there and give you the account number. As soon as I see the money in the account, I'll tell you where the codex is."

"Very well, Anna. I'll await for your call."

At the Palatin Hotel

"That was Trevor. IAA took over the dig site." Gabriel told Nicki.

"What's that mean for your work?"

"My work is over. We've got to get to the warehouse quickly. For all I know, they'll raid it again," he explained.

Gabriel threw some money on the table and both of them headed to the car.

The Director-General's Office

"Sir, I just heard from the people you sent to Gabriel's site. They have halted the Vanderbilt crew. However, Gabriel was not with them. One of his crew called Gabriel and Levi talked to him. Gabriel would not agree to come to the dig site, so he's still in the wind," said Doormann's chief internal investigator.

Doormann replied, "Well we have the site, that's the main thing. I'm not going to be screwed out of whatever else is found there. And Avi has been dispatched to the warehouse to see what's there?"

"Yes. He said he would be heading there shortly. Are you still planning to meet him there?"

"Yes," said Doormann, "and I need to get moving. I'm ready for all this intrigue to end—one way or another."

CHAPTER 51

At the Warehouse

Their rental car screeched to a stop in front of the warehouse and Gabriel and Nicki quickly got out. Looking around, everything seemed normal. Other businesses around them were being occupied as the workday was getting under way. The heat was inching up and the sky was cerulean blue and completely cloudless. Gabriel could see the padlock on the cargo door was still in place. The two of them moved to the other door and Gabriel opened it with his key. Once inside, they flicked on the lights and disarmed the alarm system. "Okay, Nicki. Time to get the pouch." Nicki headed for the area of the workshop where she had put the pouch while Gabriel stayed near the door, keeping lookout. He felt a bit silly peering through the door that was open only a crack. There was no back way out; if someone rolled up, they were stuck.

"Got it!" he heard Nicki say just as a lone car was

clearly about to turn off the street onto the ramp. Gabriel yelled,

"Stay back! Someone coming!"

As Gabriel watched he saw the DG emerge from the now parked car. Gabriel opened the door and met Doormann on the ramp. "I've got to say, you have big brass ones. First you take my dig away from me and then you show up here. Reinforcements on the way?"

"Gabby, what a pleasant surprise. With you here, it will making searching your warehouse for stolen artifacts go much more quickly. I am more sorry than I can say about how things have turned out, but the codex is still missing and we seem to be getting no closer to finding it, though we did discover a few rats along the way."

"I cannot fucking believe you think I'm involved and after all that's happened, that I'd still be holding out on you. Your men have already been here once, you'll recall, and saw the photos we took of the empty second jar. And now you think I've hidden the codex here?

Doormann looked pained as he said, "Gabby, I want to be proven wrong. I pray this search will yield nothing. But, you never can be sure in our business, can you, who is on the side of the angels? As he spoke, two black SUVs pulled up and Avi and his men began to get out.

"Damn, Doormann! All that shit back at your office about never using this fuck again was all an act. You're good, you bastard, I'll give you that."

"Gabby," Doormann said, now in a very business like voice, "if you ever want to work in Israel again you'll do two things. First, you'll show me more respect and second you'll let us in the warehouse and wait as we search it. Am I clear?"

Gabriel was sure their luck, what little they had, had just run out. Whatever was in the pouch was now going to be lost too. "You win. Help yourself," he said as he pushed the door open and Avi's men entered. Gabriel thought once about yelling for Nicki to come out, but decided not to make things any easier for Doormann than he had to.

"Gabby, please unlock the office so we may search there too," said Doormann as Avi's men were making their way slowly up and down the rows of shelves. Doormann said loudly so everyone could hear, "Call me if you find any kind of package of any size or any loose pages of parchment!" The search was slow and meticulous. The shelves were made of two by four lumber and plywood. Each bank was eight feet tall and two feet wide. Each shelf was separated from the other by two feet vertically. Searchers climbed on the bottom shelf and the second shelf to see into the top shelf. No one called out a find.

"Avi," Doormann called out, "have them look on the top of the shelves as well."

Gabriel was perspiring heavily. Not only was it warming up in the warehouse, but his sweat was also from fear. Any moment he was sure Nicki would be found and that would be that. But thirty minutes went by, then an hour. They were starting their second sweep when Avi returned to where Doormann was standing. "It's not here. There's nothing here that could be so valuable as to have been secreted away in that wall." Gabriel looked both puzzled and relieved.

"Well, Gabby, it would appear," said Doormann, "you have told us the truth. At least so far as nothing being in the second jar and no codex here. How regrettable it had to come to this, but as you know, that codex is more important than our friendship. I do hope, however, when all this unpleasantness is past, we may resume our cordial relationship."

"Sure. Yeah. It'll be like nothing ever happened." The sarcasm was not only apparent in his words, but written on his face as well.

"Please, Gabby. You'll get over this. It's just business, you know."

"Yes. Just business. I suppose even though this is all supposed to be work of the highest integrity and academic discipline, we all do things that we might not otherwise do." He thought back to the very late night phone call he, Marge and Harry enjoyed last night.

To Avi he said, "Let's go." As they left, Gabriel followed them to the door and, once they were out, he locked it. "Nicki," he said in a half whisper, half yell, "Where are you?" The office space and the restrooms were rooms within the warehouse with each having their flat roof about nine feet off the floor. From the roof of the office, he saw Nicki's head and heard her say, "Here I am. Do you have a ladder? I'm not sure I can get down the same way I got up here."

The Chancery Office

"Bishop, line three. It's Anna."

"Anna. Do you have something for me?"

"Bishop, here's the account number." She read him the account number and the routing number.

"Just a moment, Anna. I'm going to put you on speaker while I turn around in my chair to my computer." Anna could hear the quiet clicking of keys and a big sigh as the typing ended. "All right, Anna, I've finished. You should have your confirmation in a moment. Shall we stay on the line as we wait?"

"Yeah, sure. Hold it. Ah, there it is. Thank you, Bishop. You've kept your word and now I'll keep mine. A package will arrive at your office within a few minutes. It has been a pleasure doing business with you." The line went dead.

Newhouse walked to his office door, opened it and spoke to his receptionist. "I'm expecting a package momentarily. Please alert me..." As he spoke a smallish, smooth faced man, with short, light brown hair walked up to the desk with a courier bag over his shoulder. His tenor voice said, "I have a package for a Bishop Newhouse," and as he was speaking, said, "Here you go. Don't need a signature. Have a nice day," and then walked down the hall and out of the building. And with that, 'Anna' was gone. Much wealthier, perhaps even wiser, but gone.

Newhouse was focused on the package and the delivery person barely registered. He greedily picked up the small cardboard box and returned to his office. With his letter opener, he slit the tape and actually smelled the faint scent of pitch before he saw the darkened top page of Mary's Gospel. Anna had kept her word.

CHAPTER 52

The Director-General's Office

The small TV in his office was on just to provide a little background noise as the DG tried to think about his next steps. He was only half listening when CNN interrupted its regular program with a special report.

The Chancery Office

"Father, we have the codex," said Newhouse to Donovan over the phone. "The Anna woman kept her word. Come immediately to the Chancery Office. You deserve to see this wonder first hand. A knock on his door caused him to look up. His assistant silently walked in and turned on the TV tuning it to CNN. A special report had just started.

CNN Newsroom

"Vanderbilt University's Department of Biblical Archeology Dr. Stephen Gabriel, along with Mr. Harry Hanks of *Biblical Archeology Review* and in cooperation with the Israeli Antiquities Authority, have announced today a discovery of a first century codex or small book which almost certainly was written by Mary Magdalene shortly after Jesus Christ's death and resurrection. The story of this codex already reads like a mystery. Dr. Martino Fratini, the co-director of the dig in the Old City Jerusalem area was beaten and subsequently died, thought to be murdered. At the time of his beating, the codex was stolen and remains missing.

"Dr. Gabriel and his team, including an experienced photographer and videographer named Trevor Wiley, one of Gabriel's graduate students, were able to make an extensive record of both the events around finding the codex which was hidden in a jar in some ruins thought to be used by Mary herself, perhaps her home. Mr. Wiley was also able to take a number of sophisticated high-resolution digital photos of many of the pages before the codex was stolen. Using the resources of BAR and its connections, some of these pages have already been subjected to intensive study and a few have been partially translated.

We go now to Kevin Byers in Jerusalem for a report from the dig site. "Kevin?"

"Wolf, yes. We're here at the dig site where we have discovered anything but what might ordinarily be expected. Trevor Wiley, the photographer, is here with us and tells us when he arrived at the site this morning, the IAA, the Israeli Antiquities Authority, had taken over the site. Thank you for speaking with us Mr. Wiley. Tell us what happened." Trevor quickly summarized the events of the morning.

"Is this commonplace for IAA to take over a site?"

"No. But not much in the way of the commonplace has happened since we discovered the first jar, the one that contained the codex."

"Where is Dr. Gabriel? Shouldn't he be here?"

"I have spoken with him by phone, but my most recent attempt to contact him failed. I don't know where he is. I only hope he's not in danger."

"There you have it. Turmoil and intrigue here in the Old City. Back to you."

"We want to show you videos of the find of the jar which contained the codex. And as those are running, we have Dr. Harry Hanks, editor of BAR in our Washington studio. Dr. Hanks, thanks for being with us. Tell us the significance of this find and why you've released the news this way instead of the usual academic channels."

Hanks briefly summarized the importance the find for the great faiths of the world concluding by saying, "To have words we know were written by an intimate of Jesus Christ, a person with no particular agenda as some of the other New Testament writings have, is of incalculable importance to the study of Christianity and perhaps other faiths as well. We have already read passages that confirm accounts of some things Jesus was recorded as having said by the other Gospel writers, but we also have new information. This, even with only a few pages, examined. We are told we have about a third of the entire codex and we can only imagine what the rest might teach us--if we can find it."

"And why have you released the news this way?"

"Because of the theft of the codex and Dr. Fratini's murder. We don't know why it was taken nor who took it. But we can imagine it was taken perhaps to suppress its contents."

"Where's Dr. Gabriel? Why isn't he here with you making this announcement?"

"After Dr. Fratini's death, Gabby feared for his life and is keeping a low profile. We hope to hear from him soon. Let me assure you, we have published exactly what he and I agreed to. It's his find; I'm just helping."

"Before we went on the air you mentioned you had been able to read a startling piece of information. Can you share that with our listeners?"

"Yes. Let me just read it. We are about seventy-five percent sure we have the text correctly translated. It was badly damaged with oil and pitch so we've had to make educated guesses in some places. However, we think we have the essence." Adjusting his glasses, Hanks began to read from Mary's Gospel.

We watched and listened as Yeshua began the meal by blessing and breaking the bread as is our custom. But he said words different from the customary words. He said, "This bread is my body. As it was given for our supper tonight, so will I be offered up for you."

We women did not know what to make of these words, nor did the men at table. At the end of the meal when it was time for the Cup of Blessing, he prayed as is our custom, "Blessed are you Lord Yahweh. From your bounty we have this wine to offer, fruit of the vine and work of human hands."

Everyone said, "Blessed be Yahweh forever."

Then he said, "My blood will be poured out for you as this wine has been poured for you. Men and women will have forgiveness of their sins because of my shed blood. Dear friends, when I am gone, each time you eat bread and drink wine, relive these moments and these words."

The men left after supper and the other women and I began to put things in order. I knew in my heart this was a holy, sacred moment. I took the cup he had used and from which we had drunk and have always kept it with me. When we meet on the First Day of the Week to remember him, we use this cup.

Now as danger approaches, and we must leave Jerusalem for a time, I have hidden away this cup. I am afraid of taking with us, for we may be detained. When we return, we will take it out again and feel the blessing of touching our lips where his touched.

Hanks looked up. "Obviously," he said, "what we have come to call the Holy Grail actual does exist and may yet be found. This may be the reason IAA has taken over the dig site where the codex was found. To search for it."

"Thank you Doctor. If you have just joined us, we are speaking with Dr. Harry Hanks who is speaking for the team that discovered what appears to be Mary Magdalene's record of her time with Jesus. I'm told that carbon dating of leather with which the codex was tied has come back with a date range well within the time she could have been living. She would have been in the last years of her life and may have used those last days to record her memories."

"Tonight we will have a more complete report ahead of Dr. Hanks publishing the information they've uncovered. Please stay tuned for the time that report will air. We are still putting it together. Again, Mary Magdalene's journal of her time with Jesus has been discovered in Jerusalem. We return you to our regular programming."

CHAPTER 53

The Director-General's Office

Doormann sat entranced and horrified at the same time. He couldn't believe the codex had slipped through their fingers, but even more he was furious that Gabriel had outwitted him with the photos, videos and the press conference. *Oh, well. We have the site. Maybe we'll find the cup. Or something.*

The Chancery Office

Newhouse sighed. Life just become much more complicated. He swung his chair so he could look out a window. He looked at the stack of vellum sheets resting on his desk and despaired at what other surprises it held. And he wondered what else would Gabriel's team publish? How would Holy Mother Church be able to manage what people read and believed? *After we get this thing completely translated, we'll be in a better position to deal with whatever Gabriel does. At any rate, only a selected few will ever know what the other two-thirds of the codex has to say. Things have a way of getting misfiled in the Vatican Library.*

At the Warehouse

As Gabriel was placing the ladder against the office wall, he asked, "How the hell did you get up there?"

"I climbed up the shelves in the back where I had hidden the pouch. I got all the way on top. When I realized they were going to search the place, I decided to jump from the top shelf over to the roof of the office and lie down."

She was climbing down now, pouch in hand. When she was safely on the floor, Gabriel turned her around and kissed her. Then he kissed her again. And she kissed him back. Passionately. "My God, you're wonderful," he said.

"I think you're pretty special too." She kissed him again.

Breaking their embrace, Gabriel said, let's see what's in the pouch and then figure out what to do. She handed it to him and said, "You do the honors." He carefully opened the pouch, trying not to break the leather drawstring and they looked inside.

At the CPP Headquarters

"Brothers, that was the Bishop. We have the codex!" A cheer went up from the assembled priests. "The woman who had it is gone and we've been told to not try to locate her. So, we have just the loose ends to tie up downstairs and we'll be ready for our next assignment."

"Still want us to carry out the Heywood assignment?"

"Yes. I don't see how we can let these two remain free. While the tale they would tell would be too bizarre to be believed, some nuts out there will believe it anyway. Let's do with Ezra what they do in Las Vegas. His body will never be found in the desert. I'll take care of him, and then some of you dump him tonight. If you haven't already dumped Heywood, take him to the desert too."

Donovan returned to the room where Ezra lay, still moaning softly. The bleeding in his scrotum had stopped and the blood had begun to coagulate. "You know Ezra, you have learned a valuable lesson in this experience, haven't you."

Ezra looked at him through the pain and said, "Yes. Don't mess with Catholics."

Donovan chuckled, "Yes. Exactly. There is another good news bad news situation here Ezra. The good news is you will be able to apply this lesson for the rest of your life; of that, I have no doubt. The bad news is how short your life is going to be. I'm afraid we can't let you go. It's bad enough that Ellie or Anna has gotten away with something. We just can't risk it happening again."

Ezra began to whimper, "You're going to kill me, aren't you? Oh God! Oh God, why did I ever get mixed up in this?" The tears were flowing freely as Donovan said,

"Do you happen to be Catholic, Ezra?"

"No. I...don't go...to church," he was able to say between sobs.

"Pity. No point in Last Rites then. You're going to hell anyway." At that, Father Donovan, slit Ezra's throat. Blood shot several feet in the air and drenched Donovan, but as Ezra's blood pressure dropped rapidly, the flow stemmed quickly and Ezra was dead.

CHAPTER 54

At the Warehouse

"We've got to get out of here. Out of the country. And I mean fast." Gabriel was panicked and excited at the same time. "We need a plan."

"I didn't tell you this, Gabe, but I told the plane we sent to Nashville with the flash drive to come back here. I wasn't sure what might happen."

Gabriel looked at her with wide-eyed surprise. "God woman! You are truly unbelievable."

"I'm good at planning," she said.

"We still have to go through customs though, even at the private aviation terminal. How do we get the pouch through?"

"We can wrap it up like a purchase. All we have to do is go into town one more time, buy something like it and switch them out. You can put the empty pouch in your underwear."

"Really? My underwear?"

"Or I could put it in mine."

He kissed her and said, "I like that idea except for one thing."

"Oh?"

"Let me put it in there."

On A Private Jet Over the Mediterranean Sea

"I finally feel safe," Nicki said.

"Yeah. I'm just now beginning to feel the after effects of the adrenaline high I've been on." I'm starting to feel washed out.

"Maybe a nap will help us both," Nicki volunteered. "You know, this plane has a private bedroom in the aft compartment."

"No kidding. Man, I could get use to this kind of stuff. But hey, first, let's look at our treasure."

Gabriel took the cardboard box in which the contents of the pouch had been sealed and pulled it open. Inside nestled in the crushed white paper of a tourist shop, they looked at a white, lightly veined, alabaster cup with eight squared off sides. The cup was about six or seven inches high, and perhaps three and a half or four inches across. It had a flat bottom; no stem. The inside was cylindrical like a glass and stained from use. He had seen pictures of such cups from other digs. It was a first century equivalent to a water glass, but a nice one. At least it looked ordinary, but they both knew there was nothing ordinary about it. They also knew, without saying so, as the plane made its way home, life would never be the same for them. Just how different it would be was something they couldn't even begin to imagine. And not being able to imagine it—that was a good thing.

A Note From the Author

I hope you enjoyed *St. Gabriel's Gospel.* For more years than I can remember, I've wanted to write a novel in which I blended my love of mysteries with my knowledge of Christianity. This has been a blast.

You know now that Gabby's and Nicki's lives may still be in peril. To see what happens check out the soon to be released sequel, *Saint Gabriel's Passion.* It picks up where this one left off and very quickly, the action accelerates.

Thanks for buying the book. To see what else is going on or learn more about how these books develop, check my website www.JerryHarberWriter.weebly.com. There's a contact form there for you to reach me with comments or questions. I look forward to the opportunity.